Romance from
AMY LANE

I0672732

Under the Rushes
"This is an amazing tale of conflicting emotions, where each person searches for his or her own form of redemption. It's a love story, sometimes in its rarest form, beautiful, painful, forgiving, understanding, and honest."
—Rainbow Book Reviews

Gambling Men
"Oh wow, this an amazing book! It's a rare book that can have the relationship development be the entire focus but this book does it exceedingly well."
—The Book Vixen

Keeping Promise Rock
"This is such a beautifully written story of a love that can survive anything and boy is there lots of obstacles in the way here."
—The Cat's Meow

The Three Fates: Believed You Were Lucky
"…this story is worth buying the whole book for."
—The Armchair Reader

A Knitter in His Natural Habitat
"This is a touching love story, and shows some wonderful character growth…"
—Rainbow Book Reviews

By AMY LANE

NOVELS
Bolt-hole
Chase in Shadow • Dex in Blue
Clear Water
Gambling Men: The Novel
The Locker Room
Mourning Heaven
Sidecar
A Solid Core of Alpha
The Talker Collection (anthology)
Three Fates (anthology)
Under the Rushes

THE KEEPING PROMISE ROCK SERIES
Keeping Promise Rock • Making Promises • Living Promises

NOVELLAS
Bewitched by Bella's Brother
Christmas with Danny Fit
Hammer and Air
If I Must
It's Not Shakespeare
Puppy, Car, and Snow
Truth in the Dark
Turkey in the Snow

THE KNITTING SERIES
How To Raise an Honest Rabbit
Knitter in His Natural Habitat
Super Sock Man
The Winter Courtship Rituals of Fur-Bearing Critters

GREEN'S HILL
Guarding the Vampire's Ghost
I love you, asshole!
Litha's Constant Whim

TALKER SERIES
Talker • Talker's Redemption • Talker's Graduation

Published by DREAMSPINNER PRESS
http://www.dreamspinnerpress.com

BOLT-
HOLE

Amy Lane

Dreamspinner Press

Published by
Dreamspinner Press
5032 Capital Circle SW
Ste 2, PMB# 279
Tallahassee, FL 32305-7886
USA
http://www.dreamspinnerpress.com/

Bolt-hole

Cover Art by DWS Photography
cerberuspic@gmail.com
Cover Design by Paul Richmond

ISBN: 978-1-62380-537-1
Digital ISBN: 978-1-62380-538-8

Printed in the United States of America
First Edition
March 2013

To Mate, because we slogged through
restaurant work together, even if I was
the world's most inept waitress,
and he was the world's skinniest cook.

And to all of the students through the years, the ones who told me
unapologetically and without rancor, what it was like for them to be
black in a white world. Ambrosia? Sweetie, that's you too.

Locomotive Breath

TERRELL was all braced for it when he stomped into Papiano's—it was inevitable.

"Hey, T—nice teeth!"

"Get hit in the face with a railroad track?"

"If we stick a coat hanger up your ass, will we get AM/FM?"

"Yeah, yeah, yeah," he muttered, stashing his shit in the dented lockers by the bathrooms. "Like I'm shocked you degenerates got the bad fuckin' manners to bring up the rails." He'd been off for three days, and the ache in his mouth was just fading to tolerable with the help of a little ibuprofen.

"Ain't you a little old for that shit?" Percy the fry cook wanted to know. Percy was just out of high school himself, and his teeth were every bit as ugly as Terrell's.

"I don't live in the hood, Percy," Terrell snapped, suddenly irritated. "I'm planning to live long past thirty."

"You don't live in the hood 'cause you're tryin' to be white," Percy said, rolling green eyes in his café latte face. Percy's genetics were a little more mixed than Terrell's—his hair was nappy and chocolate blond, whereas Terrell's hair, skin, and eyes were dark chocolate brown—but Percy had decided that choosing to be black meant choosing to be hood, and he had all the hard-core tats to prove it. He also had an ankle bracelet underneath his chef's whites that told his parole officer he was exactly where he was in case he wasn't exactly the fuck where he should be, and Terrell didn't want no part of that.

1

"I don't live in the hood 'cause them fools think the hood is all there is," he told Percy flatly. "And I didn't spend no six years in college to look like some bush baby with these ugly fuckin' teeth."

"I like your teeth. You got a real nice smile."

At that low, slightly exotic voice, Terrell felt a jolt of awareness from the soles of his feet to the pit of his balls, but he clenched his ass, sacced up, and turned around to smile at Colby Meyers with easy sincerity. It's what he'd been practicing since the boy walked into Papiano's nearly a year ago, looking for a job.

"Hey, cheese boy—didn't know you were waiting tonight!"

Colby smiled and mirrored Terrell's actions on purpose. As they spoke, both of them pulled their aprons out of their adjoining lockers, slammed their lockers shut with their hips, and tied the strings of the worn black polyester blend around their backs. They stuffed the front with their little vinyl folders full of order tags, pens, bottle openers, and cards for the local cab companies as well as a local hotel, for easy access, and a couple of white towels for spills as well as a couple of red towels for handling hot plates. The aprons and the neon-green rugby shirts with the goddamn suspenders made up their uniform, because Papiano's was that kind of no-tablecloth place with three franchises a city.

"Yeah, well, if you're on bar, I don't want to be anywhere else!"

Terrell winked at him and turned away, afraid his expression would soften and he'd get stupid gooey and show the whole world what a fag he really was.

Fags didn't last long in Terrell's neighborhood.

Well, that was an oversimplification. The ones with the money and the balls to just flame out and the parents who got past the tenth grade, they did okay. But Terrell didn't flame, and his mother *had* him in tenth grade, and he was just smart enough to get an education and just dumb enough to get it in journalism, which meant money depended on how many tips he could charm out of his customers at the bar. Terrell had kept his little perversions and his one-nighters and his blow jobs in alleyways all to himself for nearly fifteen years, and as God was his witness, he'd keep on doing that for as long as it took, because wasn't nobody worth coming out for, not in his old neighborhood or the streets of Zanzibar or the goddamned anteroom to heaven itself.

At least that's what he told himself, anyway.

It got a lot harder to listen when his smart side said shit like that—especially when Colby came in and grinned at him, did the apron dance, and then held out his hands for a low-five-come-here-my-brother, just like any of the kids Terrell had grown up with.

The fact that he had rich blond hair complete with skinny little sideburns, a square jaw, round blue eyes, and a nose just big enough to fit his face didn't seem to matter to Colby. He never seemed to notice that even in the summer, when the backs of his hands were tanned and brown from time at the river and the lake and on his bicycle, his skin was still several shades lighter and pinker than Terrell's had ever been, even on the underside of his palms. He simply walked into work, and whether it was the end of Terrell's shift or the beginning, he managed to find five minutes, ten minutes, an hour, an entire eight-hour shift, to chat with Terrell like they were friends.

Terrell had come to think of them as friends.

He'd started thinking up jokes for Colby, because the kid (he'd just finished school, and Terrell had been out for about four years) had a love of puns. For Christmas, Colby had given Terrell an Easy button, the kind you got from Staples, and every time Terrell bitched about how hard he was being worked, Colby reached in past the servers' side of the bar and hit the button, arching his eyebrows when the words "That was easy!" came echoing through clear as day.

In return, Terrell did the kid's drinks first if he could, and he'd started designing new ones, because he *loved* to hear Colby pimp his shit.

"Yeah, so you're looking for a new drink? Our guy in back, he's got something called the Rabid Hamster—I'm not sure what's in it, but I understand it makes you want to mate like a lemming. Did you want a double?" And people ordered it too! As far as Terrell knew, Papiano's had the only bar in town that served *anything* called a Rabid Hamster—and people seemed to like that shit!

And that wasn't the best part.

The best part was that Colby treated him like a rational human being. Colby had *just* gotten a degree in sociology, and yeah, he'd been up-front with exactly what that sort of thing *wasn't* going to get him in the real world.

"I'll probably be waiting tables or tending bar my whole life," he'd said one night about four months earlier, before he'd graduated, as they'd been out on the back dock, staring at the stars and sharing a beer after shift. It had been March then, and chilly, and they managed one beer before hopping into their cars and taking off, but as always, Terrell treasured that one beer.

"You're going to school for *that*?"

"You went to school for *journalism*?" Colby mimicked with a smile, and Terrell bared his rat-nasty teeth.

"I did. Took me almost eight years to get it too, and look at all it's got me!" Terrell gestured to the back dock, with its pile of recycling, stack of pallets, and, oh yeah, the trash-masher the size of his apartment.

Colby shrugged. "Well, yeah. I just love learning about people. That doesn't mean it's going to make me any money! But that's okay. I'll be able to wait tables in Marrakesh or Vancouver, and talk to people and just see the whole damned world. That'll be all I need."

Terrell sipped his beer moodily. "I want a cat," he said out of the blue. "I mean, I want to see the world and all, but I want a place I know is mine."

Colby tipped back his beer. "And a cat's going to do that for you?"

Terrell considered. "In India, they don't move cats, did you know that?"

Colby tilted his chin and smiled. Terrell *loved* that smile. It meant that whatever came out of Terrell's ugly mouth would be thought about in Colby's pretty head. "I did not," he said thoughtfully. "Why not?"

"They figure that cats belong to a place and not a people, so if someone moves, they leave the cat in the place for the next family. I like that. I want a cat to belong to my place. That'll mean it's a good place."

Colby nodded and finished off his beer. "Well, then—a good place is worth coming back to. You let me know when you get that cat."

Terrell grinned then, and Colby's gaze darkened, and his mouth went soft, and suddenly Terrell remembered his teeth pointed in sixty-three different directions, and when he grinned, Colby could see every damned one of them. He closed his mouth and, for no reason at all, went home and spent some time on his laptop, looking up one of the three dentists in the area that took the shit-tacular health insurance offered at Papiano's.

It was stupid. Sheerest fucking folly. But he'd thrown that ball and it wasn't going to stop until the pins were knocked down, and, well, here he was, with a mouthful of metal at thirty years old and a hopeless crush on a kid whose idea of a Christmas gift was an Easy button.

Terrell couldn't even tell himself he wasn't that easy, because just shaking Colby's hand and coming in for the chest bump made him feel soft and wanting. The walking definition of easy.

Lovely.

But they had a Friday night—and not just *any* Friday night, the Friday night *after* finals at Sac State. Oh *hell* no! Every frat kid and his jerk-off buddy was in here trying to flash a phony ID!

"How you doin', T?"

Terrell looked up after he finished telling his fifth kid that he didn't take a goddamned student ID to prove someone was twenty-one, and scowled. The general manager of this particular Papiano's wasn't a *bad* guy, but he never struck Terrell as on the level, either. Maybe it was the habit he had of making sure all the young women at Papi's got taken in the back for long lessons in how to cash out, or how some of them simply quit and never came back. Maybe it was the way he'd do *anything* to please a customer, but he never fucking fronted for his people. Either way, William Templeton seemed particularly skeezy, and Terrell wasn't as diplomatic as he might be.

"We got any muscle coming in?" he asked irritably. "These white boys don't want to hear it from me that they can't drink on Daddy's dime! Jesus, can you get someone up here to check IDs for me? That would be simply fucking awesome!"

Templeton was a smooth-faced man in his early forties who obviously dyed his hair and his beard and (probably by accident) his bald spot. He scowled at Terrell before looking up at the blond frat kid and showing perfect blinding white teeth.

"I'm sorry," he said sweetly over the roar. "We really can't honor that. We could lose our license if we served you, and that would be a shame."

"Yeah," Terrell muttered under his breath while he poured two basic rotgut kamikazes, "that would really fuckin' suck."

"What was that?"

Terrell looked up at the frat kid and sighed inwardly before smiling with his lips over his teeth and saying, "Nothing, Junior. Can I get you a Diet Coke?"

"You!" the kid snarled at Templeton. "You're his boss! Can't you fire this bandy-legged little nigger when he mouths off to me like that?"

Templeton shrugged and turned away, and Terrell ignored him and focused on his next order. Templeton wasn't necessarily a racist bastard, but he wasn't going to put himself out for Terrell, that was for damned sure.

"I'm talking to you!" Geez, the kid wasn't going to let it go!

"I'm sorry," Templeton said, oozing insincerity, "but he was just doing his—"

"Ouch!"

Terrell looked up in time to see the kid jerk back, his face twisted in pain. He jerked around toward the door because someone was yanking his arm behind his back, and Terrell got a very nice—and not very welcome—view of Colby's backside as Colby hauled him away and hustled him out. Colby's voice had a deep, carrying timbre, and the entire bar heard him reading poor blond frat boy the riot act on his way out.

"Hate speech is grounds for arrest in California, and inciting violence or termination on the basis of someone's race can get you jail time."

Terrell widened his eyes in surprise. *The shit you just didn't fuckin' know.*

Templeton looked sideways at him. "Nice to have your own pet pit bull," he said mildly, and Terrell shrugged.

"You weren't doing the job," he muttered. Now see, if Templeton wasn't a skeeze, he'd take exception to that, but he didn't. He shrugged instead.

"I'm going to the back to count the safe," he muttered, and yeah, of course he was, because among every other goddamned skill needed to run a restaurant, he was also missing the one that would help him tend bar. "Let me know if you call the cops."

"We'll get right on that," Terrell muttered.

Colby was coming back through the crowd now, his shoulders square and his expression thunderous. To Terrell's surprise, he hopped up on a barstool and rang the tip bell violently and at top volume until all the chatter at the bar ceased.

"All right, college boys," he hollered, "you're having a good time tonight, am I right?"

There was a general good-hearted cheer from around the bar, and Terrell used the opportunity to keep working—he was about six drinks behind.

"Awesome! Now I need you all to do me a favor. Can you do that?"

That hearty applause again, and Terrell dimly remembered one of his college professors saying it was human nature to keep going in the same direction. Get everyone to cheer once, and they'd cheer again and again and again.

"Excellent! Now we got two bartenders, and they're working their hearts out for you, but you got to cut them some slack! Have your ID ready, and your card if you're starting a tab, and our boys can get to you. If you don't have your driver's license, you need to go somewhere else. Can you get behind that?"

And sure enough, just like Professor Nichols predicted, there was that hearty huzzah, and Terrell felt some of the tension that had been building up his spine ease on out. He glanced up at Sukrish, the other bartender, and Suk looked back, nodding and rolling his brown eyes in his thin, sallow face. Suk hadn't been tending bar very long, and if the kids were going to fuck with Terrell, odds were good they weren't going to give Suk a break at all.

They worked hard, elbow to elbow. They laughed, they joked, and apparently the stiff-necked, racist little bastard Colby had walked out wasn't going to come back. By the time twelve o'clock rolled around, the place was almost sane.

Terrell had Suk hold down the fort while he ran back to stock—they were out of their rotgut brand in almost every liquor, and it figured. In college, you ordered well. Out of college, you ordered call. Once you got your first promotion, *then* you could order your premium top-shelf shit and still make the rent. Every now and then, when one of the suppliers had some of the premium or top-shelf shit that "fell off the truck," Terrell would buy it. He didn't drink it a lot, but when he did, he knew it was the good stuff. Too many kids in his hood wasted their brains and their bodies on shit that would probably take the paint off of Terrell's beat-to-hell car.

He was in the back, grabbing a couple of bottles of Johnnie Walker, when Colby went running back to the walk-in and came out with two bottles of salad dressing—apparently the waitstaff was stocking up too. They met by the door to the storeroom, and Colby pulled back to let Terrell out first.

"They treating you okay, T?" he asked, and Terrell swallowed. You don't forget a guy standing up for you like that.

"Yeah—what'd you do to make him go the fuck away?"

Colby shrugged. "There was a cop outside anyway. He saw me shoving the guy out and asked what was up—I told him we didn't take punks harassing our bartenders. The guy went off, and, well, I hope his buddies check their messages, 'cause he got a ride he didn't expect."

Terrell stopped for a second there in the hallway by the lockers and looked at him. "You gave him to the cops?"

Colby blinked. "Well, *yeah,* T—he was trying to get served underage, was being a racist prick—why not?"

Terrell shook his head and kept going, not sure if he could articulate his bone-deep hatred of most higher forms of authority. The one exception—his *only* exception—was education. He should have said something, he thought, some sort of thank-you, some sort of appreciation, but he couldn't. He... the kid had come up like a knight in shining armor, and Terrell couldn't even fathom ever needing such a thing. He split off from Colby and trotted up the stairs to keep up with the night, and thought he might have gotten away from any sort of emotional display at all when Colby hollered after him.

"Hey, T—back dock before cleanup, right?"

Terrell nodded and called "As always!" over his shoulder before he even knew what he was saying. But of course he was going on the back dock before cleanup. You waived break times when you signed up for the job, but Colby and T, they sort of had a ritual whenever they closed together. They went out behind the store by the trash masher, had a soda, shared a sandwich—whatever. Sometimes they talked, sometimes they just hung out. Terrell always figured that if they were smokers, they'd share a smoke, but they weren't, and that was a shame, because really? Without nicotine addiction, there wasn't a name you could put on that stolen ten minutes. It had started the first night Colby closed, and he'd been looking a little beat by the pace and the noise and just all of the stupid minute-by-minute stress that came when serving in a place where the seats were designed to be uncomfortable so customers wouldn't linger and turnover would be lightning fast.

Terrell had poured them both a couple of sodas, grabbed a roll from the drawer (they weren't supposed to be free, but everyone stole them), and dragged Colby outside, made him eat, made him caffeinate, made him slow the hell down. At the end of about ten minutes, Colby had looked up at him, grinned, and said, "Ready to get back to it?" And that had been that. Colby could probably work straight through now, but the next time they'd closed together, he'd asked Terrell if they were going to take a break, and Terrell... well, he'd appreciated the boy's company. Even when they didn't say anything, he just... radiated strength and good will. It was like when he hauled the college kid out and read him the riot act on civil rights—he was a Boy Scout through and through.

Yeah. On the back dock before closing. Of course. Because he was going to just stare straight ahead and pretend he wasn't gay and hadn't noticed that Colby had a full mouth and a little turned-up nose and eyelashes that went blond at the tips during the summer and hair that grew long enough to curl at the collar. None of that meant shit to Terrell, and neither did the fact that Colby would swoop in and play Captain America for him when not a soul on the planet had ever done so before in his entire life.

Terrell recognized the thing in his stomach as he went back and forth between the bar and the stockroom. It was a buzzy, warm, fierce tingle of excitement. He remembered it from childhood—it was the feeling he got right before school was about to start.

About half an hour later, he went back for more Sam Adams (it was the only upgrade the college kids got right) when he saw Kelly, one of the Do' Hos (okay, door hostesses, but they all layered on makeup with a trowel and skirts with a Band-Aid, so Do' Ho, which was a lot more fun to say) hiding in the back corner, face to the wall, face in her hands, shoulders shaking.

Oh no.

Crap. Terrell could be a cranky bastard with men, but he hated to see a girl cry.

"What's wrong, sweet thing?" he said in his best "Tell Uncle T" voice. It got him good tips at the bar—he'd practiced!

The girl looked up, her curly brown hair falling from the clip that usually secured it at the back and her makeup running like a black bandit's mask across her eyes.

"Hi, Terrell," she said, half-afraid. He didn't blame her, really. There was a hierarchy that superseded management even. The bartender was the top-of-the-line waitstaff and the window man was the top of the line in the kitchen. Terrell had been there for eight years—he'd worked his way up from bar-back in college, and he was the most senior staff member there, including Will Skeezy Templeton, whose drawers always counted up short and who never, ever seemed to have to tell corporate about it. (Terrell counted up the bar drawers in the back when Templeton counted up the rest of the take. Terrell had heard the man mumbling to himself on more than one occasion, and since they both had to put their count slips in the same place, he'd noticed the discrepancies. He'd seen enough -$100 marks to know that something was up, and enough managers come and go to ripely not give a fuck.)

"Aren't you about ready to go home?" he asked kindly. It was getting close to one in the morning, and the few folks trickling in were heading straight for the bar since the kitchen was closing in about fifteen minutes.

She nodded and went to wipe her eyes. Terrell sighed and held out his hands. "Tch, tch, tch," he muttered, then reached into one of the freshly laundered packages of white bar towels and found one that had been through the wringer a few times. It was still fresh and white, but one more time to the cleaner's and it would disintegrate, and it was about as soft as soft could be. "C'mere, sweetheart," he muttered, and she came hesitantly. He found a bottle of soda water not far from the bar towels and dumped some of it on the towel, then got close enough to wipe her eyes carefully, taking the goop off around the lower lashes without rubbing it into the poor girl's eyes. She saw the big black crescents and let out a sound close to a laugh.

"Thanks, Terrell," she said sincerely. "That's a big mess. I'd forgotten how much makeup you put on when you're dressing for the front."

"No worries," he said softly. God, he wished this could be a kissing moment. She was a sweet kid with an open face once you got some of the goop off. You could see the roughened skin from teenage acne, but for Terrell, that just made her more accessible, more human. Well, yeah, if onlies. "So, what're you doing in here?"

She shook her head. "Have you ever been stupid?" she asked baldly. "I mean, 'don't sleep with that person' stupid?"

Terrell thought of those frantic gropes in alleyways, the blow jobs he'd gotten from strangers based on a glance and their possessive hand on his ass as he moved through a crowd. He thought of driving past Gatsby's Nick longingly, thinking of the people in there who knew what he would be there for and who wouldn't judge, and who would maybe even come home with him at night. He'd never gone in. What if someone who would know him was there? What if word got around to his hood? He never went there anymore—God knew he was going to hell for ditching his Gi-Gi for the past few years during holidays and birthdays—but he hated lying to her too. It was easier to work the holiday and the birthday and send a gift and give a phone call, and to pretend that home wasn't ten miles away in a sketchy neighborhood of people who thought he was a fool to go to school and not come out rich on the other side.

"All the time," he said mournfully, and she smiled at him with gratitude he really didn't deserve.

"Yeah," she whispered. "Me too. I shouldn't have slept with him, and I *really* shouldn't have believed him when he said I was the only one."

Terrell felt a stirring in his stomach. "Oh Jesus, sweetheart—please tell me it's not—"

"Dodge-the-bill Will?" Kelly said bitterly, and Terrell winced.

"Cute," he muttered. "And clever too."

"And true." She took the cloth from his hand and carefully wiped the crease of her eyelid. He let her do that. He'd exhausted his girl makeup skills in the first sally. "But he's going to have to foot the bill this time. You can't dodge a paternity test, you feel me?"

Terrell knew his eyes bulged, and that probably wasn't attractive, but he couldn't seem to blink. What *was* it with girls and just *spilling* that shit? "I feel you, sweetheart. That's plenty real to feel!"

"Thanks, Terrell," she said briskly, like she was regretting saying too much. "I gotta go up. Chelsea's a real bitch if I'm not there to help clean up."

She hustled out of the stockroom and Terrell grabbed his cases of Sam Adams, thinking that maybe being a spineless weasel wasn't Will Templeton's worst failing.

FORTY-FIVE minutes later he was on the back dock, sweating in the humidity and the warm summer air and trying to work up some righteous wrath, because dammit if Colby wasn't late! Terrell had busted his hump to get shit clean, and then Suk just kicked him out to his break without so much as a by-your-leave! Terrell didn't even have a chance to see if Colby was ready too, and they didn't exactly have time to burn. Damned if that kid couldn't—

The door flew open before Terrell could start analyzing his justified anger as hurt, and Terrell's shoulders and neck relaxed as Colby bustled through the door.

"Make a brother wait!" Terrell snapped before he could stop himself, but Colby just raised his eyebrows and flashed that easy smile.

"Sorry, T. Some girl was all heartbroken in the stockroom. Dammit, I hate it when girls cry!"

Terrell was not appeased. "Well, Kelly already fell apart in there. She sucked up my time, she don't need to be hoovering yours!"

Colby frowned. "I wasn't talking to Kelly, I was talking to Erin!"

"Erin?" Erin was the head waitress—she was nearly six foot tall, blonde, blue-eyed, and as gorgeous as a supermodel. "Did Erin get knocked up by dodge-the-bill-Will too?"

"Too?" Colby's voice rose for a moment. "Who else did he knock up?"

They both stopped then, eyes wide in the June moonlight that partially illuminated their little corner of the back dock, and Terrell let out a breath.

"How much do we want to know about this, really?" he asked, remembering all of his survival skills from the hood days when a boy didn't want to know nothin' 'bout nothin'.

But Colby didn't grow up in the hood. "T, if he's harassing all these girls into sleeping with him, that's… that's…."

"Harassment?" Terrell asked dryly.

Colby shot him an annoyed look. "It's illegal," he said, his voice flat and strong and brooking no argument. "Someone needs to report him or something—"

Terrell grunted. "Baby boy, if they was gonna fuck him for the girls, they woulda fucked him for the drugs and the cash already!"

Colby drew himself up, cocking his head to the side and looking very concerned. "Drugs and cash?"

Terrell shrugged. "It's gossip, right? Like, just a hunch, so don't repeat it—"

"Dude, so far we've got two knocked-up girls, a corporate manager on the rampage—"

"What?"

Colby looked behind him. "Beth Mitchell went hauling ass through the restaurant right when we were locking the doors from the outside. I have no idea who she wanted to talk to, but she was *pissed*! Now spill about drugs and theft, 'cause that's a hell of a lot more interesting!"

Terrell shrugged uneasily, his long habit of saying nothing but jack still sitting heavy on his shoulders. But Colby was looking at him with big eyes, even in the moonlight, and a little bit of eagerness, and it was clear he wanted to hash this out. Terrell was uncomfortable with the lengths he'd go to find something that would make Colby want to stay and talk.

"His drawers don't come out right," Terrell said so softly that Colby bent his head close to hear. The boy's aftershave was washed with body sweat and restaurant smells, but Terrell could still detect it over the unpleasant odor of wet concrete and the trash compactor. It was warm and sharp and musky, and Terrell bit back on a shudder. "They come out wrong in even amounts," Terrell clarified. "Twenty, forty, sixty—easy amounts to, you know—"

"Buy a dime bag of something with," Colby said seriously.

"Listen to you, being all street!" Terrell mocked gently, and Colby looked abashed.

"Yeah, well, I watched TV as a kid," he said with a shy little grin.

"Yeah, so did I." Terrell smirked. "That's where all the white people were!"

Colby scoffed. "Man, I've been through your neighborhood—there's plenty of white people there!"

"Yeah, maybe so, but they were all poor racist motherfuckers who'd as soon drop boys like you for not being white enough!"

"You're so full of shit!" Colby crowed, and Terrell had to shake his head.

"Naw, white boy, I'm serious. And what you been doin' in my old neighborhood anyway?"

Colby shrugged, and in the quiet before he answered, Terrell felt the strain of the night on his bandy legs. He exercised, ate well, and drank as much soy milk as he could afford, but poor childhood nutrition did put a damper on the old bone structure. Before Colby answered him, Terrell moved back to the wall, right by the door. They kept pallets there with stacks of boxes and crates that the delivery trucks took back to reuse, and there was a two-and-a-half-foot space between the pallets and the wall. Terrell squeezed back in there so he could lean up against something not covered by trash or restaurant grease to take the strain off his legs. He made himself comfortable as Colby squeezed in too.

"So?" Terrell asked when they were situated, and Colby turned toward him in the private dark.

"I wanted to see where you came from," he said without shame. "You mentioned it a few times—you keep telling me I'm too white to survive there. I thought I'd see."

"Yeah?" Terrell was floored. "And what'd you see?"

Colby shrugged. "You've got nice eyes," he said, and Terrell blinked them, stunned a little. Colby laughed, and now it sounded self-conscious.

"I didn't mean that quite the way… I mean, you like people. You smile and your eyes smile back. I got out to get gas, and my car's not new, and I was wearing shitty jeans and a holey T-shirt, but not one person, black or white, looked at me the way you do."

Terrell tried really hard to keep his breathing in check. "Better be careful, white boy," he said softly. "You start talking about men's eyes and they'll think you're—"

"Queer?" Colby asked just as quiet. "Have you ever seen me with a girl, Terrell? 'Cause I haven't seen *you* with one, and I've been looking."

Terrell swallowed past an arid throat. "You're not gay," he rasped.

His voice was so soft he wasn't sure if Colby could even hear him, but he must have. He smiled a faint, luminous smile that made Terrell's stomach buzz so hard in excitement he thought his balls might fly out of his chest. "Tell that to my mother and my last three boyfriends," he said, tilting his chin up like he wasn't sure if Terrell would rebuff him for that information or not.

"People aren't gay in my neighborhood," Terrell said, thinking dimly that there had to be a better way to handle this moment. He should push the kid out of their little hidey-hole, shove at him, call him a fag, and tell him to go the fuck away. But this was *Colby*, and he was one of the better friends Terrell had known in his entire life. Besides, he was nothing less and nothing more than the thing, the person, Terrell had wanted even before Colby walked through the doors of Papiano's in his nice slacks and mandarin-collared shirt and asked for a job.

"We're not *in* your neighborhood, T," Colby said mockingly, lowering his head. Colby was a good six inches taller than T's five foot six, but he never seemed to loom or throw that height around. He was usually really good at hanging back and giving Terrell space, but not tonight.

"So?" Terrell muttered, shrinking back against the wall. Colby was close now, and with anyone else, it would be an uncomfortable distance. It was close enough for Terrell to tell that his chest was rising and lowering a little faster than usual, and to almost make out the color of his blue eyes in the darkness. It was close enough to see one of his front teeth had a tiny chip on it, and that he had one of those scars below his lower lip and above his chin, like people did when they got into car accidents or fell down and their teeth busted through.

"So," Colby said softly, "if you were going to be gay, you're in the right neighborhood, and you've got someone here you could be gay with."

Terrell managed a shrug, although he couldn't stop staring at that scar. It was straight with a dip at the end, and he wanted to touch it. And while he was brushing his fingertips over it, maybe he'd brush his thumb across Colby's plump pink lower lip and…. "Why would I even try with you?" he asked, hating the self-deprecation in his voice. "If, you know, I was going to be gay."

"Because I think you have nice eyes," Colby said with that faint smile, moving in a little closer. Colby was the one who had the guts to reach up and rub Terrell's full lower lip with his thumb.

Terrell closed his eyes then, because it was such a little touch, but he hadn't been touched in so long…. Oh God, his whole body tingled, and his balls really *were* going to fly out of his chest, and the surge of blood to his groin was painful, and….

He felt Colby's breath on his face first, and that rough touch of callused thumb on his lip grew stronger. "You can keep your eyes closed, T," Colby said quietly into the charged air between them, "but you'd better know it's me."

"No one else would want to—"

"Sh…."

Colby's lips were so soft, Terrell almost couldn't feel the first brush, and he opened his mouth and made a begging noise.

"More?" Colby asked, and Terrell leaned forward, because apparently he was too much of a coward even to reach for what was giving itself to him. "I'll take that as a yes."

This time Colby's mouth was harder, and he pushed Terrell back against the wall. Colby spanned his hand around Terrell's neck, his thumb firmly against Terrell's jaw, and his other hand was at Terrell's hip, pulling him closer. Their aprons and check-folders hung in the way, and a part of Terrell mourned, because he wanted to *feel,* but most of him was caught up in Colby's mouth over his and the taste of his tongue as it plundered. *He doesn't taste white,* Terrell thought randomly. *He tastes hot and red.* For a moment he was afraid Colby's tongue would get tangled in his braces, but Colby didn't seem fazed by them, and Terrell forgot himself in the feeling of a smoldering, slow kiss.

He was lost, lost and aroused, when suddenly Colby jerked back and clutched Terrell's shoulders painfully.

"Did you hear that?" he asked, pure startlement in his voice.

"Hear what?" And only in thinking about it did Terrell realize that he *had* heard the noise. It was, in fact, a noise he was familiar with from his neighborhood, when shit was going down and his Gi-Gi had him hide under his bed. He and Colby shared a surprised look for a moment, and the door to the back dock was suddenly thrown up open with a clatter, and the patter of footsteps—plain old footsteps, in some sort of sensible shoe—hurried through the dock. The steps didn't pause at the bolt-hole the two of them were tucked into, or even stop at the chaos Terrell could hear besieging the manager's office right by the door to the back dock. By the time Colby could maneuver himself around to even see who was running by, they were gone.

Colby and Terrell shared a look over Colby's shoulder, and the two of them nodded in tandem after a moment.

"I'll go out first," Colby said quietly. "You count to two hundred and follow me. They're freaking the fuck out in there, and maybe we can keep your secret until you're ready not to, okay?"

Terrell nodded, feeling the sudden, irrational urge to cry. It was practically his first kiss—his first *real* kiss—and Colby was protecting him like he'd always secretly yearned for, and he might never be kissed again.

A Hole in the Bucket

As TERRELL waited, the panicked chatter that had built around what *must* have been a gunshot was pierced by a shattering scream. That was his cue—he started scooting out of their little bolt-hole so he could go join the party. He'd just walked in the door when he heard Colby's voice, calm and rational, start thundering over the freaked-out wail that was about to amplify the chaos.

"Anna, get Trish to the girls' room and calm her the fuck down. Jason, you call 911. Tell them we need an ambulance and the cops, because a guy's been shot!"

There was more confusion, and then Colby's voice, calm and hard, again. "Erin, go get Beth—"

"But she's not here!"

"Yeah, she's here! I saw her before I went on break! We need someone to keep the last of the customers cool, because I'm not sure if the cops are going to want to talk to them or not!"

"Okay, okay—where do you suggest I look?"

Terrell came out then and said, "The customer ladies' room. She'll be there!" He hadn't told Colby, because, well, Colby had apparently had other things on his mind, but Beth liked to toot a little sweet herself. Clinically, he'd noticed that a *lot* of restaurant managers had a thing for coke or meth—it kept them up during the twelve-hour shifts and helped them be twuntweasels when they had to deal with the staff they were supposed to be supporting.

Colby looked up at him and raised his eyebrows. Terrell rolled his eyes in return, and Colby shrugged. The boy wasn't stupid—a little misguided, apparently, but not stupid.

It didn't matter. Erin disappeared, and Colby was left squatting over…

Oh Jesus.

"Is that really him?"

Terrell looked at the remains of their former GM and wrinkled his forehead. Yeah, he'd grown up in a shitty neighborhood, but he'd been a good kid. "I ain't never seen a dead body before," he said, lost in the wonder of complete revulsion. Templeton's face was, well, bloody and sort of mashed, and he had a big pulpy spot where his suit shirt buttoned.

Suddenly, Terrell's crime-scene classes up and whapped him backside of the head. "Was he lying like that when you got to him?" he asked, and Colby shook his head.

"No, I rolled him over to see if he was okay." Colby shuddered, and Terrell was reassured. He'd known Colby was special and strong, but that total confidence with which he'd taken over the entire crew had been daunting. It was good to see the dead body grossed him out too.

"Pussy."

Terrell glanced over his shoulder and scowled at Percy. "You got something better to do?"

Percy grimaced at him. "I'm on dish detail. Ain't *nothin'* that's not better than that!"

"Well, maybe you better get back to doing that before the cops get here and think you'd look damned good with more fuckin' jewelry, you feel me?"

Percy's eyes got big, and for the first time since Percy had been led into Papiano's by his parole officer, Terrell got the feeling the kid wasn't as tough as he liked to front. "I feel you," he muttered. "I ain't goin' back to juvie—man, I'll wash all the goddamned dishes you wanna give me!"

And with that, Percy disappeared to the dish stand, and Terrell counted it a blessing. He might be a fool, but Terrell was pretty sure he was an innocent fool—at least of this. There were too many other people who'd wanted this guy dead.

All that remained in the manager's office was a bunch of other onlookers—but looking around, he realized some very important onlookers weren't there.

"Where's Kelly?" he asked the air in general. "And Suk?"

"I don't know," said a tiny blonde waitress in front of him. She turned around and looked up and smiled winsomely. "They've missed all the excitement!"

"This doesn't bother you at all, does it, Angie?"

The little one shook her head. "Nope. I'm in premed. And he was a really horrible person. If he grabbed my ass one more time, I was going to scalpel his hand off at the elbow." She smiled perkily up at Terrell and then said, "Excuse me, T. I'm going to go finish filling my condiments."

She disappeared, leaving Terrell and Colby alone in the office to exchange horrified looks.

"That woman makes me glad I don't sleep with the species," Colby muttered, and Terrell shushed him.

"What you gotta say a thing like that here for!" he muttered, looking behind him suspiciously. "Jesus, go and spread that around!"

Colby didn't even bat an eyelash. "Terrell, I know you think you're some sort of personnel god with that whole bartender thing going on, but the only one who didn't know, apparently, was you."

At that moment there was a bustle and a voice muffled by static and the cold presence of blue polyester and suspicious looks, and, holy shit and fuck me sideways, the police had arrived!

The first person they freaked out about was Colby, who stood up and offered to take a test for gunshot residue, and told everybody the same story that he and T had been leading with for nearly a year. They'd been taking a break, and they'd heard the shot and then the commotion, and Colby had come in to see if it was really that big a deal. Terrell had (of course, right?) followed when he realized that it really *was* a big deal and not something they could blow off for the remainder of their break.

Now, you'd think that after that information, they'd leave Terrell and Colby the fuck alone. Especially with the entire waitstaff there to back them up. *Especially* after Erin arrived with the short, busty, and very *stoned*-looking district manager, whom she'd managed to drag away from the bathroom and who was tottering on fuck-me spikes and trying to speak coherently when she must have inhaled half a bowl of blow in one snort, judging by her glassy stare and mile-a-minute chatter.

But no. Beth got to talk to the two detectives, both of them in nice wool-polyester blend suits, in the steaming back of the restaurant, and two flatfoots seemed to be willing to stick their nose into T's and Colby's crotches just to make sure nothing "queer" had been going on in the hallowed back dock of Papiano's.

Or at least that's what *Terrell* was hearing. Colby didn't seem to hear any of that shit.

"So," the older boy in blue was asking, "you two were taking your break. You always do that together?"

"Yeah, so the fuck what!" Terrell felt his eyes narrow. God, he hated cops.

Colby rolled his eyes at the guy—God, he was old. What? Forty? Fifty? Didn't you get to move up to a cheap suit by then? But Colby didn't see that they'd gotten saddled with the shit detail. He just grinned at the nice cop and shrugged. "Yeah—habit, you know? T and I just like bullshitting. We sit out for ten before we close."

Old Cop nodded his head and eyed Terrell with distaste. "I'll bet this guy could bullshit until the sky turns black, am I right?"

And suddenly Colby's play-the-game face got hard. "He's got a degree in journalism and I got mine in sociology—we talk about all sorts of things you might not understand."

The cop's jaw worked, and he scowled at Colby with heat. "Yeah? You want to know what I don't understand? I don't understand how someone could have shot this guy and gotten away without running right past where you and your... *partner* were standing, *that's* what I don't understand!"

Terrell surged at him, and Colby must have seen the move coming. He turned into Terrell's body, blocking him, holding his shoulders while Terrell snarled, "We ain't no fuckin' faggots, asshole! You take that fuckin' back!"

The cop smirked and held up his hands. "Hey, *you* used the word, *I* didn't! I just want to know how you could have missed—"

"You want to see where we were?" Colby snapped over his shoulder. "Come here—I'll show you."

Terrell backed off, but not before he had the impression of Colby's hard body pressed against his, and he wanted to hit something. *Great, Terrell. You talk a big game, but you and Colby both know the truth.*

The cop followed Colby, smirking as he went, but when he saw the space between the pallets and the wall, he frowned.

"What were you doing back here?" he asked, searching the ground thoroughly.

"T's back was hurting him," Colby said baldly, apparently oblivious to Terrell's glare. "He needed to lean against the wall—it's the only clean place you can lean."

The cop poked his head in and then tried to slide in himself—he was stopped by his stomach and the lack of space in general, and he pulled out and turned around to glare at the two of them.

"So you two were just tucked back in here... *talking,* is that right?"

Colby met his gaze levelly, and Terrell swallowed as the urge to punch the guy fought with the urge to vomit.

"Yes, Officer. Terrell and I were back there, talking. He said something, I turned to reply, and while I was doing that, there was a big sound and then some footsteps. By the time I could turn my body back to look, the footsteps were gone and people were starting to freak out, so I came to see what was up. Did I miss anything important? We didn't see the person running away. We don't even know for sure if that was the shooter!"

The cop scowled. "Okay. Let's go through the time line one more time."

Colby let out a sigh Terrell could feel in his bones, and Terrell gave it up and thunked his head quietly against the wall. God, could this night suck any worse?

IT WAS interminable. The cops went over and over the details, weeding out people who hadn't really seen anything (so they said) from people who really *had* seen something (so they thought) and everyone in between. Terrell and Colby were two of the last to go, and Terrell was surprised when, as he was shifting from foot to foot to try to ease the pain in his back and legs, Colby disappeared for a moment and came back with the wooden chair they kept for breaks. He slid it under Terrell's ass and then went back to his place in the jerk circle to answer the same frickin' question for the umpteen millionth time.

It all faded into babble, and Terrell found himself nodding off more than once. He'd been waking up early to work on his stupid little project, and it was getting past three in the morning. In another two hours he would have been up for twenty-four, and there was nothing going on to keep his attention except Colby, standing up and looking commanding and interested in anything that was said.

Finally, the police took a hike, and Terrell was left dozing with his head against the wall as everyone else faded away.

He was awakened by a hand on his shoulder and a "C'mon, T— let's go!"

He startled, limbs flailing, and caught someone square in the stomach. He looked up after finding his feet on the ground, his ass finally *off* that uncomfortable chair, and one of his hands up against the wall. Colby was doubled up in front of him, catching his breath, after what had apparently been a solid blow.

"Oh fuck," he muttered. "I'm sorry. God, how long was I out?"

Colby straightened, rubbing his stomach ruefully. "Long enough for me to do your closeout duties—"

"But I need to cash out and count my drawers!"

"I know you do—that's why I woke you up. Now yawn and stretch, Sleeping Beauty. I want to go home!"

Terrell grimaced. "I ain't stoppin' ya!"

Colby just rolled his eyes and shooed Terrell back behind the bar. Normally, this sort of thing happened in the manager's office by the back dock, but, well, yeah. That entire section of the restaurant was covered with police tape, including the hallway from the kitchen and the front of the dish stand. Percy had been part of the questioning (not that he'd been helpful in the least), so the dishes stood, roped off by yellow tape, growing rank and sticky, as the employees who had been there during the shooting tried to clean up and close down.

Terrell had to stand next to Beth Mitchell and count out the drawer, and he reflected grimly that it was a good thing he was an honest man, because she must have zoned out of the stratosphere at least twenty times between counting the cash and adding up the receipts. He finished up, wrote up the cash receipt for the take, and cashed out the tips for him and Suk, then shoved the receipt under Beth's hand for her to sign.

She woke up a little then, her hard brown eyes staring and glassy. "Any problems?" she slurred, and Terrell shook his head.

"Besides the dead guy in the manager's office? No. Is someone from corporate coming to deal with this mess?"

Beth nodded, looking as coherent as Terrell had seen her. "Yeah. Robin Davis is going to be here around seven. She gave me the number of a crime scene cleanup—they'll be here as soon as the CSI team is gone, and we may be able to open up tomorrow after all."

Terrell grimaced. "Really? That seems kind of wrong, doesn't it?"

Beth shrugged. "Yeah. Well. People gotta eat."

"Well, I got night shift tomorrow night. You make sure to call folks on the schedule one way or another." It was fruitless, and he knew it, because he wasn't even sure if the woman had tracked what he just said.

"Yeah. Okay," she murmured, her attention wandering to the figures he'd given her.

Terrell shook his head and trundled off, thinking that maybe, if there was a dead guy involved, people could damned well eat in their own damned houses at their own damned tables. That was one of the things he never really got about management. That shit made total sense to Beth and would have made total sense to Will Templeton—if he'd been alive. But Terrell actually thought people were more important than keeping the place open, and if Colby hadn't been scheduled the next day, he very well might have quit, just to make that opinion known.

He stumped down the stairs, feeling the night in the core of his bandy-legged bones, and blinked, bemused, when he saw Colby sitting at the table closest the door, playing with his phone.

Colby looked up and smiled softly, his expression relaxed, and well, hell. Terrell swallowed.

Tender. Colby looked tender. Terrell had seen that look on other people's faces, but never, ever leveled at himself. Not by another man. Certainly not by anyone who had just kissed him.

"Hey, T," Colby said softly, standing up. "You ready to go?"

Terrell scowled and Colby quirked up his lips. "Where're *we* going?" he asked skeptically.

"My place," Colby said, pitching his voice low. No one else could hear him, Terrell trusted that—the only people there now were the regular cleaning crew. Papiano's hired an entire tiny family of tiny people to clean up at night. Terrell wasn't in the mood to study them to see if they were as rattled as he knew *he* was, but he was relatively safe from their curiosity.

"Your place?" Terrell asked when they'd cleared the foyer and stepped out onto the walkway toward the parking lot. The night had cooled off considerably in the last few hours, and he could feel the melancholy summer predawn chilling his skin. "Don't you live with your sister?"

"We rent a house together, yes," Colby said, humor in his voice. "We get along, she makes lots of money, and we both have a pact not to make a lot of noise during sex. It works for us."

"Well, I'm real glad it works for you, white boy, but why do you think it works for me?"

Colby bumped Terrell with his shoulder as they walked, and Terrell found he wasn't heading for his own car, which he'd parked directly in the back so he didn't have to walk all the way across the darkened parking lot when the bar closed. Instead, he was heading to where the waiters parked, along the back fence, under the broken light.

"I have a hot tub, T," Colby said, his voice low and not even that suggestive. "My house, a couple of painkillers, the tub, and you might be able to walk tomorrow."

Terrell grimaced. He knew his bowed legs weren't pretty, and he could live with that. It was the back and leg pain that he didn't admit to anyone in the world, except maybe Colby, who always seemed to be there at the end of his shift, when he was propping himself up against a wall in the hopes that counter-pressure would ease the ache.

The thought of his little tiny apartment, with the window that looked at the wall of another little tiny apartment, and the ergonomic chair with that recriminating, never-ending project accusing him of doing shitty, useless work—well, it depressed him. It sank in his stomach the way not even the dead man had, or the sudden exposure of his colleagues' lives to the glaring vivisection of a murder investigation.

Colby opened the passenger door to his little Toyota without fanfare, and Terrell found himself being driven to a part of town he'd never been in, even though it was barely two miles away from where he worked.

"WHAT does your sister *do?*" he asked, sinking into the heated, *scented* water of the hot tub on the back porch. Colby and his sister, Moira (white people names, he thought with a wince; you could spot 'em on a roster a mile away), lived down Arden, maybe a half a mile from the river. The houses were small and around fifty years old, but they were nice—well maintained, with backyards like this one, with the big overhanging oak tree and the deck, complete with the hot tub that was currently making Terrell a very happy man. The whole back of the house opened up into the back porch too, from their own sliding glass doors. Step out of your bedroom and into the hot tub. *Sweet.*

"Well," Colby laughed a little from across the porch, "mostly she makes my life miserable by prying, but in her spare time, she's a lawyer who works for a judge downtown. She's overworked, underpaid, and currently making Mom and Dad so proud they'd have another son and offer him to the god of gay, just to say thank you."

Terrell grunted. "The god of gay? You got a line on him?"

Colby finished what he was doing—rummaging in what appeared to be a small refrigerator installed especially for things people might like to drink in a hot tub—and stood up with two very pricey bottles of microbrew beer. He grabbed a bottle opener from a little counter next to the fridge and popped open the tops of the beers, then walked to the side of the tub and handed Terrell one.

"A line on the god of gay?" he asked, taking a sip of his own beer and sliding out of the flip-flops he'd put on in the entryway of the house. "Nope. As far as I know, he issued a bolt of lightning to my mother's womb, and out I popped. Why?"

Terrell grunted and sank further into the scented water Colby had prepped for him after he'd put on the flip-flops and before he'd done anything else.

"'Cause I'd like to ask him to keep his goddamned lightning the fuck out of my neighborhood, that's why! It's not a picnic being black, it *sucks* growing up with the rickets, but the gay on top of it? That fucker had better have someone to pay!"

Colby made a sound—neither assent or dissent—and hopped down with his ass on the deck and his legs dangling into the water. "That sucks," he said frankly. "And I'm sorry."

Terrell looked at him without turning his head. He'd followed Colby into his room—which was a decent place, really, with framed prints on the wall and a dresser and a computer desk and all—while Colby had rooted around and come back with two swimsuits. They'd changed under the yellow glare of Colby's overhead light, and Terrell hadn't looked left or right as he'd slid on his plain red board shorts.

Now, though—well, Colby was wearing blue-and-white Hawaiian shorts, and even in the moonlight, Terrell could tell he was tan from time spent out at the river and the lake. His body was muscular without being bulky, and he had a flat and tight six-pack abdomen and bulges in the right places on his biceps. His hair was a little greasy—everyone's was after a shift in a restaurant—and he smelled like the back reaches of Papiano's, even over the floral smell of the water—but his easy smile glinted, and his long jaw and square chin looked powerful and all-knowing in the semidarkness.

"Yeah, well," Terrell said into the sudden silence. "It doesn't always suck."

Colby met his eyes and grinned. He set his beer on the deck and slid all the way into the tub, submerging completely in the hot water and staying there, scrubbing at his hair with his fingers, until Terrell's lungs burst just from watching him. He came out, gasping and flipping his hair out of his face with a little whoop, and Terrell was so irritated he splashed water at him.

"That was a piss stupid thing to do," he snapped, thinking he'd been about two seconds from reaching in and grabbing the dumbass by his hair and hauling him up for his own good.

Colby's grin was undiminished. "Worried about me, T? I was just scrubbing away some of Papi's. You know—"

"That stench? Yeah. God, first thing I do every night is hit the showers. I don't care how late it is—"

"You just can't sleep with the smell on your skin." Colby nodded. "Yeah. Me too. I know the water smells girly—"

"It's great!" Terrell said, embarrassingly enthusiastic. "It's not girly at all, really. It's just… you know—"

"Not Papi's and not chlorine?"

"Christ, yes!" Terrell relaxed further into the bubbles and took another sip of his beer. "Does she really make you pay rent?" he asked, and Colby laughed.

"Yeah. I was living in a crappy student apartment off of Howe when she got the job and went looking for the house. She told me she'd charge me the same rent I was paying on the student apartment, but this way, she could have someone water her plants and watch her cat when her hours got long."

"She's got a cat?" Terrell asked, and then wished he hadn't, because he sounded a little plaintive.

But Colby didn't seem to notice. "Two of them," he said, affection clear in his voice. "A calico with a delicate nature named Puddin' and a big honking gray tortoiseshell named Dewey Folds."

Terrell frowned. Puddin'? Dewey Folds? He wrinkled his nose and looked at Colby, almost furious that the boy hadn't told him this little tidbit before. "You mean your sister got two cats and she named both of them—?"

Colby's grin was diabolical. "Pussy? Yeah. 'Cause seriously, that's the only name they come to anyway."

Terrell couldn't help it. He laughed long and low and hard, tilting his head back against the edge of the tub and just letting the sound roll out. "Damn, Colby, I cannot be-*lieve* you didn't tell me that one before!"

Colby shrugged and then looked away, his grin softening for a moment. "Yeah, well, I didn't want to bring up girl parts until I was sure."

Terrell took another sip of his beer and then wondered if this conversation was inevitable. Was this where they'd been leading up to on the back docks, dead body or no dead body? "Sure?"

Colby looked at him sideways. "I've been dying to kiss you, T. I had to be sure, one way or the other, about whether you'd kiss me back."

Terrell tilted back his beer and swallowed the last bit, finally realizing that he'd practically guzzled the entire microbrew without tasting it, and that was a damned shame. He kept the bottle in his hand to give him something to do, and felt his sore muscles, bones, and sinews settle into the comfort of the water that even washed the smell away.

"What made you sure?" he asked after a moment, and Colby examined the blank face of the water.

"You got your teeth fixed," he said softly, and Terrell felt an absurd spike of disappointment.

"So now that I'm not gonna have a mouthful of—"

He didn't realize how close they were sitting until Colby leaned over and bumped him with his shoulder. "Naw, you've got it wrong."

"Explain it to me." He sat perfectly still, wanting that shoulder touch again but not wanting to beg for it.

There was quiet, and Colby set his beer on the deck and then turned back around. He kept his head tilted back and his eyes on the oak trees silhouetted against the almost intrusively bright June moon.

He moved his hand slowly under the water until it was on Terrell's knee.

"I told you I liked your smile about two months ago," he said quietly, rubbing gentle circles on Terrell's outer thigh with his thumb. "I was half expecting you to call me a fag and tell me to stay away, or to make a joke, or to make it perfectly clear that you only wanted girls. But you didn't. You just... every time you smiled after that, you put your hand in front of your mouth—at least in front of me."

Terrell didn't have words for what he wanted to say. But he spread his knees a little more, and Colby moved his hand up a little, curling his fingers until they brushed his inseam.

"It's a mouthful of crooked teeth," he said, compelled by that stroking hand.

"Yeah. And then, on your day off, you went to go fix them." Colby squeezed his thigh, and Terrell sank a little more, his legs spreading as he went.

"I...." *Oh God.* Colby lowered his hand and then snuck it up the leg of the shorts, his entire palm skating Terrell's inner thigh.

"What?" Colby had moved a little closer, and when he asked the question, his lips grazed Terrell's ear, and Terrell's cock, which was a little uncertain with the water and the house he didn't know and the way his friend was making a move on him when Terrell had planned to keep the entire "wants to fuck men" thing under his hat until he died, was starting to perk up and be interested.

"I wanted it to be a good smile," Terrell confessed, his voice about two octaves higher than normal. "If you were gonna see it, it couldn't just be—"

"Just be what? Just be *your* teeth?"

Terrell heard the recrimination and couldn't answer it. "The orthodontist said they woulda had to go anyway," he muttered defensively, and Colby moved his hand from Terrell's thigh and reached for his beer.

"Yeah," he said noncommittally. "It could get crowded in there."

Terrell wished rather pitifully for more beer.

"You can't be gay in my neighborhood," he burst out after a strained silence. "You can't. So I'm not."

Colby turned and looked at him, very earnestly and without any sort of pretense at all, which blew Terrell's mind. "If you're not gay, who do you kiss?"

Terrell looked away, still toying with the beer bottle between his palms. When Colby reached around his shoulder and, very carefully, pulled the bottle out of his grasp and set it on the deck, Terrell laced his fingers together and clenched his hands, because he didn't have anything else to do with them.

"Nobody," he said hoarsely. "Nobody."

Colby's lips on his shoulder coursed a shiver down his whole body. "You don't live in your old neighborhood anymore," he said before adding a little tongue to the caress.

"It's where I came fr—"

"You're certainly not there now." And he kissed the side of Terrell's neck.

Terrell tried to think of all the reasons this was a bad idea, and ended up with a blank brain while his body went and tilted his head sideways for better access.

"I fuck dirty," he warned, because that was the only way he'd ever *had* sex, and Colby's rough chuckle in his ear reassured him for a moment, because it was dirty too.

Then Colby licked the edge of his ear, just to tease, before saying, "I fuck sweet." He teased the delicate whorl, and while Terrell was still trying to control the shudders that just the boy's voice in his ear caused, he added, "And I top."

Terrell tried to tense up, but Colby had turned sideways, and Terrell had too, without meaning to, and Colby put his hands around Terrell's biceps while he was trailing kisses and nips down the back of Terrell's neck to the other side.

"You got a problem with that?" Colby asked in his other ear, and Terrell couldn't put any heat into his words.

"I'm not a fag," he murmured, but Colby ignored him, sliding his hands from Terrell's biceps to his chest and smoothing his palms across it.

Terrell moaned, which was a big deal, because he wasn't used to making sounds during sex, and Colby scooted closer behind him. Terrell could feel Colby's chest against his shoulders, and he wondered fleetingly what it would be like to have all that skin pressed up along his, naked.

"Nope," Colby whispered in his ear, and Terrell's cock pulsed, engorged, just from the timbre of his voice. "No fags here. Just two guys, sharing beers after work."

Oh good—a lie. A good one. One Terrell could tell himself out loud while he remembered—*oh God.* Colby's hand had slid to his stomach and, wickedly, under the waistband of his shorts.

"Not a beer!" Terrell gasped as Colby's hand closed around him. He grunted and pushed up into that fist while Colby continued to kiss and nibble all of those sensitive places he couldn't reach.

"We'll pretend," Colby murmured, tightening his grip and stroking some more.

Terrell grunted, his whole body tingling, but he didn't think he could come, not here in the hot tub. But the pressure in his cock, in his ultrarelaxed body, was rising, and something loosened in his chest and then broke, and suddenly he was shivering in his need to be touched all over, and his hips bucked without rhythm or rhyme because he needed that grip on his cock to be hard to the point of pain.

Colby let go and put both hands on his shoulders, murmuring shushing noises into his ears. "Here, T. Stand up. Let's get the come thing out of the way and we can do this right."

Numbly, Terrell did what he said, standing up and allowing himself to be turned around. The night air was chilly, but the water up to his thighs kept him from freezing—all the cold did was make his nipples stand up, sharp and proud, when the breeze hit them. Colby pulled his shorts down with easy confidence, and when Terrell's cock flopped out, bobbing a little, he smiled up into Terrell's face and then stuck out his tongue and licked the circumcised head.

The combination of Colby's tongue and the cooling air was lethal on Terrell's tingling body, and he threw back his head and closed his eyes. Colby opened his mouth and pushed forward, engulfing Terrell's cock in heat and wet. He pulled back and balanced Terrell's cock on the flat of his tongue, letting the chill hit the sensitive skin, and Terrell found his hands clenching and unclenching at his sides. He needed to grab something, to hold it to—

Colby grabbed his hands and put them on his own shoulders before leaning forward a little and wrapping his own hands around Terrell's thighs. "Here. Lean on me."

Terrell found his weight coming down on Colby's wide shoulders, and he felt… shored up, supported, contained, when Colby opened his mouth and took Terrell down into his hot mouth again.

Oh God! What was this boy doing to him? His head bobbed and the friction increased as Colby tightened his lips and swallowed

Terrell's erection in the back of his throat. Oh, Jesus, he knew what he was doing, even if Terrell didn't.

Terrell tightened his fingers on Colby's shoulders, and his thigh muscles shook under Colby's hands. Then Colby fumbled a little, managed a stroking rhythm along Terrell's taint, under his balls, and Terrell's head pitched forward as he tried to hang on to any part of himself. There was a fondle and a squeeze of his testicles, which caused him to buck against Colby's mouth, and then that touch moved backward just a couple of inches and teased Terrell's entrance.

"Nunnghhh...." Terrell lunged forward into Colby's mouth, both startled and aroused to the point of pain. Colby chuckled, the vibrations from his throat making *that* situation worse, and moved both hands up to spread Terrell's ass cheeks, exposing him to the chill night air and making him ever so vulnerable to just... the slightest...

Touch.

Colby's finger brushed his entrance, slid in to the point of constriction, and Terrell gasped and tangled one hand into his curling hair and, without warning, came.

Colby must have known, because he pulled away and moved his head to the side before Terrell's body convulsed. After that moment, that still moment of trembling that Terrell hadn't ever experienced with another human being, he opened his eyes and looked down to see Colby blinking and clearing his face from a white glaze of come.

Terrell was having trouble with his breathing, but after another minute of getting his chest under control, he reached to the side of the deck for one of the towels Colby had brought with them. He offered it to Colby silently, and Colby nodded thanks before wiping off, getting the corner wet so he could get the stuff near his eyes, especially. Terrell stood for a moment, feeling dumb, and then Colby smiled at him again.

"Well, back up and let me out, T. Do you think we're done?"

WHEN Terrell was twelve years old, he almost got raped in the boys' room of his middle school.

It started when he was gazing off into space, thinking sweet thoughts about Will Smith and wondering if a rich black family in Bel Air would ever adopt *him*, when Cameron Wilkins walked in front of him. Terrell had pulled himself out of his reverie enough to smile, because him and Cameron, they hung out at lunch and talked video games—they were cool.

But Amos Coolidge must have been watching Terrell, because suddenly he set up a whoop and a holler and a "Oooheeee! Lookit you, Terrell—you is sweet on that boy!"

Terrell wasn't stupid. In middle school the lines had been drawn—there were color lines, but everybody could see them, and the teachers made you work with the browns and the yellows and the pinks. Couldn't do nothin' about that, so Terrell didn't sweat it. But the one line you could not cross was the line that made you a fag.

"Don't be stupid," he snapped, thinking that Amos was already nearly six feet tall at the age of fourteen and that he'd flunked eighth grade twice. Terrell was who he'd always been: small for his age, slow because of the bandy legs, and quicker with his mouth than with his hands. "If I was gonna crush, everyone knows I'd do it on you!"

The class laughed and made cracks about Amos for the rest of the day, but Terrell knew better than to celebrate. He'd poked a rattler in its hole, and one way or another, Terrell was gonna get bit.

He'd seen Amos's crew in detention at the beginning of lunch and made the tactical error of thinking it was safe to go to the bathroom. He'd never been in detention. He didn't know you could get a bathroom pass out of there, same as any other fuckin' class.

Amos was waiting for him as he came out of the stall, and shoved him up against the dirty wall between the two urinals.

"You think I'm a faggot?" he snarled. "You think I'm a faggot? How you like it if I fuck you up the ass?"

It was hard to talk because his mouth was shoved sideways, but his mouth had always been his best hope. "You fuck me up the ass, Amos, what's that make you?"

He couldn't remember what Amos said after that. He woke up in the urine on the bathroom floor with a concussion and a teacher anxiously shaking his shoulder. When the whole story came out, Amos had gotten three days of suspension, and Terrell had been cautioned strongly against looking at guys like that.

Cameron Wilkins hadn't talked to him for the rest of the year.

So now Terrell was looking into Colby's face, with shaking hands and breath that *still* hadn't caught up in his chest, and he was thinking that Colby was offering to do what Amos had threatened way the hell back in the eighth grade.

Colby looked nothing like Amos. Besides the fact that Colby was lot paler than Amos, with blue eyes and dark-blond hair, Amos's face had been broad and wide, and his jaw had been squat, just like his nose. And his black eyes had been rattlesnake mean. Colby was meeting Terrell's gaze with a resolution to his long jaw and compassion in his eyes.

And a vulnerable quiver to his full mouth.

Terrell did the brave thing this time and cupped his jaw, rubbing a pink thumb pad over that dark-pink lower lip. "I can't see us when we do it," he whispered, closing his eyes against his own cowardice. "It's secret."

He opened his eyes to see Colby nodding seriously, and the thing Terrell loved about him was that he understood without questions or psychoanalyzing things or going all white on Terrell's black ass. "It's secret," he said soberly. "I won't tell a soul."

Terrell nodded and took a step back. Colby stood, and they clambered out of the hot tub and wrapped up in the towels to ward off the chill. Colby stopped to turn off the tub and throw on the cover, and Terrell followed him back through the sliding glass door to his room.

Colby left the light off when they walked in, but he also left the drapes open so that the light from the deck and the full moon lit up the room with secret shadows and quiet lambent glows.

Terrell walked in and eyed the bed suspiciously. "You know, I don't have any idea how to—"

Colby was right behind him, and without warning, he whirled Terrell into his arms. Colby's mouth was hot and wet over his, and Terrell gave himself up for a moment, closed his eyes, and let Colby take over.

The boy did know how to kiss.

While Colby's mouth was moving, invading, plundering, his hands were busy too, stripping Terrell's trunks off and then his own. Terrell made a noise then and said, "You gotta hamper?" and Colby kissed him again, murmuring, "We'll do laundry tomorrow."

For a moment Terrell was caught up in practicalities and how he'd be able to wash his uniform and maybe borrow some of Colby's sweats and—

"Ahh...."

Colby had dropped his head to suckle one of Terrell's nipples into his mouth, and, oh God! Colby moved to the other side and pushed backward until Terrell was lying on the bed, naked, with Colby covering his body with kisses.

For the first time, Terrell realized how passive he was being. He put his hands on Colby's shoulders and stroked, but he was mesmerized by the picture of the black backs of his fingers contrasted with Colby's tanned white skin. It didn't belong, he thought, almost panicked.

"You shouldn't be doing this," he muttered as Colby made his way down again. He shoved Terrell's thighs up, exposing Terrell to the air and the world at large, then peered up over Terrell's short body.

"Shouldn't be doing what?" he asked, wholly practical. "Does something not feel good?"

Terrell reached down and massaged his fingers through Colby's hair. "You're a good boy," he rasped, trying for words. He was a journalism major. He could speak white when he wanted. Colby just never made him feel like he had to. "You're a good boy, and I'm—"

"You're a good boy too," Colby said wolfishly before delicately taking one of Terrell's balls into his mouth.

Terrell moaned and arched his back until Colby put the flat of his hand on Terrell's stomach. "Don't do that. It'll hurt later," he cautioned and then parted Terrell's ass cheeks and dug in with his tongue.

"*Oh my God!*" Terrell had *never* felt anything like that. It was slow and dreamy and *amazing,* and he was untethered, ungrounded, flailing with his hands onto the fine white sheets underneath. Colby brought one hand up, caught at Terrell's, and laced their fingers together, and Terrell managed to put the other hand on the back of his head again to clench his fingers in Colby's dark-blond hair.

Unbelievably, Terrell's erection returned, and every time he jerked his body in arousal, it flopped on his stomach. He found he was gibbering, wanting to reach for it, to stroke it, but not wanting to let go of Colby, not even to touch himself, for fear he'd never touch ground again.

Colby came up for air smiling and then slid up over Terrell, his body lean and fit, covering Terrell's with ease.

"You're so tight," Terrell muttered, liking the feel of Colby's biceps, his triceps, his lats and deltoids under Terrell's wandering hands.

Colby grinned and wiped his glazed face on his shoulder before kissing Terrell without shame, and Terrell had to take that kiss, because it was Terrell on the boy's mouth and nothing worse.

But all it tasted like to Terrell was Colby, and he started to think about it as the best taste in the world.

He was drugged by that taste, hazy with kissing, and he missed the presence of Colby's body over his own acutely.

"Where you going?"

"Being safe," Colby said, reaching across Terrell's body to the end table. He pulled out a tube of lubricant and some condoms, and Terrell tried to wrap his head around that.

"You're not...," he said, pulling back, frowning.

Colby shook his head and rolled over to sheathe up. For a moment, Terrell felt robbed—he should have explored that before it was covered. He wanted to touch it, to—ohmygod, it wasn't cut! He wanted to play with that and taste it, if they were going to do this one night, pretend it didn't happen, and continue on their way!

"Not according to my last test," he murmured. "Habit, Terrell. I'm not asking questions about your past yet, so we need this." He turned his head then and kissed Terrell soundly before rolling back on top of him.

Yet? God. How was Terrell supposed to own up to that past? Back alleys, privacy booths, sucking strangers off under stairwells?

Terrell blessed the condom, thought wretchedly about taking his own test, and then reached down to spread his cheeks and make it easier for Colby to shove himself inside Terrell's body. He hadn't done it much, but he remembered the red taste of pain.

The pain never happened.

Colby's fingers came first, and they were so soft, so slick with lube, that it was almost like they weren't there at all. His cock came next (oh *Lord* it was there—the boy was huge!), but Colby didn't shove. For a moment, it was like he wasn't moving at all. The head of his cock just sat at Terrell's sphincter, nudging, nudging, until Terrell's entrance relaxed and relaxed and relaxed and stretched and…

Simply let him in.

Terrell gasped, his eyes flying open, and realized Colby was right there, right on top of him, looking at him, his jaw clenched tight with control. This wasn't pretending, he thought wretchedly before he had to close his eyes against Colby's intensity. This was real. He was lying naked in bed with Colby, and his body was being… slowly, ever so slowly, invaded by Colby's. The first gentle thrust went on forever, and when Colby was fully sheathed, he buried his face into Terrell's neck and groaned.

"We good, T?" he asked, and Terrell stroked his hair and closed his eyes.

"Yeah," he whispered. "You can move, baby. Move."

Colby did, and it was nothing but gentle, so gentle, and for a moment, Terrell wanted dirtiness and pain. He didn't know what to do with gentle. It made his hands shake and stars swim behind his eyes and it made the pleasure, the slow, excruciating pleasure in his ass, at his groin, so much bigger than he ever thought possible.

Colby pulled up and kissed him again, and again, and his thrusts inside Terrell grew stronger and harder, and it was better than fast and dirty and so much better than pain. Terrell couldn't help it—he kneaded Colby's chest with his hands, cupped his cheek, his jaw, the side of his neck, wrapped his ankles over Colby's thighs and drove him faster, *oh God, faster, please, Colby, please, faster, faster, I'm going to explode and I want you with me, I ain't never done this with someone with me, I ain't ever done this any way but alone!*

Colby pushed himself up until he was kneeling and grabbed Terrell's hips tight so he could slam into him harder. Terrell reached for his prick, stopped, and was rewarded by Colby's hand on his, guiding him home.

"C'mon, T, help a guy out!" he panted, and Terrell opened his eyes enough to see Colby, in the selfish part of sex now, his head tilted back, his eyes closed, his hips pistoning without thought.

He was beautiful, Terrell thought, his heart in his throat. So beautiful. His own hand hardly needed to squeeze his cock before he closed his eyes vise-tight and exploded.

Colby groaned—in fact he *growled*—and fell forward, his hips still locked in that after-come spasm that had always made Terrell feel helpless and frightened.

Not Colby—no, not T's boy. He groaned and buried his face in Terrell's shoulder and shivered and climaxed and came and came and came. He was still shuddering when he pulled back a little and beamed into Terrell's eyes.

"Good?" he asked, kissing the sweat from Terrell's jaw and his temple.

"Good," Terrell confirmed, but it sounded like a lie. It was disastrous, catastrophic, and annihilating. God, oh God, he wanted so badly to do it again!

Silent, Still, and Warm

THERE was the inevitable cleanup—getting rid of the condom and wiping up Terrell's come, and the sweat too, in spite of the fact that the room was air-conditioned. Terrell stood up gingerly, unsure of how his insides felt after that, because it was as thoroughly as he'd *ever* been reamed, and in spite of his education, he still had fears of finding his internals had become externals because he'd been doing something bad.

But he was fine—well used, well stretched, and a little achy, but fine.

When Colby threw a pair of striped knit boxers at him, Terrell caught them one-handed and put them on. "God, white boy, even your underwear is high-end!" He'd never worn anything with Andrew Christian around the waistband. He wasn't even sure if Wal-Mart *sold* high-end drawers.

Colby looked over his shoulder, his expression inscrutable. "Yeah," he said. "Spoiled and white, that's me." He pulled on his own underwear and then disappeared outside for a moment. The deck light went off, and the sliding glass door opened and the screen shut, letting in the breeze.

"Crawl in," Colby said as he crossed the carpet toward the hall. "I'm going to turn the AC off since it got so nice outside."

Terrell lay down in the bed, pulled the sheet up around his hips, and turned on his side. He ached, both from the long night at work and from the thing he and Colby had just done, but the sheets were relatively clean, and he felt absurdly afraid of asking for anything more from the night.

He didn't have to ask.

Colby came back with a couple more ibuprofen for his legs and back, and a heating pad. Terrell looked at him mutely as he stood over the bed in his underwear and shooed Terrell toward the middle of the bed.

"Scoot. Here, sit up and take these."

Terrell complied, then rolled over like Colby told him to and was immediately greeted by the heating pad, right... *there* on the small of his back where everything in his nervous system went to hell. Terrell moaned and murmured, "Kid, you are *spoiling* me. Thank you."

Colby made a little purring sound and then straddled his ass and started rubbing his shoulders.

"You're welcome, T."

Terrell went very still, and Colby's sigh literally shook him to his ass cheeks. Colby bent low, hands squashing at Terrell's shoulder muscles in a decent massage, and whispered in Terrell's ear. "I get that you don't want to reciprocate," he said quietly. "But you need to at least *articulate* whether you want this or not."

"It feels good," Terrell was forced to admit. "I just don't...."

Colby sighed again and swung off his back, and Terrell missed the hell out of him. "You don't owe me shit," Colby muttered and then reached over Terrell's shoulder to turn off the lights before rolling away to his side.

It was easier in the dark. Their breaths grew deep and regular, and some of the strangeness of the bed and the shapes silhouetted against the moonlight coming from the deck eased into the familiar.

"You're just so kind," Terrell said softly, knowing he was a coward because he figured Colby was asleep.

"You just...," Colby said, startling him badly. He jerked a little, and Colby laughed, but not bitterly. "You're nice, Terrell. You're fun. You never complain. I just wanted to be kind to you. I've wanted to be kind to you for a long time."

Terrell closed his eyes, thinking about all those breaks, the funny Christmas gift, the trips to the river they'd taken in the summer and the trips shopping they'd done in the winter, and the way the boy always seemed to make time for him, no matter how different their shifts were. "That's not honest, is it?" he asked, knowing he should probably look at the thing they'd just done head-on.

He heard Colby swallow. "You're the only one who never guessed I was gay, Terrell. You know perfect strangers' drinks, who's dealing to who, and I watched you once predict that a ten-year marriage was going to break up *in the restaurant* just by the way she wouldn't let the guy hold her hand when they walked in. And you never, not once, asked me why I wasn't there with a girl. Why is that?"

Terrell swallowed and remembered that sigh and the perfect, gentle way Colby had eased into his body. *I'm not gay. I could dream. I wanted to smile at you and not have you wonder. I could pretend....* But even the pretending was a lie.

"Sometimes," he said carefully, not sure what thing he could say here that would neither hurt Colby nor expose more of himself than he was planning, "sometimes, it's just enough to have a friend."

There was a rustle behind him as Colby rolled back over and inched a little closer to Terrell's back. Terrell felt his hand, long-fingered and warm, settling on Terrell's hip. Terrell scooted back into Colby's body and the hand slid down to his stomach. Terrell covered it with his own and settled in to sleep. Outside the window, the sky was waxing from gray to gold with morning.

Terrell woke up sometime around full light to a sudden sound. His whole body stiffened and he threw his elbows out, hearing that gunshot in his dreams.

A warm hand on his shoulder calmed him down. "Sh, it's just my sister, closing the door before it gets too hot."

Terrell groaned and rolled over in the bed, covering his head with a pillow, and then some blessed angel of the cool dark pulled the blackout drapes, and the searing white light of midmorning ceased to torment him. "God," he grumbled from under the pillow, "what time is it?"

"Eight. We can sleep for a few more hours."

"Thankya Jesus," Terrell muttered and fell mostly back asleep with the pillow over his head.

Colby started to move then, and Terrell grunted and reached out for him. Colby patted his hand and lowered his head to Terrell's little space under the pillow. "I'm just gonna talk to her, okay? I'll be back—I'm thrashed."

"'Kay," Terrell sighed, and relaxed. Thrashed was the operative word. It really would have taken a gunshot to get him out of bed.

He heard Colby's voice, low and sleepy, and then his sister's voice, a little higher in pitch but still considerately lowered. He was just conscious enough to make out their conversation.

"Nice," Moira said, and Colby grunted.

"Sh—he's skittish."

"He looks dead!"

"No, that would be our boss who got murdered. The cops didn't let us go until almost four."

"*Get out!*" Her voice rose, and thinking he was being evicted, Terrell tried to push himself up and comply.

"What? Jesus! I'm getting!"

"Go back to sleep, T!" Colby snapped and then hissed at his sister, "Jesus, could you suck any worse? Do you know how hard it was to *get* him here?"

Terrell was melting into the bed again, and that thought made him pause. Colby had *tried* to get him there? Yeah. That was true. Colby had *seduced* him. How cool was that?

"Well, congratulations. You've managed a seduction. I'm proud. Does he know about—"

"I don't even know about," Colby said harshly. "Don't mention it."

"But *Colby*! You worked for that for—"

"And I get to change my mind! Now could you, you know, go away? Did I mention the late?"

"Yeah, yeah. Hey—do you want me to use my contacts? I could find out a whole lot more than the paper will tell us."

Colby's laugh was low and sort of evil. "Yeah! Actually, yeah—that'd be great. I totally want to figure it out before the cops do."

"You wish! That only happens in cop shows."

"Yeah, well, a boy can dream."

"Yeah, well, go back to sleep, little boy—I think that guy's the only dream you're gonna get this time."

"Hey, Moy—"

"Yeah?"

"You got time to go get us some orange juice and bagels?"

There was a long-suffering sigh, and Terrell wanted to smile. Apparently it was a family sound. "You got any cash?"

They hadn't left their aprons in their lockers the night before—it had felt like *nothing* was safe at Papiano's, including their stupid polyester aprons and tip trays. Terrell heard Colby move to the chair where they'd draped their aprons the night before—neither of them had moved their tip take to their wallets either.

"Grab mine," Terrell muttered from under the pillow. "And get the OJ with the calcium. And pie."

Moira giggled. "For breakfast?"

"I ain't getting' up 'til twelve," he said, still under the pillow. "OJ for breakfast. Pie for lunch."

"I like him," Moira chimed, her voice not in the whisper mode anymore. "He's buying me pie on a Saturday. Night night, baby brother!"

Colby grunted and, a minute later, slid back into bed. "Did you have to buy her pie?" he grumbled. "She's going to eat half of it before we wake up."

"Good. I don't want you to get fat." It was a silly thing to say—a sappy, stupid, gay thing to say to the man in bed next to you—but Colby was suddenly draped over his back, planting little fish-darting kisses on Terrell's shoulder.

"Won't happen," Colby promised. Then he yawned, and Terrell peeked out at him from under the pillow.

The room was still dark, and Terrell was *definitely* going to fall asleep again. But he was relaxed, and happy as he rarely was. He rolled over to his side toward Colby. "Turn over," he said. "I'm big spoon this time."

"Deal." Colby backed into him, and when Terrell draped his arm over Colby's middle, Colby twined their fingers, and they slept.

BY TWELVE O'CLOCK, it was over 100 degrees outside. Colby's house had *awesome* air-conditioning—especially compared to Terrell's apartment, which had weak, half-assed, bootsy air-conditioning that wrapped you in pit stink the moment the thermometer got above eighty—But that didn't stop the heat from being a... a *thing* that sat over the house and made you sweat, air-conditioning or not.

It was the sweat that woke Terrell up at twelve, not the light, or the need for more sleep, which he most definitely had.

Colby was coming out of the bathroom with a towel wrapped around his waist and one he was using on his longish hair. Terrell blinked sleepily at him, smiling, seeing the long, tanned lines of him, the vee cut to his abdomen where it dipped below the towel. He realized that he hadn't *seen* what was underneath the towel, at the end of the gold-furred treasure trail. He'd felt it inside of him, but he hadn't *seen* it, and now, in the daylight, that seemed a damned shame.

Colby caught the laser focus of his eyes and smiled, raising his eyebrows and dropping the towel. "You seem curious about something, T. Anything you want to ask me about?"

"You got a turtleneck," Terrell said with a blink, trying to make it casual as he swung himself out of bed and looked anywhere *but* where the towel had been. "I've been in enough locker rooms to know *that* is unusual!"

Colby shrugged and twisted his lips ironically, like he knew *exactly* what Terrell had been thinking, but he answered. "My parents were liberal—still are. The kind with money who could stand up to a doctor and say, 'Oh, noes! Don't do that to my baby!'"

Terrell chuckled. "I guess my mom figured since we were on the state dime, they could do anything they wanted to me."

Colby laughed, but not a lot. "When did you start living with your grandma, T?"

"Oh hell no! No life stories!" Terrell tried to laugh it off. They'd shared a lot on the back dock during break time—that wasn't the Terrell he wanted to be here. "You know plenty about me, cheese boy—it's time for me to shower so you don't know how stinky my ass can *really* get."

Colby nodded as though he'd been put in his place—as he had, Terrell had to admit—and started rummaging in his drawers. "I'm going to do laundry—it just makes the water a little cooler, and that's actually not a bad thing right now, so don't worry about it. I'll leave you some shorts and a T-shirt and put your tips and stuff on my dresser so I can do your apron, okay?"

Terrell nodded. This was easy. It was casual and work. Amen. "Yeah, thanks a lot for that. Appreciate it."

Colby's smile was a little bit self-deprecating. "Yeah, well, I'll make some man a wonderful wife someday," he said and turned around to put on some clean underwear before Terrell could object. Terrell was treated to his backside—covered in sparse light-brown hair, and tight and cut from all the activity Colby seemed to use to keep himself grounded—and Colby glanced at him to see why he wasn't moving.

Terrell startled and headed toward the bathroom with purpose, but Colby wasn't fooled.

"You can have an encore presentation tonight, Terrell," he called over his shoulder. "I promise I won't charge a piece of your soul."

Terrell snorted, not fooled for an instant. "You say that, brotha, but there ain't nothin' that good come without a price—you know that."

Colby turned around, his underwear still at his thighs, and Terrell took a quick, deep breath through his nose and just looked.

God, the boy was big. He was. Terrell had always felt a bit cheated—black men had all this mystique of being hung like gods, and he got the average six-inch pecker and made do. But Colby... God. He was probably five inches flaccid, and hardening in front of Terrell's eyes. Terrell's mouth went dry, and he clenched his hands to fight the compulsion to kneel down before that marble god and worship.

"Terrell?"

"Yeah?" He jerked his gaze upward.

"You've got a goddamned bachelor's degree. If you want me to believe I don't mean that much to you, you need to remember to either speak white to me all the time or stop hauling out the street when you're trying to make me feel small. You've already shown your hand here, T. And so have I."

Terrell swallowed hard, mortified, and Colby pulled up his undershorts and took two steps toward him, put a hand on his shoulder, and kissed him softly on the cheek. "Let's try this again, okay? You get an encore presentation tonight. I don't work, but I'll be there to pick you up after shift."

Terrell looked at him, mesmerized by his blue eyes, by the thick brown lashes around them, by the way his lip curled up to show his chipped tooth every time he said "I" or any word close. His heart thundered in his stomach and he had to swallow six times before he could actually think about speaking.

"I'd like that," he said quietly. "Thank you."

Colby kissed his mouth this time, just long enough for Terrell to open his lips and hope. "My pleasure, T. Maybe this time, you can look your fill."

Terrell nodded and then broke the mood heading for the shower. He didn't want to open his mouth, because if he did, he'd say something stupid like he could look at Colby's body until it shriveled with age, and he didn't think it would ever get old.

COLBY'S clothes were a little loose on him, and the shorts went down to his knees, but he figured this was as casual as things got. Colby had set him out a new toothbrush, which he was grateful for, especially with the new braces. He scrubbed carefully and for a long time, to make up for the lack of dental floss or a pick, and thought that caring for this (achy!) mouthful of metal was going to be a full-time job.

But he had a hazy thought, just him and Colby on the back dock, him laughing at something Colby had said—and not wanting to hide his mouth behind his hand. It was worth it. That smile, unashamed, unafraid—*that* smile would be worth it.

He wandered down the hall and into the open sitting room/kitchen after that, curling his toes in the nice, plush cream-colored carpeting.

God, everything about this house was so damned classy. The windows were all clean, and the bookshelves (a *lot* of them!) weren't dusty. The pictures on the walls were all framed, even the movie ones. (Colby liked action-adventure movies a lot—Terrell could ask himself now if that was because he liked the action or if he liked the hot guys who starred in them. For Terrell, it was a toss-up, but he thought he'd keep that to himself.) The yard outside was neatly kept—green, which meant they could pay the water bill—with pruned roses and a mowed lawn. Colby had mentioned doing yard work before; that must have been part of his unspecified rent, but he did a good job of it.

Colby was sitting on a stool by the counter that divided the kitchen from the living room, drinking orange juice and eating a bowl of Grape-Nuts with a banana cut up inside.

Terrell looked over his shoulder before taking the stool next to him, the one with the pie in the clear plastic grocery baker's box sitting in the spot. Colby was right—his sister had eaten about half of it—but she'd left a clean fork and a glass of OJ. As Terrell sat down, she turned and grabbed two halves of a bagel as they popped up from the toaster, and set them at the edge of the pie box.

He looked at them, trying to decide if they were health food or not, and then looked up at "Moy." She was not what he'd expected.

For one thing, she was fat. He felt guilty about thinking that particular word, so he amended it to "plump," but she was very much of it—although she wore it well. She had round, shapely calves, soft thighs, a big bubble butt, and a rack you could hang clothes on. She also had her brother's dark-blonde hair pulled back into a wavy ponytail down her back, a very rounded oval-shaped face, and blue eyes. Her lips were full, and she had a definite tummy, which you could see because she was wearing a tank top and exercise pants.

She moved in the kitchen with a fluid, unconscious grace that made Terrell think of a dancer, big-girl build notwithstanding. She was also short, with pale skin that had tanned from being outside, but on her, you could tell how porcelain fair her skin would be if she hadn't been active.

Maybe it was cultural—being skinny was not as big a thing in Terrell's neighborhood as it seemed to be on white TV—or maybe it was the fact that Terrell could appreciate a girl who unapologetically ate pie for breakfast. Maybe it was the fact that she'd named her cats for a dirty joke or that she toasted the bagel for him and didn't set it down on a plate but used the pie box instead.

Maybe it was the way she'd woken him up that morning, getting as excited as a kid about gossip, and had gone to get them pie and bagels and whatever the hell Colby was eating, as cheerful as a person should be, at eight in the morning.

Either way, Terrell took one look at her and wished he loved women, because unlike Erin at work, who was a bitch, or that freaky chick Angela who seemed to scare the crap out of Colby too, Moira was someone to be adored.

"Thank you," he said from a full mouthful of bagel, and she grinned at him. She even had her brother's smile, with the corner of the lip pulled up over the teeth. It made her look as tough as any guy and twice as smart.

"Yeah, well, if you're like me, the pie's great for breakfast until the sugar gives you a headache and then charges through your intestines like a runaway train."

He laughed. "Well, yeah, sometimes it does leave you a bit bubbly, but it's worth it." She'd gotten cherry pie, and he blessed her. "As long as it's fruit pie—you read my mind."

She smiled again. "Speaking of minds... you guys want to—oh no." Her voice sank, and Colby turned around from his single-minded approach to nuts, berries, and raw twine, and smiled.

"Battle stations, everybody. Here it comes."

Terrell turned around in time to see what they were talking about. A gigantic gray tortoiseshell cat was lying on the back of the bright-red couch, pretending to sleep. Pretending was the operative word. The cat's green eyes were open, glinting demonically in the sunlight streaming in from the sliding glass door, and its tail was whipping on the couch hard enough to make a solid thwap sound every time it landed.

He was staring, vulturelike, at the delicate little "kitteh" confection who had padded in from the hallway.

"Five bucks on the little one," Terrell said, watching, and although he was immersed in the impending Armageddon, he caught Colby's appreciative grin over his shoulder.

"No deal. That's why he's all freaked out. He's been waiting for his advantage—oh no!"

The tiny gray-and-orange calico blurred into motion across the floor and up to the top of the couch. Once she got there, she landed a series of solid blows across the gray cat's head, tagging him hard on the nose before dashing off again to hide behind the love seat, and the battle was *on*.

"Oh *hell* no!" Terrell chortled, watching as the gray cat leaped from the couch and landed with a hard thud before taking off after his antagonist. He hauled his large body up to the love seat and over the back. When he got to the top, he crouched, obviously looking for his enemy in battle, his tail lashing outrageously.

And that's when she struck, bounding in the air and over the arm of the love seat to leap on top of the gray cat's back, thwack him a couple of times on the head again, and go tear-assing to the back of the house.

And she would have gotten away with it too, but Colby stuck out his foot.

The little calico tried a hasty bound over it, but she timed the jump wrong, got her back legs hung up on his foot, and then went tumbling across the living room.

"Puddin'!" Moira squealed. "Colby, you dick!"

But Colby didn't even look at her. "She had it coming," he said, laughing as the cat recovered from her smackdown. She rolled over on the floor, looking dazed, when the thundering of giant cat pads shook the floorboard.

"Oh my God!" Terrell was laughing so hard he couldn't breathe. The giant gray cat loped across the floor, leapt, and landed on the tiny calico with enough force to flatten her.

"Dewey, you pussy! She's just a baby!" Moira squealed, and she was running around the divider to rescue her kitty when there was a furious feline shriek from under the bulk of the gray cat's body. Suddenly Dewey flopped over on his side, then rolled to his back while the little calico chewed at his neck. Dewey growled and jackrabbited his back legs furiously, but he was so long, he didn't even touch Puddin' as she seriously dominated his giant tomcat ass.

After a moment the tension flooded out of the two of them, and those pumping back legs went limp. Puddin' started licking Dewey's neck, and then his ears, and then he rolled onto his stomach again and she collapsed on top of him, licking his whiskers back while he purred in gratification.

"Show's over, folks," Terrell chuckled, and they all turned back to their early afternoon breakfast.

"She's something, isn't she?" Colby asked, grinning, and Terrell agreed.

"Where'd you find her?"

"Shelter," Moira said, reaching across the counter and snagging one more piece of pie. "Dewey was Colby's choice—he was this tiny little abandoned thing at the PetSmart, and he was so lonely, we thought he needed a friend."

"Didn't expect a dominatrix, didja, big guy?" Terrell asked the big gray area rug. The cat twitched his whiskers in reply, and Terrell figured that was the cat equivalent of "don't knock it 'til you try it."

"So," Moira said after a friendly silence had fallen, "do you guys want to hear what I know about your ex-boss?"

Terrell looked at his cherry pie and contemplated being revolted, but he couldn't manage it. Walter Templeton had been no friend of Terrell's, and, well, pie was pie. Judging by the way Colby was still plowing through his jute, sawdust, and shredded newspaper, he hadn't been that attached either.

"Yeah," Colby said, catching Terrell's eye and nodding eagerly. "Hit us with it. I want to know who did it!"

Moira rolled her eyes. "Well, we don't know that yet—but you guys saw more than you told me this morning, and I want details. Apparently this Templeton guy donated money to a lot of politicians, and everyone wants this solved!"

Terrell grunted. "Politicians? Man, he couldn't possibly make *that* much money, could he?"

Colby shrugged. "He'd been a manager for five or six years. He didn't have any family, and I think he was blowing somebody in corporate."

"Really?" Moira asked, wrinkling her nose. "The police say he was straight."

"Well, it could have been a she," Colby said defensively. "And it might not have been literal. But something was going on, because his drawers kept coming up short, and nobody ever called him on it."

"You knew that?" Terrell asked, surprised.

Colby shrugged. "Beth brought it up in our little circle jerk last night, when you were dozing off. But even beyond that—Suk told me that every time he did inventory and Templeton worked, he came up short on bottles of high-end booze."

Terrell grunted. "Didn't happen to *me!*"

"Yeah, that's 'cause you're sharp, T. You don't let that shit happen. Suk's easy to pick on, and he didn't want to admit it to you, because he's sort of scared of you."

"Scared of me?" News to Terrell!

"He looks up to you—and when you see someone being stupid, you're not afraid to tell 'em!"

T scowled. "Well, he doesn't have to list every goddamned top-shelf liquor we have every time someone asks, dammit! I know he knows them—by the time he's done with the list, the customer's eyes have glazed over and he just wants a goddamned Coke!"

Colby cracked up quietly and then picked up his cereal bowl and drank down the muck in the bottom. When he was done, he set the bowl down and looked up at his sister expectantly. "Okay, so Templeton's skimming drawers, selling stolen liquor, and knocking up waitresses left and right—"

"I didn't know about that last part!" Moira said, leaning against the counter with salacious delight. If Terrell didn't know better, he'd say she was watching an episode of *Tosh 2.0* or *E!*

Colby snorted. "Yeah, Moy—I'm gonna tell you that he's screwing girls in the manager's office, because *that's* a fun conversation." Colby pitched his voice up as he mimicked his big sister. "Gee, Colby, why don't you report him for sexual harassment? That's illegal! Well, I don't know, sis, maybe because he's never put his dick in *my* cooter, so I'm not the one who's gonna dial the damned phone—but I'll pass your regards to the next waitress whose ass he grabs!"

This time both Terrell and Moira cracked up—but in between laughter, Moira was shrieking defensively. "That's not *fair!* It *is* illegal! He *shouldn't* be getting away with that! That's what the law is *for!*"

Terrell calmed down enough to roll his eyes. "Yeah, the law is all for that, but people are what they are. This guy was a sleaze, and you can only tell someone so many times that they don't have to be victims before it's up to them to believe it."

Colby nodded and sent Terrell an inscrutable look from under his brow. Terrell's face heated for no reason he could think of, and he turned his attention back to Moira.

"So, we know Templeton's greasing politicians, and I'm pretty sure he's hooking up the DM with her nightly pick-me-up—"

Moira did a spit-take. "He was *dealing?*" she asked, and Terrell shook his head.

"Naw—it's probably the one thing he *didn't* do. But...." Terrell shook his head again. "She's getting high in the bathroom, and he's getting away with, well, not murder, but *somebody* is. You can't tell me that's not connected!"

"Yeah," Colby said thoughtfully. "But how?"

"Well, what did you guys see last night?" Moira asked. Randomly, she started picking up things to clean—Colby's cereal bowl, the orange juice glass Terrell had emptied. He realized he had barely touched his pie and started to eat so it wouldn't be wasted.

He looked at Colby, and they locked gazes over that first big mouthful of pie.

"Nothing," Colby said, grimacing. "We were tucked back behind a stack of pallets, leaning against the wall. We heard the shot, the door to the back dock opened, and we heard footsteps. The door was in the way, for one, and by the time we'd started to slide out of the bolt-hole, the footsteps were gone. We wouldn't have been chasing them anyway—all the action was inside the manager's office!"

"Behind a stack of pallets?" Moira said suspiciously, and Colby shook his head at her in warning while Terrell stared at the refrigerator and stuffed pie in his face. He tried to tell himself that it didn't matter: she'd seen him lying in bed with her brother, both of them wearing underwear to keep their balls from flapping around their thighs and no other reason, but that didn't help. The past half an hour, laughing, eating, talking—it was like it had never existed, and in its place was Terrell's driving need not to be gay.

It was horrible. He wanted that time back. That had been good time. But he couldn't seem to get it. All he could do was stare at the refrigerator and pretend Moira wasn't looking at him in confusion and Colby wasn't trying not to lose his patience.

In a moment it was done. Moira held her hands up and said, "Okay, fine! I won't ask! But I can't believe the cops let you get away with that bullshit either!"

"They didn't," Terrell said, because he could see the dull red flush on the tanned skin of Colby's neck and knew that if he had to answer one more question, his temper was going to snap. "We had to show them—once you see the spot, you understand."

Moira nodded, and Colby looked at him and seemed to pull some composure and good humor back around him. "Okay—so you guys aren't witnesses so much as...."

"Fate," Terrell supplied, "hidden in an auger hole, ready to...." Well, the rest of the quote didn't fit, did it?

"Maybe 'ready to rush out and seize the killer'!" Colby intoned dramatically, and Terrell grinned at him, absurdly pleased that Colby knew that play too.

"You have Adams?" Terrell asked, and Colby nodded.

"Best Brit Lit teacher *ever*!"

And their moment was *back*.

"Great." Moira snorted. "So you guys can quote Shakespeare, but you didn't see the killer. Was there anything special about the footsteps? Were they... I don't know, magical footsteps?"

Terrell chuckled around another bite of pie. "Just average footsteps, running fast. Soft footed, I guess. Like tennis shoes, or something with a soft sole."

"Yeah," Colby said, obviously thinking hard. "You know, we're all wearing tennis shoes on the floor—something soft soled. Even people with orthotics are wearing them." Foot problems, back problems, leg problems—you spent enough time on your feet, carrying heavy trays around, and you were going to get some sort of problem that dealt with pain and feet.

"Okay," Terrell said, raising his eyebrows and thinking about it too "That's good. That actually eliminates some folks."

"Beth, for one," Colby said, and Terrell nodded. "She was wearing those fuck-me pumps, and Erin was wearing those things that *look* like fuck-me pumps but are easier on the feet."

"Yeah, yeah, exactly! And it pretty much takes out anyone from the kitchen—"

"Don't they wear tennis shoes?" Moira asked. She'd about cleaned up most of the kitchen by now, and Terrell would have felt bad except she'd seemed to do it on automatic, like she needed to move. He could respect that. He needed to be still to think. It helped.

"Yeah," Colby said, "but the grease and the soap residue on the floor makes their shoes slippery. They wouldn't have just gone running off like that—we would have heard something different. You can tell when you watch them walk that they're moving careful."

"Gotcha!" Moira had clearly never thought of that, but she took their word for it.

Terrell was really starting to enjoy himself. He'd had some deductive reasoning classes in college, and while he'd never set out to be an investigative journalist, he felt like he was stretching long-neglected muscles. "And it rules out someone from the front of the house, right?"

Colby and Terrell both jerked, and Terrell shook his head. "Front of the house couldn't have made it back there without someone seeing them."

"Seriously," Colby added. "It's like, the cardinal rule. Customers can get hurt back there. Half the store would have been spazzing out before someone got back to the manager's office. Even if they were *with* a manager, the whole frickin' store would have noticed."

Moira grunted. "God, you guys. It's like a cult. Makes me glad I worked retail through college. So the girls on the fuck-mes are out—"

"That's the Do' Hos," Colby said, and Terrell nodded.

Moira grimaced. "Lovely. Do' Hos. Excellent. The customers are out—who's that leave?"

Colby grunted. "Whoever it was, they didn't have to be that big. I know those were hollow points, because the hole in the back was smaller than the one in the front, but as gross as those holes in Templeton were, they could have been a whole lot bigger. It couldn't have been bigger than a .38—probably more like a .22." He shuddered, and Terrell was almost assaulted by the sudden urge to touch him. Cover his hand, massage the small of his back, kiss his shoulder—

something—because Terrell remembered that moment too. That horrible, jarring disconnect between *this was a person I know* and *this is shredded flesh.*

He would have done it if they hadn't... *done* it, he realized. He would have patted Colby's back, palmed the back of his head, bumped his shoulder, *something.*

He was almost as surprised as Colby when the palm of his hand hit Colby's bare thigh. Colby jerked and Terrell was yanking his hand back when Colby closed his fingers around Terrell's and held them there.

Okay. That was done.

"It was ugly," Terrell said from a rough throat, remembering the way he'd startled out of sleep that morning. "Nightmare ugly."

Moira grimaced. "Sorry, guys. My bad. I didn't mean to come across so bloodthirsty."

Colby flashed her a wicked grin. "We *like* that part of you, Moy—you wouldn't be nearly as much fun playing *Borderlands* if you weren't!"

"What's *Borderlands*?" Terrell asked, and Colby grimaced.

"Yeah, I forgot you and your unfounded prejudice against video games."

Terrell remembered talking about this before—he'd never seen the appeal.

Moira let out a hurt whimper. "But... but...," she said, with a mock quiver to her full lip, "I... I thought we were *friends*!"

Terrell rolled his eyes. "Yeah, yeah, pick on the guy who'd rather play Ping-Pong—you do that!"

"I *love* Ping-Pong!" Moira gasped, excited. Then she sort of deflated. "We keep talking about getting a table for the garage, but with Colby lea—"

"We'll get one this Christmas," Colby said shortly, and Terrell looked up to see him and his sister having some sort of titanic eyeball death match.

Colby broke it off to look at him sideways and then yanked on Terrell's hand—which he'd never relinquished—and pulled Terrell off the stool.

"C'mon, T—my gym is right around the corner. Let's go swim some laps before you go into work."

Terrell actually went to a different branch of the same gym for just that reason, and Colby knew it. "What about our uniforms and shit?" he asked, allowing himself to be towed away from the kitchen and the pie and the murder investigation and the thing Colby didn't want to talk about.

"We'll throw 'em in the dryer before we go. Come *on!*"

Thinking on Your Feet

THE hoped-for call canceling work never came, and Terrell found himself getting out of Colby's car and running for the front door without a kiss or a touch on the hand or a backward glance.

He wanted to give all three, but you just didn't do that to a guy who'd put you up for the night and nothing else.

He wondered if Colby wanted that kiss as badly as Terrell did.

He'd felt it especially when they were changing. When they'd changed in Colby's room, putting on their trunks and grabbing towels, Colby had moved behind Terrell to get something out of his drawer, and he'd put a hand, simple and intimate, on Terrell's hip. The touch had been brief and meaningless, but it had burned there, accusing, inviting, until they'd both plunged into their adjoining lanes at the pool and started to swim.

After their workout, they'd air-dried in the Sacramento heat on the way back to move Terrell's car from Papiano's (where they'd seen the open doors and business as usual) to the covered spot in his apartment complex. He hadn't gone inside—there was nothing to check, really, and he was already self-conscious enough about his neighborhood. Two blocks away were houses like Colby's, small, single family, nice yards—the kind of thing you'd *expect* to find near the river. But not Terrell's block. No, Terrell had managed to find himself a tiny one-room airless shithole of an apartment in a building that looked like a leftover from a demilitarized zone in non-Western country.

He parked his car in his spot and hopped into Colby's old beater, and they went back to the nice house in the suburbs with all the air-conditioning and the spa.

"God, it's hot," Colby bitched and then smiled. "Stupid, right? It's gonna be one-oh-six today—of course it's hot. It's just that when I'm in the river or something, it doesn't seem so bad, but when I'm stuck driving, *crap*, it sucks!"

"Listen to you! Aren't you the one who gave me crap about having the college degree?"

Colby cracked a smile. "Just like you, I can talk white when I want!"

"Yeah, when's that?"

"When I'm talking to my folks, for one thing, and trying to convince them the education was money well spent!"

Terrell laughed like he was supposed to, but Colby's face had darkened for a moment, and he had time to wonder at the thing Colby wasn't saying. But then, Terrell couldn't complain about holding shit close to his vest, could he?

"So why aren't you leaving me at my apartment again?" Terrell asked as they neared Colby's house. It was a big freakin' circle, yeah, but they had to go get Terrell's work clothes from Colby's drier.

Colby glanced at him before turning his attention back to the road. "Because," he said shortly. "Last night wasn't a fluke. I'll drop you off, I'll pick you up, we'll do the thing again. Maybe, a little practice, you won't obsess over every time I touch you."

Colby's face went grim when they'd had a good afternoon, actually. Their swim had been competitive and companionable, and Terrell had appreciated the chance to work out. Water was easier than a regular workout regime on joints that had been damaged by childhood malnutrition, and Terrell worked out at least five times a week to build up those muscles and give his back a break. Colby was a fun swimming companion, delivering one-liners whenever they stopped for water or while they were toweling off at the end. For a moment Terrell missed that easiness, and then Colby relaxed a little.

"Don't you want to do that again, T? I do."

Terrell shrugged and tried to be nonchalant. "Well, you know. You're a friend. Anything for a friend, right?"

Colby looked at him sideways and smirked. "Yeah, well, dig deep, Terrell. I'll hold you to it."

When they were back in Colby's room, Terrell had just pulled his polyester work pants on over his freshly cleaned underwear, and Colby walked behind him and paused again. He bent his head and kissed Terrell's shoulder, and then his spine, and then his other shoulder. Terrell closed his eyes and let him, wanting more, knowing that even if he had the nerve to ask, he had to be at work in twenty minutes and it was time to go.

"Well," he said breathlessly, "like I said—"

"Anything for a friend," Colby breathed into his ear, and then he was gone, and Terrell was left wondering how many chances he was going to get to touch that boy like he wanted.

It was sobering, and it haunted him through the beginning of his shift.

"Hey, T! How're they hangin'?"

Terrell looked up to see Sean, a regular, leaning over the bar in his fine suit, nursing a Glenlivet neat. Sean was one of those tall, broad-shouldered black men who could wear an expensive linen suit, shave his head bald and sport a goatee, and live with *fine* women—the kind with tiny waists, big boobs, and top-shelf manicures—draped over his back like silk scarves. Because they were black together, Sean liked to think they had something in common, but Terrell was reasonably sure Sean's old neighborhood was a damned sight better than Terrell's old neighborhood, and the only thing they had in common was that they had to visit the barber once a week and it was hard to tell when they blushed.

But you didn't say that to a customer, certainly not one who ordered Glenlivet and tipped 25 percent!

"Low and inside," Terrell cracked, and Sean gave him a courtesy laugh. "How're you tonight?"

"Thinking," Sean said, sighing heavily like those thoughts were deep indeed. "Man, I'm gonna miss old Will. You?"

Terrell shrugged. "Yeah, was a shame what happened to him."

"Who's gonna take his place, you know?"

Another shrug. "Corporate will come up with someone. Erin might—she's a good house manager, she could be GM."

Sean shivered. "That woman is one cold, skinny bitch. I saw it when she walked in tonight. She was *glad* old Will was gone!"

Yeah, well, if she'd made the mistake of being one of Will's harem, Terrell didn't blame her—but you didn't just spill that out to someone you didn't know. "He wasn't as good to her as he's been to you," Terrell said delicately. "He wasn't... *respectful* of the women, you know?"

Sean's deep brown eyes opened wide, and he held out his hand to the warm and willing trophy on his back. He turned to her and smiled, and she leaned forward and rubbed noses with him. "Well, you've got to be respectful of the ladies, now don't you?"

Terrell nodded sincerely. "Yeah, yeah you do!" He wondered if this particular lady knew how many women Sean actually brought *in* to Papiano's. "Speaking of, sweetheart, can I get you another mai tai?"

The woman—Terrell had needed to card her, because she was barely twenty-one—giggled and said yes, wiggling a little in her tight pink dress and trying to keep her coffee-colored cleavage from escaping and smothering the masses. Sean leaned forward and whispered in her ear. Her eyes went to half-mast, and Terrell hoped he didn't have to break up what *that* turned into before the night ended. God, the man had the morals of an alley cat and the libido of a leg-humping schnauzer.

Weren't there any *decent* black men in Sacramento?

Decent gay black men?

Why would he care?

He closed his eyes for a moment as he turned around to get change, and remembered Colby's feathering touch across his back, his simple promise that there would be *more* touching where that came from, and wondered why, if he was going to be gay, he was even worried about whether it was with a black man or a white man. It was with a *man*, and at least with Colby, he already knew it would be...

Gentle.

And very probably monogamous.

God, of all the things to worry about, maybe being dumped while Colby went and banged some other guy was something he could check off the list!

He turned back around to give change and asked the next guy what he could do for him, and he didn't realize how much lighter his expression was until Sean spoke up.

"Look at him, Stacy—doesn't he look perky? What you thinking about, T, that got you all lit up like that?"

"Only one thing makes a guy look like that!" said the blond guy Terrell was pulling a draft for. "He's thinking about getting *laid*!"

Terrell kept his face even and his words light. He'd had practice with this. "Of course I am! Your sister called—says she's free and easy!"

The guy chortled—he was another regular—and Terrell spent the rest of the night feeding the two of them the myth of the sexually insatiable black man. God, what would they think if they knew?

Do I care what they think? They don't want truth tonight. They want some drinks and they want to forget how bad their lives suck.

He knew the blond guy had a wife he doted on—but whom Terrell was pretty sure he'd seen in Papiano's with other men. He knew that Sean would probably *love* to settle down, but he'd brought his sisters in one time, and they'd teased him unmercifully about being a player, and he was probably just living up to their expectations. His mom and dad had come in after that, and they'd given him the same deal.

So here Terrell was, doing the same thing they were, putting up a front to live up to someone else's expectations. The difference was, Terrell thought as he spun off to another customer and got *his* order, that while Sean's front was all about impressing people while he lived a lonely life, and white-blond guy's front was convincing himself that his life wasn't crap, Terrell's front was to keep them off his back while, for the first time in his life, he thought about a good life, one that didn't hurt, and wondered how to make that come true.

The night went quickly—the undercurrent of curiosity may have been pretty low class, but it did seem to be drawing a crowd. By the time the last customer left, Terrell and Gina, a bartender who had the good fortune *not* to be on shift the night before, were both tired.

"God, T," Gina muttered, "I was hoping for some time to do homework tonight!"

"Are you signed up for summer school?" he asked incredulously, and she nodded, looking embarrassed.

"Just a couple of classes on the computer. School by the pool!"

Terrell laughed. "That's *your* bad. I don't know *anyone* who wants to sign up for a slow shift but you!"

"Yeah, well, I don't plan on doing this forever," she snorted, and Terrell rolled his eyes. She was young. Plain, stocky, brown hair, freckles, brown eyes, no bullshit, but still—twenty-four. As young as Colby, but maybe a tad more driven. Ending up behind the bar was the Papiano's version of climbing the corporate ladder. Colby probably could have ended up tending bar, but he'd been more content to schmooze customers and organize shit.

"I didn't either—but then nobody ever told me that joke before." What do you call a college graduate in journalism/sociology/humanities/Renaissance poetry? Hey, bartender! Yeah, it wasn't funny the thousandth time you heard it, either.

Gina winced and pulled out the elastic holding one of her insufferably perky pigtails. "Yeah, sucks to be you."

"And Colby and Diana and Erin and—"

"Yeah, yeah—but I'm getting my degree in a growth industry!" She pulled out the other elastic and tunneled her fingers through her hair, then combined the elastics and put her hair up in a slightly more relaxed ponytail.

"Computers, Gina. Go you. Rub it in the face of all the journalism majors in the world. Do you want me to stay late and count the drawers?"

Her smile took some of the plainness from her unremarkable face. "You're the best, Terrell." She took a step toward him and kissed his cheek, and he shook his head in mock bashfulness. "You're going to make some woman very, very happy," she crowed, handing him her stack of receipts and her checkout sheet for the night. She didn't waste any time after that, grabbing her knapsack from under the bar and trotting down the stairs to the floor level on her way out to her car.

"Hey, Percy!" Terrell called as the boy cleared the kitchen on his way to the same place. "Follow her! She shouldn't be walking out alone!"

Gina stopped and looked over her shoulder. Her face lit up a little when Percy came walking down, and Terrell pulled back his head and thought, *Huh?*

"Hey, Percy. You were awesome on window tonight. Man, we didn't have to wait once for bar food."

Percy ducked his head and preened a little, and Terrell actually felt good for the kid. Calling window meant Percy had been keeping his nose clean more than Terrell gave him credit for.

"Thanks, Gina," Percy said shyly. "I really sorta sucked most of the night, but, you know, had T's back." Of course it didn't hurt that bar food was a priority, but Gina was looking at the kid like he was some sort of hero, and Terrell bit back a warning. God. If she ended up getting laid instead of doing her homework, it was no skin off his nose, right?

Besides, her taste could be worse. Percy was a punk-ass eighteen-year-old one step out of the hood, but at least he wasn't a sleazy drug-dealing manager who'd knocked up half the waitstaff, right?

Beth came teetering up the stairs, and he pulled his attention from impending disaster as he watched her wander around the bar in the obligatory checkout. For form, she lifted the register to make sure he'd wiped underneath, and ran her fingers underneath the liquor shelf to make sure he'd gotten that part too. Of course, if he didn't get these places, the bar would be rank, sticky, and stinky in a matter of days, and that was just plain gross, but it was her job too.

The side of the fruit cooler, the fingerprints off the brass bars, yeah, yeah, yeah. She was being thorough tonight. Excellent. He wasn't all that sure she would have been this thorough if Gina had been the one counting the drawer out instead of Terrell, but that could have been sour grapes. Truth was, he didn't know Beth all that well.

"Did you stock the top shelf?" she asked, looking up from her diminutive height.

"Yes'm."

"Did you cash out your food tickets and your comps with the floor manager?"

"No, Beth, we don't do that at this store, remember?"

Beth blinked at him. Her eyes were bloodshot, and she was teetering a little on her FM pumps. He wondered how much sleep she'd gotten the night before, and how much coke (or meth—her complexion was getting a little yellow—it could have been poor man's coke) she'd done to make up for it. "Don't get rude, Terrell, I was just asking—"

"You were just seeing if you could dodge out of one more thing and blame the black guy for being stupid," he retorted. "We count with the GM. We have always counted with the GM. Will was the head GM, but he wasn't the only GM, and maybe you should have called Shelley or Dawn or given Erin a quickie promotion, but you didn't. Now here's my counts, here's my drawer, do your job."

Beth scowled at him in distaste. "Jesus, Terrell, don't get uppity—"

He took a deep breath, but it didn't clear the red haze from his eyes. God, tonight? He'd been having these great fucking dreams about what he was going to do when he and Colby got private time together, how maybe this time he was going to take his time, touch that boy's skin, see what made him close his eyes and gasp.

"Yes'm. I'll keep my uppity mouth shut, ma'am. I'll just sit here on your leisure and let you do your goddamned job."

He tried to pretend his hands weren't shaking. See, that's the way the rage took you. Unawares. Just when you started thinking you were a person, and you got dreams, the world hit you with the double whammy. And he'd seriously dared to hope.

Beth looked at him suspiciously, shifting as she stood in her heels and tapping her pen restlessly against the drawer checkout sheet.

"You're short twenty-five cents," she said, and Terrell raised his eyebrows. The house wiggle room was two dollars. He reached into his pocket and pulled out a quarter, which he flipped to the counter. She reached out quickly and caught it before it rolled into the trough that circled the bar.

"Can I go now, ma'am?"

"Terrell, I'm going to be here awhile. I know you may not like me—"

"I liked you fine until about five minutes ago."

"Well, like me or not, I'm your boss, and you're going to have to put up with me. It's not like you're going anywhere else."

Terrell thought about his shitty little project, his one concession to maybe not working in this piss-ant town for the rest of his life, and scowled. "You have no idea where I'm going," he bluffed. "I've got more education than you, more smarts than you, and I *don't* have a monkey on my back." Her mouth dropped open a little, and he nodded meaningfully and went on. "And I could have been a friend, ma'am. I could have been a friend."

He looked away and fumed, and saw Colby walk in the door. For a moment his stomach dropped in fear. At just about the time he found his footing and realized that friends picked each other up all the time—in fact, Colby had picked him up on more than one occasion when they'd been going out to the lake or the river after work—he realized that the two-ton weight that had been pressing on his shoulders, squashing his chest, making his arms shake, had gone helium balloon on him and floated away.

So Beth was a racist bitch. He knew they existed, had met more than a few of them, many of them teachers. He'd gotten his degree anyway and had met a whole lot of nice people on the way.

Colby was one of them.

"Can I go?" he asked, and she shoved the signoff sheet in front of him with an unfriendly hand.

He looked it over, initialed the totals—which matched with the receipts—and then fixed the end total to reflect the quarter he'd pitched into the till.

"I didn't mean to offend you," she said stiffly, and he rolled his eyes.

"You wanted to put me in my place," he said, not willing to let her off the hook. "I know my place, bi—Beth. And it's not being dissed by some tweaker who couldn't get her business degree." He swung on his heel and rattled down the stairs, not even stopping to see how she'd responded. "Hey, Colby—man, I'm right here."

Colby looked up and smiled warmly, and the ice in Terrell's stomach thawed a little. It was that good of a smile.

"Hello, Colby," Beth purred from the bar behind them, and Colby's smile thinned and iced over like a puddle on the sidewalk.

"Hiya, Beth. Is T out of here?"

"Yeah. You two got plans tonight?" she asked, and Terrell stared at her because she had the sort of tone a woman had when she was going to try to insinuate herself into someone's plans when she wasn't invited.

"Nintendo and a beer," Colby chirped, and Terrell heard the false brightness same as anyone else could—anyone but Beth, that was.

"Sounds mellow—you want some company?"

Terrell had to fight the terrible compulsion to plant a kiss on Colby that would burn through the floorboards. *Bitch, moving in on my*—oh hell. No. He couldn't do that. Not in front of this bitch, who he would rather not even know he was black, if that was the sort of thing a man could hide.

"Sweet of you to offer, darlin'," Colby drawled, "but it's my sister's house. She knows Terrell, but she's not really big on strangers coming by."

"Oh." Beth's voice dropped in disappointment. "Some other time, then?"

Colby made a polite noise, and Terrell led the charge out the double Tiffany doors.

"Oh *hell* no!" Colby thundered in that sweet deep voice of his.

Terrell looked at him, a little surprised, because those were going to be the words out of *his* mouth, but with a little more heat. "You don't want to share Nintendo and a beer with Lady Beth?" he asked, playing calm to Colby's het up, because it was funny.

"*Fuck* no!" Colby snapped. "*God!* You would think that woman would have better sense than to try to hit on you—"

Terrell almost swallowed his tongue. Oh God. The night had sucked so badly. He'd been so angry, so disillusioned, and now, ten seconds with Colby and it was all better.

He remembered the other times Colby had done this for him. Had taken the drunk frat boys off his hands or insisted Will Templeton call him Terrell and not T-Bone on the rare nights Templeton was trying to be funny.

"She wasn't picking up on *me*, cheese boy!" Terrell laughed, feeling relief wash him to his toes. "She was picking up on *you*! She all but called *me* 'boy' and asked me to shine her shoes! God, you're clueless!"

Colby stopped still. "She *what*?" he roared and spun on his heel back toward the swinging doors of Papiano's.

"Stop, stop, don't get your knickers knotted." Terrell was laughing, and it was a gentle, easy thing compared to what he'd felt before. "There's assholes everywhere, Colby. She's an asshole, but we don't need to bother with her, okay?" He took a couple of steps out into the night and took a deep breath. Papiano's was close enough to the river for him to smell it—willow trees and oak, along with blackberry bushes and (mostly) clean running water. The breeze had started up again, but the day had been so hot it barely touched the balm of the air. Colby's skin would be a little moist if Terrell ran his fingertips over it on his back deck. It would probably taste salty, especially in the crook of his neck or the crease of his thigh.

Terrell turned around, grabbed the boy's elbow, and hauled him back toward the darkened parking lot. They got back to Colby's car, and Colby managed to say something past his anger.

"My knickers?"

Terrell knew his face heated, and it was silly because he was a thirty-year-old man who had just finished telling a bar full of people he could fuck a sorority for breakfast (not one of his finer moments) but who blushed at the thought of this boy's "knickers."

"I gotta thing for your drawers," he said, his voice low and teasing, and Colby laughed back.

"That's, uhm, promising," he said, his voice throaty. They looked at each other evenly, the shadows so dark Terrell almost couldn't make out the glint of Colby's blue eyes. They were close and secret and Terrell wanted nothing more than to taste the inside of Colby's mouth again, and see if it was hot and red, when a sudden sound broke the silence.

Terrell wasn't sure which one of them jumped higher, but they stood, back to back, scanning the parking lot. For one silly-assed moment, all Terrell could think about was that set of tennis shoes pattering into the night, and he had a sudden nonsense vision of a tiny inhuman gnome in oversized black tennies, crouching with a cannon in the June night.

He was searching the smallest possum-sized shadows with his eyes when he heard Colby exhale in relief.

"Well, that's Gina's car," he said, a little bit of humor lacing his voice, "but I'm not sure who's—"

"*Oh no!*" they both cried out in tandem as a full moon blossomed in the steamed back passenger window of Gina's old SUV.

"Percy," Terrell said, wide-eyed. "That's Percy." Well, he was the only other black man working that night. It was a safe bet.

"Oh my *God*," Colby said, his eyes as big as Terrell's felt. "He's hung like a fucking *donkey*!"

"Wonderful. Do you need that notch on your bedpost next?"

Terrell's hands were in his pockets, and without warning Colby reached down and tugged until he could lace their fingers together. "No," he whispered, his voice intimate. "It was an observation, nothing more."

Terrell blew out a breath and shook his head, turning away from what was going on in Gina's ride and letting Colby take him to the little beat-up car they'd been heading for.

"Man, I hope that boy knows what he's doing. She's way out of his league."

"Maybe they were both lonely," Colby said, opening Terrell's side and then moving to his.

"Yeah, but summer hookups—they don't ever last that long. You know that."

The summer before, the two of them had spent the hot months watching the progression of couples hooking up, splitting up, fucking on the back dock or in the bathroom or in cars, and then never speaking to each other again.

"Sometimes," Colby said quietly. "Angie met her boyfriend here last summer. He doesn't work here anymore, but they're still together."

Clark had graduated and actually gotten a job. Angie still had five years to go.

"Yeah," Terrell said, feeling ready to hope, ready to do anything, just so this night with all its promise could end well. "Fine, whatever. Do we need to watch a chick flick, or can we go now?"

"Chick flicks are hopeful," Colby replied while starting up the car. It clicked a few times before turning over, but Colby insisted it had been doing that since he got it way back when he'd graduated from high school, and it had been over fifteen years old. Terrell had always thought it was sort of cute, the way the boy held on to his car, but that's not something one man really said to another, was it?

Well, after they'd slept together it might be.

Terrell tried to backtrack in his head and take that thought back, but Colby looked behind him and gunned the car so that it looped crazily in the almost empty parking lot before he could, and before he knew it, Terrell was hanging onto the Jesus bar while Colby buzzed out of the parking lot like the ghost of Will Templeton himself was after them.

Colby's driving didn't get any saner—he sped up to make green lights, buzzed around the few cars still out, and executed a series of right-hand turns that was so tight and so fast, it left Terrell dizzy from the E-ticket ride, all to avoid a red light. When they got to the street Colby's little house was on, Colby zoomed right past it, and Terrell was afraid to even break his concentration before they ended up at the tiny dirt parking lot that took them to the river.

Terrell looked around, surprised.

"There's no bar across it," he said dimly, and Colby, who had thrown the parking brake on and was currently hauling himself out of the car with the same manic energy he'd just shown, paused long enough to look at him.

"No," he said, and his voice was incongruously gentle for all of that vehicular violence. "This place is sort of secret. Locals only."

Terrell smiled widely at that—he liked the idea. Like the back dock at work, the little place behind the stack of pallets, or under his bed back at Gi-Gi's. He pulled out of the car feeling like that little kid, knowing that he was safe in his little blanket fort. It was perfect.

There was a little red dirt track that led between two head-high stands of blackberry bushes.

"Careful here," Colby warned. "Moira's got someone on line to cut these down, but they'll getcha."

"So," Terrell asked, sidestepping between the encroaching thorns, "did you plan this, or was this a bee that flew up your ass?"

"The second one," Colby muttered. "Ouch, fuckin' thing is out to get me! Here, T, watch yourself."

Typical that he'd hold the offending whippet back so Terrell could get through safely. Terrell took it from his fingers and slid sideways right into Colby's body. Very carefully, Terrell put the branch back and turned to him, for the first time cursing that the kid was so tall.

"I don't need a nursemaid," he said mildly, but inside, he was thinking that he couldn't decide when Colby was more beautiful, by sun or by moon. Silly—stupid and sentimental—but God. He had that long jaw, strong, which meant when he smiled, there were grooves on either side of his mouth, and the nose that was just barely large enough for the face. He was handsome—every movie star in the world had hoped to look like Colby when they were growing up.

But it was more than that. It was the whole Captain America thing.

Terrell knew from past conversations that Colby had some convoluted plans to make the world a better place. He hadn't said much about them as his graduation had neared, and in spite of Terrell's assertion that he'd go watch Colby walk the stage, Colby had worked the day of the ceremony like it was any other day.

But some nights, like the night before, when he'd been bent on saving Terrell's bacon, or like this one, when he just swooped out of nowhere and took them both to a secret spot on the river—some nights, he made the world a better place just by breathing.

And now, in another cozy little hole, with the moonlight as a witness once again, Terrell couldn't stop looking at him.

"It's wrong," he said, his throat dry, and Colby's eyebrows lifted. Someday, when he was in his fifties, they'd be overgrown scary-old-man eyebrows without some manscaping, but right now, they were just bold.

"What's wrong?"

Terrell swallowed, but he seemed unable to stop talking. "You look... I mean... you're such a good-looking kid, and I keep thinking, maybe I should be looking at another black guy like I'm looking at you, right?" Because hell, even Sean, for all his failings, didn't take home white women by the scores, right?

"Why should it matter?" Colby asked, and his voice had that simple faith that only the best of Terrell's teachers had ever managed. It was the sound of someone who really thought it *shouldn't* matter that Terrell was black and Colby was white, or that they were both men.

"It shouldn't," he said, wanting to cup the side of Colby's jaw, to see his dark skin like a shadow against the pale skin of Colby's neck. "It shouldn't, but it does."

"Why?" Colby asked, and God, how did he read Terrell's mind like that? He cupped the side of Terrell's jaw and stroked, like he was looking at the contrast of moonlight and darkness that made up Terrell's face.

Terrell held very, very still, and not just so he didn't snag himself on a blackberry briar, either. "It... what would your family think if they knew me?" Terrell asked wretchedly, and Colby drew a little nearer, his smile gentle.

"You've met me, Terrell. You've met my sister. Did you think we sprang up like mushrooms? Out of nowhere?"

Terrell thought of Gi-Gi, who gave him an earful about not getting a business degree every time he called. He thought of the faceless father his mother wouldn't or couldn't name on his birth certificate. He thought of his mother, who as far as he knew was still living fast and cutting hair and giving blow jobs to afford the dresses and the nails and the weaves that had made her seem so glamorous when she'd left him with Gi-Gi as a baby.

"I did," he said, and nothing could keep the bitterness out of his voice.

"Naw," Colby said, disbelieving. "You came from somewhere. Somebody made you."

There were flashes then: a procession of teachers—the non-racist ones who smiled at him. There was his Gi-Gi, who hugged him on holidays and got her useless son to scavenge a computer for him when there wasn't money for it by any stretch of the imagination. There was the track coach, who ran him on the relay even when his times sucked because he said anyone with Terrell's heart deserved a shot. There was the off-duty cop who worked the after-school programs when Terrell was young, and who told him he was smart and needed to go somewhere with all of that.

"Maybe," he said, absurdly grateful for people he hadn't thought about in years. "Why's it matter?"

Colby's smile was sweet in the moonlight. "I want to know who to thank," he said softly. "I like the way you came out in the end."

Oh God. Something in Terrell *hungered* to introduce Colby to his Gi-Gi—something in him *yearned* to say, "Look at this man. *Look* at him. Isn't he fine? He's damned fine, and he *wants* me!"

But what if his Gi-Gi didn't want him because Colby was a man?

"I'm a rank fucking coward," Terrell said, ripping his chest raw with the shattered mirror of the truth.

"Sh… breathe deep, T. What do you smell?"

Blackberry bushes. Water. "You."

Colby's mouth was soft and warm, and Terrell opened up for him so easily, it was like they'd been kissing all their lives. Colby slid one hand from Terrell's neck and then down to his hips while he rucked up Terrell's shirt and smoothed a palm across his ribs, his waist, the small of his back, and Terrell shivered all over.

He pulled away long enough to whisper, "My balls smell like Papiano's—how far you want to take this?"

"Just a kiss, Terrell," Colby said softly. "We'll go home, shower. I'll smell your balls then. Right now, it's just a kiss."

Colby took over the kiss again, and there, in that tiny space of safety, Terrell was forced to cling to his shoulders, squashing his body against Colby's, pleased that he'd left his apron in the car. It was amazing, the two of them in a secret world, the intimacy of Colby's mouth on his. When Colby pulled away, Terrell's grip on his shoulders stayed, and Colby dropped a kiss on his forehead.

"Want to see the river?" he asked playfully, and Terrell looked up at him and nodded.

"Yeah. Why not?"

Colby took a step back and grinned shyly, then turned around and continued through the briar tunnel. When they emerged, Terrell had to blink as his eyes adjusted to the difference between the dark and the light.

And it really was light.

There were a few great willow trees by the near bank, but the far bank was open for about fifty feet—plenty of room for the moonlight to settle in all the available nooks and crannies, to run off the ripples in the water, to glint tiny off the windows of the houses far across the way.

It was secret and magical, and very private, and Terrell turned his face up, closing his eyes against the silver brightness on his lids.

"Nice?" Colby asked uncertainly, and Terrell nodded.

"Yeah. Real nice. How'd you know about this?"

Colby shrugged. "All the houses pay an upkeep fee, import criminals to pick up the trash, keep the blackberry bushes trimmed—it's sort of like a community park. In the day, the kids come and swim—it's pretty sandy to about waist deep, and it moves slow enough." Colby shrugged. "It's too slow for me—that's why I always take you upstream to Folsom, so we can float down. A lot more fun that way."

Terrell nodded. He loved those trips. There was a company that specialized in dropping people off on inner tubes with a floating cooler of beer and then picking them up at a narrow place in the river. The previous summer, when Colby had first proposed they spend their day off that way, he'd been skeptical—and prepared to exact a promise from Colby that they would *never* do anything that wholesome and outdoorsy again. But the river had been cool and the sun had been warm and the beer had been good (Terrell had brought it—he knew his microbrews!), and by the time they'd reached the pickup spot, he and Colby had told each other every bad pun known to man.

"Hey, Terrell—what did the ghost say to the vampire?"

"Oh Christ. What?"

"Don't try to hypnotize me, I can see right through you!"

"Save me, Jesus. Why'd the vampire with the hangover bite the werewolf?"

"'Cause he needed some hair of the dog! How many surrealists does it take to screw in a light bulb?"

"A fish!"

"You knew that one!"

"No, seriously, there's a big-ass catfish about three feet down— he just swam under your tube!"

"You're fulla shit!"

"No, seriously, he's—"

"Oh fuck! What was that!"

And at that point, Colby did something distinctly nonheroic and pretty much kersplanged that long body the fuck out of the inner tube and flipped it. He came up sputtering while Terrell laughed so hard he couldn't breathe.

"So tell me, T," Colby panted, clinging to the tube and wiping the water out of his eyes with his hand, "was there really a fish?"

"Oh man!" Terrell whooped, practically rolling his own inner tube. "Who the fuck cares? Yeah, there was really a fish!"

Colby laughed then, and no, in the end, it hadn't mattered. Fish or no fish, it had been a helluva time.

"You know the best spots," Terrell said now, admiration in his voice. There was something brave about Colby—he was the guy who knew the fun things and the different places. He was the kind of guy who knew a secret magic spot like this one, where he and Terrell could sit on an old dying tree and hold hands.

They were holding hands.

Oh God, how had that happened?

He looked over at Colby, who was sitting close enough that their thighs touched, and realized Colby had been stroking the inside of Terrell's wrist with his thumb since they'd sat down.

"Why'd you bring me here?" Terrell asked gruffly, looking back out over the water and pretending his hand wasn't in Colby's lap and his nerve endings weren't being settled and smoothed with every stroke of Colby's thumb.

Colby was looking straight out over the light, the water, and the darkness, just like he was. "You wouldn't let me up to your place," he said, and Terrell heard the hurt there and didn't know what to do about it.

"It's a real shithole," he said truthfully, squeezing Colby's hand unconsciously, not wanting him to pull back because of this.

"It's your place," Colby said, and Terrell, with all his inside bullshit, could hear that Colby was trying hard to keep his voice casual. "It's yours, and you don't want me to see—"

"It's a shithole," Terrell said again wearily. "It's... it's embarrassing, Colby! I've lived there for eight years, and there's not even a poster on the walls!"

"It's your place, T—why no poster?"

Terrell closed his eyes, saw the room which had maybe one window and basic white-painted walls. There was a kitchenette and a computer table and a single bed, with a tiny attached bathroom with a shower cubicle.

"No room," he said, laughing softly. "And…." How to put into words?

"You like your places secret, safe, and small," Colby supplied, bringing Terrell's knuckles up to his lips and placing an absurdly tender kiss there. "I know, T. It's half the reason I brought you."

"What's the other half?" Terrell said. Without even conscious thought, he leaned up against Colby, seeking out some of his warmth.

"I'm showing you mine, T. We've known each other for a year. You told me about your mother, 'bout your childhood, 'bout your shitty tenth-grade teacher and your rocking twelfth-grade one. I learned more than I ever thought I would about being black in America, and suspect more than I think you'll ever tell me about what it's like being gay. Don't you think I've maybe earned your trust?"

"It's a tiny room," he muttered, but he didn't break contact. "It's an auger hole."

"Where our fate is waiting to rush out and seize us," Colby quoted and then sighed. For a moment his gaze shifted restlessly across the water, his brow knitted, and his jaw was set so stubbornly Terrell thought he might have to kiss the boy to see that smile again. The thought was exhilarating. *His* kiss could make that happen.

But then Colby straightened, smiled, and let go of Terrell's hand just long enough to put his arm around Terrell's shoulders.

What part of this wasn't being a fag? How could Terrell worry about that when the moon on the water was just so damned pretty and Colby's body heat seeped steadily into his bones?

The Bones of Men and Summer

TERRELL got out of the shower to find Colby lying in bed, naked, one hand behind his head and the other on his cock. The quiet light of the bedside haloed his already golden body.

Terrell clutched the towel around his hips and, for the first time, looked his fill.

Colby's chest was broad, but his body was long and his waist tapered so he didn't look like a refrigerator. His nipples were a dark, dark pink, almost a plum color, and his hipbones might have poked out a little, but the boy had a set of devil's shoulders Satan himself would be proud to claim.

His pubic hair was golden brown, and he moved his hand slowly from base to tip, the lubricant he was using leaving a fine sheen in the lamplight.

For a moment Terrell was hurt—he'd wanted to taste it! But then, how was Colby going to know that? Terrell hadn't done much for the past two days but absorb this quiet upheaval of the life he'd always planned to have.

Colby's eyes were hooded, and he looked at Terrell with a sleepy, sexy smile.

"You want to touch?" he asked, and Terrell nodded like a shy schoolkid. He reached out one finger like he was petting a rabbit and stroked it along Colby's smooth chest, looking at the contrast between his skin and Colby's paleness.

"What do you see?" Colby asked, looking on soberly as Terrell added all of his fingertips to the stroke.

"A vain white boy who waxes," Terrell said drolly, and Colby grinned.

"Little bit, yeah," Colby said, and he rolled his eyes. "My ex liked twinkies, and I sort of got into the habit then."

Terrell blinked suddenly, brutally reminded that he didn't have exclusive rights to all of this. "How long ago did that end?" he asked, feeling a surge of possessiveness he couldn't seem to allay.

"Well, he was sort of the reason I left the Olive Garden," Colby confessed, laughing a little. "He was cheating, I was not, I found out he was doing... well, *everybody* at work, so I just took myself off the menu."

Terrell laughed, finding the fur below Colby's belly button and rubbing with his fingertips. God, it was so soft. Terrell's was too, even though it was kinkier, the curls tight and nappy—it was still soft.

"You didn't wax here." It was easier to state the obvious than it was to crow over something as petty as not ever knowing the last guy Colby had slept with. Colby was his, all his, and together they would crouch in their secret little world where nobody would ever see them.

"No," Colby said, gasping a little. "It felt... too personal. Like if someone didn't like me hairy down there, they wanted an eighteen-year-old and not me."

Terrell shivered. "You're young enough as it is."

Colby's blue eyes were bright on Terrell's. "Twenty-five. Spent a little bit of time getting the minor in lit and the master's in soc."

Terrell jerked back. "I thought you just got the BA!" he accused, and Colby shrugged and grabbed his hand, putting Terrell's reluctant fingers right where they belonged.

"I didn't get that. I sort of had a fubar thing with my... oh God. Do we have to talk about school *now*, Terrell? Are you just gonna play with my pubes?"

Terrell grunted and started a full stroke of Colby's abdomen, enjoying the play of skin on muscle, enjoying the way the boy's cock jerked whenever his hand came near. He felt the shininess of the skin and frowned. "That's not lube?"

"It's precome," Colby panted, stroking himself again. "And I could do this all night!" He grunted a little, and when he pulled his foreskin back, revealing the pinkness of the head, there was a tiny spurt at the end.

Terrell stared, mesmerized by the thick clear droplet clinging to the slit. He brought up a thumb and rubbed it, and Colby kept his foreskin out of the way while Terrell ran one finger around the head. Very carefully, he brought up his fingertip to his mouth to taste.

"It's sweet," he said analytically, and Colby let out a low moan.

"You never gave a blow job?" he asked, and Terrell bent his head and licked across Colby's exposed crown.

Colby moaned again, and Terrell pulled back long enough to say, "Not that I want to remember," before opening his mouth and taking the head of Colby's cock gingerly inside.

The crown rubbed on his palate, and he swallowed, wanting to taste some more. Colby made "mmmmnnnn" noises, soft and not showy, but still... hot, while Terrell moved his head up and down, liking the taste, wanting the fullness, open and vulnerable to this man's cock in his mouth like he'd never been to a stranger's. He pulled back and Colby put a hand on his shoulder, kneading, and Terrell dropped the towel at his waist and lowered his head again, sucking harder.

Colby gasped. "Your tongue," he directed. "Use that when you can... *God*!"

Terrell braced some of his weight with an arm across Colby's thighs and used his other hand to squeeze Colby's erection. He paused for a moment, looking at the contrast of their skin again—black hand, white cock—but he was too hungry for the taste of Colby in his mouth to dwell on the differences much longer. Then Colby moved the hand on his shoulder to his backside and started kneading, and he had a different thing to worry about.

His knees were going weak.

He moaned, the back of his throat vibrating, and Colby moaned in return. Colby's fingers dug in tighter, and his fingers barely brushed Terrell's pucker and his balls, and Terrell lunged forward in response, taking half of Colby's shaft down his throat, wanting more, shaking from the sudden arousal of the actual touch on *his* private parts.

Colby wrapped his hand around Terrell's thigh and tugged. "C'mere, T," he muttered, and Terrell allowed his back end to be maneuvered until he was leaning against the side of the bed. Colby wrapped a strong hand around Terrell's cock and stroked a couple of times, until Terrell's whole body started to shake and he let Colby flop out of his mouth while he tried to catch his breath.

"I can't do this with you doing that!" he panted, and Colby's low, evil laughter didn't stop his bold caress of Terrell's erection.

"Of course you can—that's what the sixty-nine is *for*! Now c'mere and straddle me!"

Terrell's body was moving at the same time his brain was short-circuiting. "But... but, I need to... oh *hell* no!"

He'd washed really good in the shower, every nook, cranny, and crease and even beyond, because he'd had a pretty good idea that all of his dark places were going to be exposed, and he wanted Colby to be comfortable going there.

But still, his rough scrubbing touch on his own privates was *nothing* in comparison to the heat and the pressure and the pleasuring pain of Colby's mouth on his cock. Terrell's breath shuddered out and he tried to concentrate on Colby's body, on how much he wanted to enjoy it, on the way it seemed to glow in the softened light of the bedside lamp.

It was hard to do when Colby squeezed Terrell's cock in his spit-slickened fist, lifted his head off the pillow, and started licking his crease and asshole with aggressive, probing little tongue thrusts.

Terrell's half crouch on the bed sank until most of his weight was resting on Colby's stomach, and Colby's erection had to be content with Terrell's hand as Terrell buried his face in the crease between thigh and pubic bone and groaned.

"God... oh God... what are you *doing* to me!"

Colby's chuckle was muffled, and Terrell's vision went black he was fighting his climax so hard. With a heave and a flop, he was lying next to Colby on his back, panting, shaking with arousal.

Colby rolled to his side and put his hand on Terrell's upper thigh. "Too intense?"

Terrell sucked in breath and nodded. His eyes were tightly closed, and his entire world boiled down to the feel of his cock aching in the darkness and of Colby's warm hand on his thigh.

"Too bad," Colby said playfully, and then he rolled over between Terrell's legs and engulfed his cock in one playful thrust. One, two, three strokes, that's all it took, and Terrell barely had the presence of mind to grab him by the hair and pull him off before he came, helplessly, biting his palm to keep from waking Colby's sister and half the neighborhood.

"Why'd you *do* that?" Terrell panted, and Colby scooted so that his head was lying at the foot of the bed along with Terrell's.

"Did you have fun exploring my body?" Colby asked, wiping stray come spatter off his face.

Terrell nodded, still shaking, grateful for Colby's hand on his arm. "Yeah."

"You can do that now. Your woody will come back again, you know."

Terrell rolled his head sideways, and Colby matched him stare for stare. "Maybe for you, young'un," he said, trying to be hard.

Colby grinned at him—just that, *grinned*—and the only thing half-hard about Terrell was his twitching cock.

"C'mon, T," Colby invited softly. "Don't you want to touch me?"

Terrell looked at him, sweaty, erect, undulating his taut ass against the comforter, and thought, oh *hell* yes!

"I ain't never done it like this" is what he said.

"How've you done it?" Colby asked, those blue eyes so earnest.

Terrell rolled to his side, near enough to kiss Colby's shoulder, because that was the closest thing and his want was overriding his caution with every minute. "Dirty," he whispered. "Don't ask about it, white boy. It was dirty."

Colby's hand on his chin pulled him up short. Terrell looked up and saw Colby was looking back at him soberly, all trace of play gone.

"Dirty doesn't have any place here," Colby said. His lips twitched a little. "But no one said anything about 'hot'. Suck on my nipples, T— I might come from that alone."

Terrell laughed and kissed down Colby's collarbone to his neck, which fascinated him. Colby didn't have five o'clock shadow, but there was a definite dividing line where his stubble stopped and the smooth skin started. Terrell stroked with his tongue, trying to find that place, and then suckled where Colby's neck met his shoulder. Colby palmed his shoulders while he worked, and made... noises. Good noises. Noises with a lot of liquid consonants in them.

Terrell found he was working for those noises.

When he sealed his lips around one of those dark-pink nipples and suckled hard, he got a bonus "Auuunngggghhh...," and he stayed there for a while as Colby rubbed the flattened half-inch hairs on Terrell's head. When he was done with the first nipple, Terrell moved on to the second, and Colby's noises got even better.

Colby's hips also started wiggling uncontrollably, and Terrell reached down and grasped his cock tightly again and stroked, suckling and arching against Colby in arousal.

Colby's sweat—clean and showered sweat—even *smelled* like sex, and God, the boy was so good at giving Terrell clues as to what to do next. Terrell fought the urge just to bury his face against his throat and hump his side until he came again. He didn't like to think he was a coward, but something about the tight binding he felt with every touch frightened him.

But the thought of running away, leaving Colby confused and wanting and, God help him, *hurt*, scared him even more.

Colby was bucking now, and Terrell was going to move his head down, take the next logical step and try sucking him off again, but Colby pulled a surprise move and captured his chin to pull him in for a kiss.

Terrell opened under his mouth and Colby bucked inside Terrell's fist, and his best noise of all was when he groaned and spilled, hot and wet, over Terrell's hand.

It was the vibration and the heat and the sound—that's all he needed. He'd succeeded, he'd pleasured this beautiful boy, and his second, quick and searing orgasm was his reward.

He rested his head on Colby's shoulder and Colby nuzzled his cheek, his ear, his neck.

"You did good, young Padawan," Colby intoned, and Terrell chuckled weakly.

"Aw, man, shut up."

Colby laughed some more, and they lay there, on the wrong end of the bed, dozing lightly in the breeze coming in through the sliding glass door.

EVENTUALLY they roughly toweled off and lay under the lightweight comforter. (It was blue—a color that looked horrible against Terrell's skin, but since it looked awesome against Colby's, Terrell decided not to care.) Colby was on his side, sliding graceful fingertips along Terrell's bicep and punctuating it with little kisses.

Terrell looked around the room appreciatively. It was basic—IKEA furniture on cream-colored carpet with framed pictures on the walls. But one of the walls was painted blue with tan trim, and the prints on the walls were vibrant posters of rock bands. Colby seemed to like Maroon 5 and Pearl Jam the most, and that made Terrell stop and think.

Colby had plugged his iPod into the iPod jack playing music softly in the background. Terrell closed his eyes, opened them, and looked sharply at Colby.

"Jesus, kid, what are we listening to? *Motown?*"

It was one of the first times Terrell had ever heard Colby actually *sound* like a kid. He giggled into Terrell's shoulder and said, "Honestly, T?"

Terrell started laughing helplessly. "It's the only black music you know?"

Colby hid his face some more. "It's the only black music I know."

Marvin Gaye started playing "Heard it Through the Grapevine," and Terrell nodded in time to the gentle thud of the beat. "Not a bad place to start. Why'd you bother?"

Colby pulled back, no longer hiding his face. "You worry that I'm not black," he said quietly. "Like I won't get what it's like when you say you're not supposed to be gay. I... I guess I just wanted you to forget about it for a little."

Terrell grunted. "Kid, the music ain't—" He corrected himself, because he realized Colby had been right about this. "It isn't gonna make you black like me."

"I know," Colby sighed, and he rolled over to his other side, hurt.

Terrell lay there for a moment, staring at the ceiling—it was textured, and he wondered if it would start to fall apart like the one in his apartment. "I'm not a good bet for a relationship, Colby," he said after a moment. "Us, here? It feels so good, but half the time I'm thinking I just found a good way to screw up the best friendship I maybe ever had."

Colby grunted, and Terrell guessed that wasn't welcome news. "What did you mean?" he asked, his voice sounding tinny and distant. Marvin Gaye was still playing softly, and Terrell was starting to think the boy's taste was fucking prophetic.

"When?"

"When you said it was dirty."

Terrell rolled over on his other side and wished he were somewhere else—wished *they* were somewhere else, if truth be told. The secret place between the blackberry briars, the little spot behind the pallets at work. Under his old bed as a child.

"You don't want to know that about me," he all but begged.

"Sure I do," Colby said, and there was a rustle and Colby kissed between his shoulder blades. So much for Terrell's newfound bravery, making the boy come to him like that.

"It was just… you know. You'd catch someone's eye, they'd follow you behind a bar or a classroom, and there you go. They're blowing you or fucking you and then they're history."

"That's awful," he said, but he was only assessing—not judging.

"Yeah, well, it's what I got."

"It doesn't have to be. You could have me."

Terrell laughed without humor. "Kid—"

"I've had three relationships," Colby said, his voice a study in stung pride. "Four. And I know how not to make them dirty. Kids get blow jobs behind bars, T. Men look their lovers in the eye."

Terrell rolled over, face-to-face, eye to eye, and without meaning to, he flinched back.

Colby's eyes were shiny in the lamplight, the lashes around them clotted and wet.

Terrell swallowed and cupped his neck, then leaned forward and touched their foreheads together. "I am a bitter, mean old man," he whispered. "I have… so much anger inside me. I would give *anything* for you to not know that part of me."

Colby's laugh was almost as bitter as Terrell professed to be. "Do you think I don't know?" he asked softly. "Do you think I don't see your face when Beth talks to you? When Templeton didn't have your back? When the customers start throwing their weight around? When someone tells you to get a real job? Do you think I don't see it? We've been talking for a *year*, Terrell! Every time you call me 'white boy' or 'cheese boy' or, hell, just 'boy'—do you think I don't know what you're saying to yourself?"

"Yeah, and what's that?" God, it hurt to be so transparent. What was all his hidey-hole bullshit for if this—*fuck!*—if this *man* had seen him all along?

"You're saying 'He can't understand me, because he's too white! We could never happen, because he's too white!'. You are reminding yourself of all the things that make us a bad idea."

Later, Terrell would ask himself why he didn't get up out of bed and leave right then. It was maybe three miles to his apartment—walking it wouldn't have been that bad.

"Yeah? Well, you think you know so much, can you give me an answer that makes it a good one?"

Colby's smile was... God. Pure sunshine in that midnight room. "You are *happy* when you're with me. You want to know why you haven't shown me your dark side, T? It's because that side is a whole lot lighter when you're here with me."

Terrell closed his eyes, but that smile already sat there, in his brain, where it couldn't be blocked out.

When his eyes were closed, Colby kissed him, and kissed him, and kissed him, and Terrell opened his mouth and let that man in because his soul was as naked as his body right then, and Colby was the only blanket he had.

THEY worked together the next night, and Colby insisted on Terrell borrowing Moira's bicycle that morning so they could take a ride on the bike trail down by the river. It would have been a great ride if the sun hadn't been trying to kill them dead, and they both got to work sweaty (because their shower just didn't take), dehydrated, and starving, because Colby needed to shop. He'd been *planning* to shop after the bike ride and the shower that didn't take, but Terrell had showered first and, well, things had happened when Colby had gotten out of the shower.

Things that had ended up with Colby on his knees in front of Terrell and Terrell pulling out so he could pump his come all over Colby's face.

Terrell had wiped him off tenderly afterward, sinking down to his knees next to him on the soft cream carpeting, and when Colby could open his eyes without fear of the sting, he grinned.

"T, you ever think about getting tested?"

Terrell's erection softened at triple speed. "Why?"

"'Cause I'd really like to swallow. I'm *good* at swallowing. And it feels *awesome.* But first...?" He batted those innocent blue eyes at Terrell, and Terrell grunted.

"Is it covered in our bootsy-ass health insurance?" he asked to buy time, and Colby grimaced.

"No. Is that going to be your excuse not to do it?"

Terrell glared at him. "You think I'm looking for an excuse?"

Colby raised his eyebrows, and Terrell found himself shifting uncomfortably and offering Colby a hand up.

"I'm... I mean, you know."

"Yeah, T. You can't be gay. Gotcha. But just because you can't be gay doesn't mean you can't be positive."

The thought of carrying around a load of something evil and giving it to Colby twisted his stomach. He started rooting around the clean laundry pile for his boxers, unable to look at Colby anymore. "If you think my thing's dirty, why do you keep putting it in your mouth?" he snapped, hating himself with a particular viciousness.

Colby's hug over his back was the last thing he expected. "I don't think it's dirty," Colby said into his ear. "And regarding HIV, we've been pretty safe. But that's not the only thing out there, and I'd like us to start out clean."

Terrell swallowed and took that comfort as it was offered. Without meaning to, he tilted his head sideways and shivered when Colby kissed his temple.

"You're getting prickles," Colby said, and Terrell grunted. He usually kept it cut real close but not shaved bald. You let it grow out too much and the half curls would start to feel like bad wool.

"I usually go to the barbershop on Sunday," he confessed.

"I've got an electric razor," Colby said, not letting up on that comforting hug. "How about we call up, make an appointment for the two of us, and while we're waiting, I buzz your hair close again."

Terrell looked at him, pleased without knowing why. "You'll go with me?" God—he'd said he'd been tested before. That was a hell of an expense.

"Yeah. Why not? My test last year was negative, but there's that whole window thing. I don't need the whole panel, but I'll get the HIV."

Terrell nodded, swallowing. God, he was so matter-of-fact. "Did you ever think that if what we're doing means we need to be tested for disease, then maybe it's wrong?"

Colby pulled back and smacked him on the back of his head. "There are plenty of straight men with crud on their peters, T. Jesus, don't overthink things. It's a disease, not a moral judgment!"

Terrell turned around in time to see him shaking his head as he ambled to the kitchen in his basketball shorts, which is what he'd managed to put on before Terrell had gotten out of the shower. The thing Terrell had chewed on in his head until it was bloody healed, shifted, became a simple critter in the dark instead of a ravening monster.

So Colby put off shopping and the two of them got to work starving, but without thinking too hard about what the results might mean for him and Colby, Terrell thought maybe it would be worth it.

Sunday nights in the summer were a crapshoot. Sometimes they were rocking and sometimes morgues had more fun.

This night would give a morgue a run for its money, and when Colby came up with his drink order through the waitstaff window, he looked mischievous and social.

"They're talking Club Papi's tonight, T. You in?"

Terrell grimaced. One of the things that sucked about closing the bar down was that very often, employees of almost anywhere liked to gather after shift for a drink. You couldn't buy from Papiano's after they closed because the place would get shut down, but you *could* send the guy who got off first out for some beer at the liquor store across the street, and he could share with his buddies in the darkened parking lot, as long as you didn't make enough noise to attract the cops.

Voilà! Club Papi's was born!

"You first off tonight?" he asked, because Colby tended to get off-the-wall shit when he was buying. Last time he'd bought for Club Papi's, around three weeks ago, he'd had the whole crew drinking Advocaat, which was this weird-assed liqueur from Holland, and mixing it with that marshmallow-flavored vodka, of all things! The results had tasted very… desserty, in a way that had made pretty much everyone want to throw up and get the whole thing over with.

"No," Colby said, looking a little disappointed. "Angie and Kim are."

"Good, then! I'm in! Tell them to get me one of those pale microbrews—something blond, okay? I like that shit!"

Colby was the only one at the back bar, which was a good thing, because his chuckle, low and dirty, pretty much sent Terrell on silent erection for the next hour and a frickin' half. "Something blond? Gotcha, T. I'll make sure you've got something blond after work."

Terrell didn't like getting caught flatfooted, but as Colby took his appletini and Captain & Coke downstairs, Terrell found he was staring after the man, thinking that he wanted to tell the whole world that Colby was talking about himself, and Terrell was going to get *him*.

He managed to refrain, but he was still standing there, staring off into space, when Percy came up to refill his big plastic cup with Dr Pepper and ice.

"What you lookin' at, T?" Percy asked, and Terrell grunted in disapproval.

"You should drink water, Percy. It's better for you.

Percy rolled his eyes. "You just like being old," he said plaintively. "Just because I'm old enough to enjoy the hell out of life doesn't mean—"

"You have to abuse your kidneys because they *will* stop working for you one day."

Percy's chuckle was low and evil too, and Terrell had a moment to wonder if that was just the noise a man made when he'd gotten him some the night before. "As long as other things keep working, T, I'm going to be a happy man!"

Terrell shook his head. "Yeah, you're a boy and she's a woman with shit she gotta do. What makes you think *that's* gonna work?"

Percy was apparently too self-involved to question where Terrell got his info, and too shameless to care that it was true. His smile was self-satisfied and arrogant. "I'm a man," he said, his chest puffed out, and Terrell rolled his eyes.

"You're a kid with a dick," he said grimly. "If that's what she needs right now, it's not what she's gonna need forever."

Percy shrugged his shoulders. "No one lives forever. I might not even live until thirty!"

Terrell shivered. "Jesus, Percy—can't you see bigger than the hood you grew up in? Those fools might not live past thirty, but you live with your auntie, and she lives on a different block. There's no reason to hang with motherfuckers who'll get you killed!"

"Man, why you care?" Percy sucked down his soda and then refilled it, like his disgust gave him more need for a bigger sugar/caffeine rush. "It's not like you give a fuck about the hood *or* me! You got your college education and shit, and you think that makes you so much better than me, but I got news for you, fucker. We work in the *same place*!"

Well, Terrell couldn't argue with that. "Yeah, that's right. We work in the same place. But I at least know how far I want to go. I can *see* the stars. All you seein' is the lid of the box you in."

Oh hell. There he was, dropping his endings, fucking up his pronouns. All that time in school, practicing the talk, learning the code of the professors and the administrators so he could walk through any door and speak the language, and this kid was reminding him of who he was with enough emphasis to steal that away.

Yeah, Percy was right about one thing. They both worked in the same goddamned place.

But still, that conversation with Percy couldn't sour the idea of Club Papi's after work. For one thing, he'd sort of caught some of

Colby's excitement for solving the murder of one spineless weasel and all-around douchebag, and he figured that if anywhere was a good place to gossip, behind the restaurant where it happened would do the trick.

For another, well, they weren't going to hold hands, and they weren't going to neck. He wasn't planning to stand any closer to Colby than on any other given night, and he certainly wasn't going to go public. But even if they just stood together and leaned on the hood of Colby's car and listened to everyone talk and watched their expressions in the warped light from the one working street lamp, they would talk about the conversation and mull it over and discuss the holy hell out of it. It would give him a way to be with Colby without having to think in his head, *We are going to have sex.* He wanted to be with Colby. He *ached* to be with Colby, and the sex wasn't even necessary.

An excuse, any excuse, please *God* let there be an excuse, so the self-confession wasn't necessary either!

God, wasn't it enough just to be at a party with the guy?

And it was.

It was just like all the other times they'd had Club Papi's out in the lot, except the gossip was a hell of a lot more interesting than just who was banging whom and who was snorting what.

"Yeah," Trish said, poking her black work tennis shoe into the earth planter behind the curb and taking a quick drink of her beer. "Man, I just came out of the bathroom when I heard the shot. Beth had just torn me a new one for… God—*something* stupid. I think my boobs weren't big enough on Friday." That got her a laugh, and she took another sip of beer. She was one of those quiet, studious girls who waited tables subtly and efficiently. She didn't get *huge* tips, but she did get *steady* tips. Terrell thought Beth probably hated that about her. Trish wasn't flashy, and she wasn't cocky, and she wasn't loud. She was just competent, and God forbid that be a virtue.

"Did you see anyone?" Colby asked, and Trish shook her head.

"No. I was the first one out in the hallway, and I saw the door to the dock swing shut, but by then, you could smell the gunpowder and the manager's office was just sitting there, wide open." She shuddered. "Yeah—good thing I want to be a schoolteacher and not a cop. I mean, I can probably do violence, but the dead bodies, not so much."

"You didn't even see it when it was turned around!" Percy said excitedly. "Man, it was gross—they used hollow points and it looked like a big ol' bloody watermelon!"

Terrell grimaced. "Hey—who gave that kid beer!" he snapped.

Gina said, "I did—why? He's twenty-two, right?"

Half the little group standing around the back of Angie's truck groaned.

"No, sweetie," Erin said, condescension dripping from her voice, and wasn't that nice. Who invited the manager? "He's eighteen."

"Aw, fuck!" Gina sputtered. "Percy, you *weasel!*"

Terrell and Colby met eyes and wondered if anyone there guessed she was talking about more than underage drinking.

Percy must have, because the face he presented to her looked like more than a basic apology. "I'm sorry," he said quietly and then handed her the beer back. "Here. I don't want to get you in trouble."

Terrell looked at the sudden earnestness on the boy's face, and the vulnerability, and he wanted to bang his head against the tree. Suddenly, he was rooting for *Percy*, of all people!

Gina hadn't said anything back yet, but she and Percy were having one of those eyeballin' conversations that looked like it was an entire library in one long look.

Terrell threw the boy a bone and spoke up to give them a little breathing space. "Yeah, that reminds me. Who uses hollow points? I mean, for anything *but* killing, right?"

"Well, they're better for controlled shooting," Colby said next to him, "and they're the go-to ammo for a Saturday night special."

Terrell shot him an incredulous look. "You mean they're more accurate?"

"No, not unless they're teardrop shaped. I just mean short range, that's all. But yeah. The cops said they were .38s—they were Saturday night special bullets, I asked my sister."

"What's your sister know about it?" Percy asked, apparently done with his eyeball wars *and* with his time in the doghouse. Gina was leaning up against him, and Percy had his arm draped around her chest. Well, wasn't that special and sweet? That was making all sorts of peace in this world, wasn't it?

"She's an attorney—she works for a judge who tries criminal cases. She comes home with all sorts of interesting shit."

"What?" Suk wanted to know. Terrell had never seen him drink, but he always did enjoy nights like this, where everyone gathered around and he was treated equally and invited into the conversation. "What does your sister get to know?"

Colby looked around and then turned a quick wink in Terrell's direction. "Well, like, you know how Will liked his coke, right?"

Most of them nodded, and Terrell wondered if Templeton had realized how discreet he had *not* been during his lifetime. "Well, she told me he was into dealers for some cash—but too much cash for just one guy, so he was buying for someone else."

"Oh man!" Jason said, and Terrell raised a skeptical eyebrow.

"This surprises you?"

"No! Man, he asked me if I had a source! I told him no—I'm just naturally this hyper!"

Colby started to laugh at the guy—who was barely twenty-one, six three, and weighed maybe 150 pounds. "He seriously asked *you* where to get drugs?"

Jason was, among other things, a strict teetotaler. He was *very* Mormon, but not in a sanctimonious way. Jason was actually one of the few people whose religion Terrell totally respected, because Jason simply lived his faith by being sweet to other people. Like tonight, he was with Suk in the drinking diet Coke for company department, but sure enough, if someone got too drunk to drive? Jason was the guy taking them home.

Jason shook his head in disgust. "He seemed to think that's why I stayed so skinny!"

Colby laughed. "Yeah, you stay skinny from clean living, my friend. That is your only secret!"

Jason mumbled something, blushed, then looked at his toes, and Terrell glanced at Colby sharply. Did Colby know? he wondered. Or was that just maybe Colby's magical superpower—he made guys who weren't supposed to be gay want him.

Worst. Superpower. Ever.

"So," Colby mused out loud, "he wasn't just buying for himself, he was buying for someone else. That's interesting. I can't figure out if it spreads the motive or narrows it down."

"You trying to solve the crime?" Mark the window dick asked, and Colby shrugged. Mark was still in his chef whites (not so white at the end of the shift), and he was in his last year at school.

"Well, I'm curious, you know? 'Cause you know,"—he looked around meaningfully—"it had to be one of us. Maybe not someone here *now*, because not everyone who worked that night is here, but it had to be an employee at Papiano's, and I'm wondering why we haven't all been questioned more than this."

"What do you mean?" Kelly asked. She'd worked this shift on half cylinders—Terrell had heard the waitstaff bitching about her all night.

"Well, my sister says Templeton was greasing people up at the capitol," Colby said. Terrell might not have been the only one to notice the girl's hard-eyed interest. Colby cast a covert look at Terrell, who took the cue and started studying the people around them as Colby talked. "So I figure if he's asking Jason here who to buy from, and he was still functional, his usual supply must not have been enough. I think maybe he was buying for someone high up."

"What kind of fool would do that?" Percy wanted to know. "You're risking a whole lot of bad just buying for yourself."

Colby obviously thought about it hard before he answered. "He wanted people to think he was important," he mused. "Well, he didn't seem to have a lot of time or energy for us peons, but he wanted important people to value him."

Percy snorted. "Man, you buy for someone, you've got about as much value as a drive-through window!"

Oh hells! "Percy, that is about the smartest thing I have *ever* heard you say!" Terrell told him in admiration. *Oh thank you, Jesus, this boy might make it yet!*

Percy ducked his head behind Gina's. "Yeah, well, two years in juvie oughta teach a guy *something*."

"Well that's a damned sight more than Will Templeton ever learned," Colby said, and there was a universal grunt of assent.

"I just wish he'd learned to wear a rubber," Kelly grunted. She took a long pull from her beer to punctuate that sentiment, and Terrell wondered if that meant she had a doctor's appointment in her future. He hoped it was that and not a trip to the local Planned Parenthood—those places had been picketed a lot recently.

"You're not the only one," Erin muttered, and Kelly looked at her in surprise.

"Seriously?"

"What?" Erin snapped. "We were here 'til three one morning, checking out the drawers. I was tired, he was horny…."

"Yeah, for a guy doing so much blow, he sure did fuck everything with legs!" Angie said, and they all looked at her. She blushed, her skin so fair you could catch the darkening of it under the iffy light. "My apologies," she muttered. "He just got a lot of tail."

"Does anyone know if he got Beth?" Suk asked, and his voice had the same analytical tone as Colby's. "They did have… well, one bad habit in common."

"Naw," Percy said. "Not the same habit. Beth's doing meth, Will did coke."

"How do you know that?" Mark asked, and Percy shrugged.

"Coke may shrink your balls, but it does make you horny before that happens. Meth makes you zitty and yellow, and she's got that going for her right now. Pretty soon, her teeth'll go bad. You'll see."

They all grimaced. Yeah, they could see that coming.

"She won't have a job by then," Gina said. "She's pulling from the till to buy, just like Will did."

"Oh Jesus!" Erin exclaimed, and even though she was still dressed nicely, in her high heels and short skirt, she turned around and kicked the tire of the truck she was leaning against. "God, I'm stupid! Fuck this shit, I'm gonna go back and live with my parents and go back to school!"

There was a bemused silence, and Erin's pretty model face twisted, and she wiped her eyes with the back of her hand. "That's why we were here until three in the morning," she said, sounding humiliated. "He stole money from the fucking till, and I was dumb enough to think it was my fault. Fucking *Jesus*! If he wasn't already dead, I'd kill him myself!"

"Now you don't mean that," Jason said, his Adam's apple bobbing nervously. He took a few steps sideways and put a bony arm over Erin's shoulders, and Erin tucked her face into his chest.

"No," she mumbled, lost in misery. "But I just told the whole world I let a dead douche bag knock me up. You let me know how I can fuck up my life any worse—obviously I need to be told what not to do."

"You could have been doing blow when you got knocked up," Kelly said, and everyone stared at her in horror. She shrugged. "Jesus, people—that shit's everywhere!"

"God," Gina said passionately, "was there anyone here he *didn't* hit on?"

"Colby!" Jason said cheekily, and to Terrell's shock, Colby rolled his eyes.

"I wish! Naw, as soon as he knew about me, he grabbed my ass. Equal opportunity douche bag, our boss—and proof that karma works!"

"And bullets," Terrell said sourly, garnering a laugh. Terrell wondered if they'd be laughing if they knew how badly he wanted to dig that fucker up, resurrect him like Frankenstein's monster, and then hunt him down with a pitchfork and a shiv so he could gut him again. Grab Colby's ass? Terrell would kill him twice.

"Yeah," Jason said over Erin's head, "he tried with me too—and I'm not gay!"

"You're not?" Erin asked, jerking back.

Jason grunted and locked her against his chest again, and to Terrell's amusement, she stayed. Well, it was nice that Erin believed it, because Terrell wasn't buying.

"Wow," Gina said, and she sounded like Terrell felt: caught between laughter and horror. "So, we know he hit on white boys—Percy? Terrell? What about you guys?"

"Naw," Percy assured her, digging his chin into the top of her head. "Besides, everyone knows ni—uh, hoodrats ain't gay, am I right, T?"

"If that's what everyone knows," Terrell said, carefully not looking at Colby. He saw the guy anyway, and the fact that the boy *didn't* look disappointed in him actually depressed Terrell further.

He glanced away before he started babbling all their secrets, just to make him proud.

"So do we think the person he was buying for killed him?" Angie asked with nothing more than curiosity, and Colby shrugged.

"No. I think one of the rich people he was buying for got someone here to do it."

"I think you're wrong," Terrell said before he knew the words were coming out of his mouth.

"Why?" Colby asked, but he didn't seem hurt.

"Because it was so damned close," Terrell said, and Colby shrugged.

"Yeah, but it was in the back. It was impersonal. And whoever it was, they were cool enough to run *immediately*. None of that 'Oh my God! What have I done!' bullshit. They just hit him twice and ran."

Terrell thought for a minute. "Yeah, you're right. Damn, that's cold. But as bad as he was screwing with everyone? Could just have been cold rage."

Colby nodded. "Yeah. Not worth it to me."

"What do you mean?"

Colby's grin was wicked. "If I was gonna risk getting arrested, going to jail, it had better be for something I damned well gave a fuck about."

"Hey!" Kelly said suddenly, and they both jerked their attention across their little people circle to her.

"Is for horses," Colby said cheekily, and she sneered.

"No, this is serious—you guys *really* didn't see anything?"

Colby laughed and Terrell followed his lead.

"Really really," Colby said. "We were tucked back into that little bolt-hole so T here could lean up against the wall, and all we heard was the gunshot and footsteps!"

Terrell shook his head. "We didn't even really register the gunshot—"

"*You* didn't know it was a *gunshot*?" Percy asked incredulously and was immediately back on Terrell's shit list.

"No, asshole, I didn't register the gunshot. It's been a long time since I heard one of those!"

It had been too. His ugly apartment complex wasn't really in a shitty neighborhood, just a tacky one.

"Okay, okay!" Percy held up the hand that wasn't wrapped around Gina's shoulders. "I just thought you might have, I don't know, heard a frickin' gunshot! What were you two talking about, anyhow?"

Without missing a beat, Colby said, "Cats!"

The whole crowd laughed.

"No, seriously! Cats! Tell him, T—we were talking about my sister's cats."

Terrell's laughter was spontaneous and relieved. "Man, you would not be*lieve* what his sister named their cats! And it's not fair, either, 'cause both those animals are—"

"Damned fine pussies," Colby intervened drolly, and Terrell slugged him in the arm while he bent double and cackled until he couldn't breathe. While Colby did that, Terrell explained about Puddin' and Dewey Folds, and the rest of the group laughed until *they* couldn't breathe, and the matter of Will Templeton's murder—and Terrell and Colby hidden in the bolt-hole—was dropped.

It wasn't until they were in Colby's car, heading back for—praise God—his place, that Colby brought it up.

"I'm sorry," he said.

Terrell jerked his attention from his fascination with the soda-lamp shadows passing through the car windows as they traveled. "For what?"

"I forgot. Digging into that night might get you outed. I never meant to do that."

Terrell grunted. "Man, I wasn't even worried. Fucking hated *myself*, but I wasn't worried."

Colby's car was stick shift, so his hand on Terrell's knee was a fleeting, hard squeeze. "You're doing your best," Colby said. "I just wish…."

"What?" It would be better if he said it. Terrell deserved to have him mad, deserved to have Colby call him a coward.

"I wish you could see the world as a bigger place, is all," Colby said, his voice sort of lost in the darkness, like he was searching for just the right words.

Which was odd, because the words he used were *hauntingly* familiar.

"Bigger?" Terrell asked, but his voice didn't catch the first time. He cleared his throat. "Bigger?"

"Yeah. I mean… Sacramento's not a small place, but it's not the *only* place. There's places all over the world—a lot of them are a damned sight friendlier to gay people than we are here."

"I know it," Terrell said. "Germany, Belgium, the Netherlands—"

"Yeah, you *say* that because you learned it in school, but have you ever thought about what it means?"

Terrell frowned and turned to imprint Colby on his eyeballs some more. "What what means?"

"That you don't have to live in this town! You could get out! *We* could get out. Not forever. Just long enough so that when we come back, only the people who don't give a shit about us being together will matter."

Blink once, and the world shifted from Fulton to Eastern. Blink again, and it shifted from Sacramento to Belgium. Blink again, and they were piloting a starship shuttle to a galaxy far away.

"What would we do?" he asked, fascinated and dizzy from the space exploration they were conducting from the front seat of Colby's car.

"I don't know. You're a journalist—haven't you ever thought of traveling?"

Terrell caught his breath. No. No. His project, his one old, tired project, was to show life from his perspective. He'd worked on it in little tiny increments, little stolen packets of time, little, bitter, corrupted moments that had left him feeling acrid and soiled with the venom he was spewing instead of cathartic and relieved.

He'd never thought of leaving that all behind.

"No," he said, his throat thick with his own blindness. It was terrifying. It was *exhilarating.*

"Will you?" Colby asked, his voice low, pulsing with something Terrell couldn't identify, and Terrell wanted to reach out and touch it. He was missing something, he knew it. Missing something basic to who Colby was and what he was doing with his life.

"Think about it?" Terrell asked, half-afraid to know that missing part. What if it was the part that Terrell couldn't have?

"Yeah."

"Yeah," Terrell muttered, sure he'd be able to think of nothing else. "Absolutely. I'll think about it."

The car was at a light, so Colby could reach out again and squeeze his knee. Terrell captured his hand for just a moment and let go in time for Colby to drive. His knee tingled, and suddenly he remembered the hot tub and the scented water and the promise of Colby's bare skin against his own.

He wondered when that promise would get old, when it would cease to slug him in the solar plexus and make him struggle for breath.

Later, as Colby was pushing inside his body, battling for space, kissing him repeatedly and squeezing his most sensitive places until Terrell had to scream to let it all happen, to let out enough Terrell to let Colby in, he had the dim thought that it was not getting old. It was not getting familiar. It was gorgeous, terrifying and new, every goddamned time.

Heat and Flesh

COLBY worked the day shift the next day, and Terrell worked the night. Colby dropped Terrell off in front of his apartment, and Terrell—without thinking about it because, really, who knew him here?—leaned over instinctively to kiss Colby's cheek before he went in.

The look of pleased surprise on Colby's face carried Terrell for the rest of the day.

God, what he wanted to give that boy. He wanted him to look like that all the time. Terrell wanted to wake him up like that in the morning and do things in bed at night that made that look inevitable.

Terrell imagined saying *I love you* and seeing what Colby's face looked like then.

For a heartbeat this was an exciting thing, thrilling in ways Terrell didn't know he could be thrilled, and then....

Right when he put his hand on his doorknob and realized he was wearing Colby's basketball shorts and his T-shirt and his underwear, and that he hadn't been home in three days, *that's* when the full panic of what he was thinking hit him.

His palms started sweating so bad, his hand slipped on the doorknob like a fish in a grease bucket. It was a few painful moments before he could let himself in.

Oh God. Sweet Jesus, *really?* Terrell—bandy-legged, crooked-toothed Terrell, with the nappy hair and the flat nose—*he* was going to tell *Colby* that he loved him?

For a moment his heart quailed so badly he wanted to call his Gi-Gi and ask her advice.

He barely got himself into his apartment after that, and when he *did* get in, he just lay there on the bed and shook for twenty minutes, trying to get over the terror, the recoil on her face, if he ever went over to her house and told her that he and a white boy were in love.

Gi-Gi never did have no use for those people who went against God.

Terrell eventually pulled himself together. He had his uniform in a bag, and it needed washing, and he had the clothes from three days ago (ew!), and they needed it too. His apartment needed airing out, and he needed to dust and sweep and dump out the rancid orange juice and shop for groceries.

He had things to do.

They didn't take long.

In three hours he had clean laundry, cold cereal, and a clean one-room apartment. That left him three hours in the heat of the day before he had to get ready for work, and he figured he could spend an hour and go swimming, and that would be fine.

But it didn't take a genius to realize that his tiny apartment, with its brown carpeting and its one bed with the brown bedspread, the brown couch, and the little coffee table where he ate—it was now too small and too plain to contain him anymore.

He couldn't even *look* at his computer, where all of the bitterness of growing up black and gay was festering. He was almost afraid he'd see the surface of the screen and the tower blistering from the poison he'd planted inside.

Trying hard not to think about it, he pulled his suit out of the bathroom and a towel out of the clean-clothes basket, because he just wasn't ready to face this thought yet.

On his way out the door, he stopped at the counter that divided his tiny kitchenette from the rest of the place and checked his phone messages.

Terrell? Honey, you there? It's your Gi-Gi. Honey, I was gonna call you anyway 'cause everybody's comin' here for the Fourth of July, and we wanted to see you this time. You gonna be too busy for us again? We ain't seen you since Christmas, honey! Your cousins all miss you, and you don't hardly live that far away. But anyways, your cousin Monique, she's gonna have a baby soon, and you're always so good about sending a present. She's not out of high school yet, so the baby's gonna be here. I sure could use a new crib, hon. The last one was falling apart when we put it in the garage, and I think it'd be a danger now. So anyway, if you wanted to give her that for the baby, it would be a blessing. She's due at the end of June. Love you, honey! Call me back. I sure would love to see you!

And with that, the message ended.

Terrell thunked his head gently against the doorframe.

Lovely. Terrell's mother had been the oldest girl, and the youngest when she'd gotten pregnant, so Terrell's cousins were *all* younger than he was by at least six years. There were ten of them, and they had all, at one time or another, spent time at Gi-Gi's. Terrell was sure that if he asked Colby, he could find the statistics or the reasoning or the cultural necessity of the young parents leaving their children with not-quite-so-young grandparents (Terrell's grandmother was sixty-five, maybe), but all Terrell knew was that Gi-Gi was getting too old to be raising all these children. Monique was one of the younger ones, at sixteen, and damned if Terrell knew where her mother was or why Ashanti couldn't be bothered take care of her own kid, but Terrell, as the oldest, got the joy of providing when Gi-Gi's resources fell short.

The fact that Terrell only made it to the neighborhood twice a year to visit was obviously allayed by the fact that he sent money and things like baby cribs and food and clothes for the younger cousins when Gi-Gi needed him to. Terrell knew there were white families like this, and black families that lived like Colby's family and put their kids through college and called them just to see how they were doing.

But not in Terrell's neighborhood.

God. If he told Gi-Gi he was gay, would he get to go to her for advice? Could he get something back from this relationship? Because that sure would be nice at this point, oh yes it would. And if he didn't, could he break all his ties then and not feel like a monster for not providing for the people who couldn't barely send him a thank-you card when he did?

He didn't want to think about it. He wasn't *ready* to think about it. He went to work out instead.

HE SLEPT in his own bed that night, and hated it. He closed his eyes and remembered the sound of Colby's breathing, the creak of the cats as they wandered around the house (or, sometimes, beat the holy hell out of each other), and even Moira's voice as she talked to herself over paperwork.

But mostly the sound of Colby's breathing.

He'd liked this place when he'd first gotten it—had chosen it because it had fit his student budget at the time and because it *was* small. Tiny and unadorned, it wrapped him up and kept him safe, like his spot under the bed at Gi-Gi's.

Weird, wasn't it? How safe didn't seem as important as Colby these days?

He fell asleep around 2:00 a.m., dreaming about Colby's breathing.

He woke up around nine because Colby was on the phone.

"You up?" God, you could give a white guy a deep velvet voice, but you couldn't take the fucking chirp out of it at ungodly a.m., could you?

"Am now." Terrell swung his legs over the edge of the bed and stretched carefully. If he didn't stretch before he stood up, his leg muscles might cramp, especially after a late shift, when he stood up for seven hours and then went home and crashed.

"I can hear you making your morning sounds. It's fucking sexy. What's your apartment number?"

"Two-oh-six," Terrell responded automatically. "Why?"

"Hang on a minute." He heard the sound of Colby breathing and moving fast, and then the call ended.

Terrell blinked. Wait. *Hang on a minute?* Oh hells. Oh *fuck*!

About the time he was struggling to his feet and thinking about getting dressed so he could go outside and catch Colby on the way in, somebody pounded at the door.

Terrell looked around frantically for a pair of sweats or sleep shorts or something to put over his boxers, and Colby shouted, "T, you don't need pj's, it's me! Now come on! Open up! I brought coffee and pie!"

Oh Jesus! "Come in! Come in before the whole apartment complex comes out to see—" Terrell opened the door, and Colby, dressed in a tank top and cargo shorts, came inside, kicked the door shut with his foot, and then leaned forward and captured Terrell's mouth with his own. His hands were both full, so it was just that, his mouth, and Terrell closed his eyes and let that boy kiss him senseless.

Colby pulled back and smiled, his eyes half-lidded and sexy as hell. "I missed you," he said easily, and Terrell made himself step back and turn to the dresser under the bed to find some clothes.

"It was damned quiet here," he acknowledged, and Colby stopped and put the pie and the carton with the coffees on the counter.

Terrell straightened and Colby stepped behind him, hands on his hips, lips on his ear. "Is that all you missed?" he whispered, and Terrell kept a smile under wraps with extreme effort.

"Well you know, I did miss the cats."

"The cats!" Colby's voice cracked with indignation, and Terrell cracked up. "The cats!" Colby repeated, swinging Terrell around to face him. "I sex you up for *three days* and all you're missing is the—"

"Hush," Terrell whispered, and this time he kissed Colby.

Colby reached around and pulled Terrell closer until Terrell ravaged his mouth, tried to climb inside, framed Colby's face with his hands, stood a little on his toes, and gave Colby everything he had.

Colby groaned, went pliant, sagged against Terrell, and Terrell was surprised when he found he could catch him. He backed up a little, hit the bed, bent his knees, and went over backward, still kissing Colby as aggressively as he could. Colby was still his, still following his lead, and Terrell rolled them over so he could be on top, undulating his nearly naked body on top of Colby's.

Oh God, he wanted. Colby smelled like shower and sun, and Terrell hadn't breathed him in like this for nearly an entire day. Colby kept kissing him, kneading his hands on Terrell's bare back and then sliding them under Terrell's boxer shorts.

"Nunng...." More. He needed more.

Colby fumbled, finally managing to shove *all* the pants down, his *and* Terrell's, and they were cock to cock, naked. Terrell shoved his hands under the tank top, which was offending just because it was *on,* and Colby captured their cocks in his hand and squeezed them together. Terrell hit the brink of orgasm at a speed of Mach six, no turning back.

Terrell thrust against Colby, driving into the friction created by his hand, craving the soft skin and hard length of his erection, needing all of it hot and dreamy and... oh God, not enough.

Colby let go of his own cock and gripped Terrell firmly, anchoring Terrell's hips with a hard hand in the small of his back. A groan ripped its way from Terrell's balls, past his taint, and up through his stomach. He buried his face in Colby's neck and let that sound out, and Colby panted in his ear, "God, you're hot. Let that out, baby, c'mon... c'mon...."

Terrell pulled back and kissed him again until the pressure and pleasure at his groin shivered their way up Terrell's spine. It was coming, surging, surging, building—he couldn't even *think* about kissing anymore, so he pulled away as his orgasm took him over. He latched his mouth over Colby's neck and sucked, hard, to keep from screaming.

His come spilled hot and slick in Colby's hand, and Colby took both their erections again and started to thrust frantically, frenzied, while Terrell grunted and kept spilling into his tightened fist.

Colby squeezed some more. Terrell *did* scream, keeping it muffled against Colby's shoulder, and Colby palmed the back of his head and buried his face in Terrell's throat and let out a long-drawn-out grunt as the heat of his come spurted between them.

"So that," Colby panted after a few minutes, "is what you missed, huh? The cats?"

"Yeah," Terrell panted back, too spent even to chuckle. "You know—" Gasp. "—me. I'm all about the pussy."

Colby managed half a laugh then before they went back to catching their breath.

Eventually they showered, squeezing into Terrell's tiny shower compartment and rinsing off. Colby looked at Terrell's special skin wash and made a "woohoo!" sound, and Terrell shrugged and looked away.

"You don't shave right, you get the big pink bumps," he said, and Colby's eyes widened.

"I wondered!" he said, avid as a little kid, and Terrell got over himself.

"If you were any whiter, your eyes'd be red and we wouldn't let you out in sunlight," he said dryly.

Colby's chuckle was low and evil. "So you'd keep me in the basement, right? I'd be like your white sex slave?"

Terrell smacked him upside the head, but that didn't stop the man from keeping up that irreverent barrier-breaking laughter as they got out and dried off and got back to caffeine and pie.

"So," Colby asked as they sat themselves on the couch with coffee and pie on the little table between them. "What are your plans for today?"

Terrell was leaning over the pie box, wiggling out his first forkful, and he stopped with it halfway to his mouth. "What do you mean what are my plans for today? You're the one who came by with food, all hot to do something!"

Colby was all with the laugh-crinkled eyes and wicked chuckling today. "Well, we just did something hot! I stopped by to see what your plan was and to join you!"

The pie was awesome. Cherry, with just the right amount of tart to sweet. "Seriously. You got this from the *grocery* store? This is some good shit!"

"Yeah, and you're stalling. It's our day off. Did you have plans?"

"Our day off? Don't you work this morning?"

Colby narrowed his eyes, all of the wicked laughter gone. "I traded it off to be with you. And yes, I've got some shit I want to do with you, but damn, Terrell, you're stalling and it's stupid!"

Terrell tried to be casual, but he was pretty sure Colby saw through this like he'd seen through everything else, so he might as well just blurt it out. "Man, you're the one who made us go get the damned tests. Shouldn't we maybe go find out how those went?"

Colby nodded. "Yeah, and that was on my itinerary. We'll go together—it'll be fine."

Terrell forced himself to take another bite of pie. "You say that— you ain't done the things I done."

"Yeah, I know," Colby said quietly, and for the first time, Terrell had a sense that Colby really *did* know. It was both reassuring and frightening.

"Yeah, well, I'm sorta... I mean, I didn't have any plans for after that. I figured if it was bad, you know, you wouldn't have any plans with me."

Colby dropped his fork, and Terrell looked up from his careful contemplation of his large caramel frozen latte to see Colby wiping his mouth with a hand that looked like it was shaking.

"So that's it?" Colby asked, and it wasn't Terrell's imagination. His face had gone pale. "You... you test positive and, what? I'm just gonna... I don't know. Go home? That's it? We go back to being break buddies?"

Terrell frowned. "Well, a whole lot of things would suck, wouldn't they? No use you getting sucked into all of that...." He flailed for words.

"Suck?" Colby supplied, some of the color coming back to his face.

"Yeah. Suck."

"God, Terrell. I thought you liked me or... I don't know, at least thought I was worth your fuckin' time!"

Colby stood up, banging his knees on the coffee table, his movements jerky, all elbows. He took two steps out from the coffee table and turned his back, obviously trying to get his breathing under control.

Terrell grunted. "What—what's going to happen if that test comes back positive? You think you're going to want to touch me—"

"It's not a death sentence, asshole! It hasn't been for years. Jesus, read a fucking newspaper or something."

"Yeah, but... you know. You don't need to be doing it with some dirty old n—"

Colby whirled. "Be careful how you finish that sentence, T, and then decide if it's a word you want me to use or not."

Terrell took a deep breath. "Okay, okay—I just... as fucking awesome as this all is, I just... man, Colby. You brought me coffee and pie and a hand job. I just don't know what I'm bringing to the table here!"

Colby laughed a little. "Jesus, you're stupid," he said. Some of the starch seemed to leach out of his sails then, and he returned to the couch and flopped down.

"I've been sayin'," Terrell said, suddenly embarrassed. He sat down too and took a big drag off his frapped coffee. "What am I stupid about now?"

"I've been rearranging my schedule to spend time with you almost since I started working at Papi's. Didn't it even occur to you that I thought you were special?"

"No," Terrell said shortly. "And now you're the stupid one."

Colby let out a wounded noise, and Terrell was shocked into looking him in the eyes. God—was he ever going to stop hurting this man?

"But since, you know, you're planning to spend my day off with me and all, maybe I should stop rubbing your nose in that."

Colby shook his head. "Yeah. Yeah. You do that." He sighed. "Terrell, you are the nicest guy. You help the new people, you smile at all the regulars, you're honest as the day as long. That's why I wanted to spend time with you. That's why I... I waited so long to actually kiss you! You're such a good guy, you really are—but I swear to Christ, baby, you hurt me every day."

Terrell swallowed. "I never want to hurt you, Colby," he said sincerely, and he was not reassured when Colby rolled his eyes and took another piece of pie.

"So," Colby said, "after that?"

"What do you mean, after that?"

"Well, we get the results, they're negative, everybody's happy, we can do it without rubbers, yay! Or we get the results, you set up a time for a consult and a drug regimen, which will suck, but I'll be there for that, and it's not happening today either way; bummer—what do you want to do with the rest or your day? It's our day off, man. Let's fucking do something!"

Terrell looked at him. Just looked at him. Making plans for what they were going to do—together, mind you—whether or not he found out he was negative. "I don't know," he said, feeling fuzzy and disoriented. "I thought maybe I'd get a crib for my cousin Monique. The one Gi-Gi has in the garage is gonna fall apart through one more baby."

Colby's eyes widened, and he took a hasty sip of coffee. His gaze darted to Terrell, and Terrell looked back blandly. "So," Colby said, meeting that challenge with a scowl, "you want some company with that?"

Terrell shook his head and laughed. "You know, you could have just gone to the fuckin' loony bin and tried to pick up on someone there. I guarantee they'd have less baggage."

"Yeah, well, crazy people only have less baggage because they tend to throw all theirs away. You're on, buddy. Let's go have ourselves a domestic partnership day."

And now Terrell was the one who widened his eyes. "That sounds really fucking serious, you know that?"

"Hey, I'm volunteering to help you with your meds for a potentially deadly disease, genius. If that doesn't declare that I'm really fucking serious, I don't know what does."

Terrell shook his head and finally started enjoying his pie. "Jesus," he muttered. "When you first showed up, I was really hoping for a trip down the river with some beer!"

Colby's scowl eased up, and his usual eye-crinkling smile took its place, just that quick. "Well, I'm pretty sure we both have tomorrow off too. We can do that then!"

Terrell nodded, then closed his eyes and savored before he swallowed the most excellent pie. "Yeah, but first let me get in on some more of this, okay? You and your sister, you've got this pie thing *down*!"

NEGATIVE.

All clear.

No viral load, healthy baseline white-cell count.

All was good.

Terrell looked at the little piece of paper, and then at the doctor, and smiled just enough to show his braces. "Thank you," he said courteously and hopped off the table. His knees gave a little wobble then, and Colby grabbed his elbow, and together they prepared to leave the exam room where the doc had consulted with both of them and given them the good news.

"Now, you boys know what to do to keep those results negative, don't you?" the doctor asked seriously, and Terrell nodded.

"Yeah," he said, a little bit of emotion seeping into his voice. "Not have sex with anyone but him." He nodded at Colby and then realized what he'd just said. Out loud. To a stranger.

A stranger who didn't appear to give a flying rat's ass.

"Yeah," the doctor said, making a notation in his chart. "Well, monogamy is a perfectly acceptable way to stay disease free. You gentlemen have a good day."

Terrell looked quickly at Colby, to see if he noticed that big fucking momentous thing that just happened, and Colby rewarded him by mouthing, "In bed!" and making Terrell giggle. Together, they laughed their way out of the clinic and into the stunning summer heat pounding the crap out of Colby's car.

"Whew," Terrell said, feeling about six zillion pounds lighter. "Dodged a bullet there!"

"Yeah, well, you know how not to ever even see that gun again, don't you?"

Terrell wondered if the heat had fried Colby's brain. "Well yeah! I just said! Don't have sex with anyone but you!"

Colby squeezed his eyes tight. "Yeah, well, that's great, and I'm going to have a little faith that that's possible, T, but what if it isn't? People break up all the fucking time. What are you going to do if you wake up one morning and decide my feet are too big or my laugh is too loud or there is something about me you absolutely cannot *stand*?"

Terrell's stomach went cold and he suddenly had to pee. "I'll never have sex again," he said soberly, and he was completely serious.

Colby whapped him upside the head.

"What in the hell—"

And he did it again.

"What in the hell was *that* for!" Terrell asked, backing up against the window so he couldn't do it again.

"Don't be piss stupid, T! If we break up, you're going to have another boyfriend—"

"No I'm not!" Terrell snapped.

"You are too—"

"The hell I am! I am *not* gay with *anyone* but you, do you understand that?"

Colby blinked like he'd said something earth-shattering, and then Terrell blinked because it occurred to him that he had.

"That is one hell of a thing to put on my shoulders, T!" Colby snarled, but Terrell wasn't paying any attention to the fact that he was pissed.

"Oh my God, I actually said it," he muttered, and Colby stopped whatever was going through his head and coming out his mouth and turned on the car (which was good because the heat was making them both pissy), and by the time Colby actually thought to say whatever was on his mind, Terrell had managed to close his mouth before he caught any flies.

"Say what?" Colby asked cautiously.

"Said I was gay," Terrell muttered.

Colby blinked again, and maybe he saw that the world had come apart and been reformed too.

"Congratulations, T," he said, with only a little irony and mostly a gentle sort of acceptance. "You're out for me!"

Terrell narrowed his eyes. "What does that mean?"

"It means you need to read something besides nonfiction. I'll lend you some books or something. You'll love 'em. Here, let's go to Sears—they'll have the crib delivered if you've got the address."

Terrell perked up. "Then we don't need to drive to Oak Park!" he said, happy for a moment, and then Colby rolled his eyes.

"Oh you wish. We're going to bring something for your cousin and you're going to introduce me to your Gi-Gi—I don't care if you're introducing me as the help, I'm going to see where you grew up, okay?"

Terrell scowled. "You know? You showed up this morning and I thought, 'Hallelujah, we're gonna get us some sex!' I had no idea you were going to push me off the deep end and make me swim!"

"T, we sort of witnessed a murder together. We've *been* in the deep end. It's time you learned to keep your head above water."

"Nice metaphor, cheese boy. Maybe *you* should be the journalist."

"Yeah, well, we'll save the conversation about what we're going to do when we grow up for another day. Here we are. Arden Fair. Let's go buy us a baby crib for a baby you don't ever plan to go see." Colby swung the car into a parking space in front of the Cheesecake Factory, and Terrell got out when he did.

"How do you know I won't see this baby?" he asked, and then looked around quickly-- he didn't want people to assume it was *his* baby he was ducking out on. That sort of thing pissed him off.

"Because," Colby hissed, drawing up alongside of him. "There's a reason you don't go back to your old neighborhood. Probably a couple of them. Do you want to talk about those reasons now, or do you want to go fork over a chunk of your tip money for something you shouldn't have to buy?"

Terrell grunted. It was on the tip of his tongue to argue that he *should* have to pay for the crib, because it was a family obligation, when he remembered that he'd been asking himself the exact same question, and shut up about it. Should or shouldn't weren't going to factor into this equation. He was *going* to do it, because that's just the way things were.

"Man, are you sure you wouldn't rather go inner tubing?" Terrell asked wearily. He was tired already.

Colby took pity on him and bumped him with a shoulder. "I'll tell you what. After we buy the damned crib, I'll take you out to eat, my treat. We'll act totally straight and only you and I will know it's a date."

Terrell's smile reached his eyes. He could feel it. "It *is* a date," he said soberly, and Colby grinned tightly.

"So that's good for today," Terrell conceded. "And then tomorrow?"

"Us, on the river, with beers, after a mind-blowing night of sex with your gay boyfriend. How's that?"

It hit Terrell, then, all of the things Colby was doing for him, all of the ways he was trying to make Terrell's life easy, when the fact was, Terrell had a decent life, but it hadn't been *good* until just this last week. "That's more than I deserve," he said quietly. "Someday, maybe I'll earn all that, but right now, I'm just going to be grateful."

Next to him, Colby sighed. "You know, T, I really want to hold your hand right now."

"Yeah. Me too."

But by then they were inside Sears, and the blessed, blessed air conditioning had kicked in. Well, some things were just that easy, weren't they?

SEARS said it could deliver the crib in a week, and Terrell figured if the whole baby thing was more pressing than that, maybe Monique shouldn't have told Gi-Gi at the last moment like *all* the women in his family.

They went for food then—Terrell picked Pizza Kitchen and couldn't believe all of the many ways that place managed to fuck up a perfectly good American food. While they were there, at Colby's insistence, he called Gi-Gi.

"Yeah, G, it's me," he said, darting a glance at Colby, and the next few minutes while they waited for their food was a frantic tap dance of dodging all her questions. "Yeah, well, I got the crib, it's coming next week. I don't know about the fourth—that's a busy day sometimes, G, especially at night. Yeah, you can see the fireworks from the restaurant. People like to eat there on the patio. It's usually insane." (People actually preferred to *drink* there on the patio. He just didn't want to get into that. But he was being truthful about the insane part.) "Well, actually, you know. I was thinking about dropping by today. I've got a friend who wants to meet you. No, not a girl—"

"Then I don't want to meet him," Gi-Gi said, interrupting the perfectly good rehash of every one of their previous conversations.

"But, Gi-Gi, he's just a—"

"I got no use for no thug friends of my boy!"

Terrell actually looked over at Colby with bug eyes to see if the man had suddenly devolved into a knuckle-dragging, gang-tatted criminal.

"Gi-Gi, he's just a friend! He's got a degree—"

"Is he black?" Gi-Gi asked, her voice sharp, and Terrell crossed his eyes.

"No."

"Yeah, then he's no one I want to know."

Terrell swallowed. "Gi-Gi, why would you even ask that?"

"If he was black, you would have already brought him, and it wouldn't be no big deal. If he's white, well, he's not the kind of friend you ought to be having, and you know that."

"Gi-Gi, he's a white guy. It's not illegal—"

"It should be, for boys like you. You can bring home a white woman but not a white man, Terrell, and that's just the way it is."

Terrell had never been quite this confused. "Boys like me?"

"You know what you are, Terrell. That's between you and God, but don't you bring home no white boys."

Terrell hung up, looking at Colby blankly. "She, uhm." His face heated. There was no good way to say this.

"She doesn't want to meet no gay white boys," Colby said, his mouth twisted, and Terrell shrugged.

"I don't know how she got to 'gay' from 'white'—I really don't. There's enough colors of folks down in Oak Park that my cousins brought home more than just black kids when they were growing up. I'm... I'm at a loss, sort of."

Colby regarded him levelly. "Terrell, have you ever brought home a girl?"

Terrell shook his head and looked away. God, college was hard enough. Bootsy teeth, full-time job—it was just easier being the guy everyone went to for advice than being someone's real friend. Girls didn't befriend him. Guys assumed he was just totally self-sufficient.

"No," he said. "Twelve years, I ain't never brought anyone home." And there was the street in his mouth again. But Colby didn't call him on it. He must have known it wasn't aimed at him.

"Well, T, if guys in your hood ain't gay, then maybe she's afraid guys from not in the hood are going to do it for you. She knew you as a kid, T. I'm assuming you weren't always the guarded fucker you are now. At some point in time you must have shown her your heart, and she's been trying to make you forget it ever since."

Terrell fidgeted, wondering what about him had given it away. "Maybe it's just the no girls part," he said, hating the thought that this thing—this miserable thing about him that he'd never wanted to acknowledge—had been on display for the world, or even just his Gi-Gi, to see.

"And maybe, whatever it is, it shouldn't be a bad thing," Colby said, but he looked upset. Suddenly, it was incumbent upon Terrell to make that look stop.

"Man, this is so not your problem," he said, laughing to lighten the mood. "This is my own family bullshit. And I don't know what made her think or suspect or whatever the hell. You know the one thing I know?"

Colby looked at him, his eyes still pinched—and holy hell, they were red too—and shook his head.

"I know I'm working one more goddamned Fourth of July!"

Colby's reluctant laughter set something low and real thrumming in the pit of Terrell's stomach.

"You know what *I* know?" Colby said, then paused for a moment while the waitress put the shitty excuse for pizza in front of the two of them. She left after casting a wistful glance in Colby's direction, which he returned with a playful—and platonic—wink.

"What?"

"Our day just opened up, and the river is calling my name!"

Terrell smiled, the full metal jacket, and he couldn't even make himself hide it. "It's a little late for the tubing service, isn't it?"

"Yeah, but we can go up to 49er Canyon, drive down the gorge—they've got water boards set up there."

Terrell just looked at him. "Isn't that some sort of torture they're trying to make illegal in foreign countries?"

Colby grinned. "It's also a lot of fun that *is* illegal in this one, because it's hella dangerous. C'mon. Let's go get your shit so you can stay two nights running, and then go break some laws!"

Terrell couldn't seem to stop that grin. It was like when there'd been flooding in Sacramento and they'd closed all the schools down. Yippee! No school, no homework, and no one to make you feel guilty for ditching! He'd always known he dreaded the hell out of the old neighborhood and Gi-Gi's, but he never realized how much.

"Yeah," he said, taking a bite of cold, artistically awful pizza. He chewed and swallowed and wondered how long it would take to get the green shit out from between his braces. "Sounds like a plan. And maybe on our way up the freeway, we can get us some fuckin' *food*!"

Colby paused, in the middle of shoving about a quarter of the pizza in his mouth. "Wha's wong wi' dith?" he asked.

Terrell shook his head. "I would have to eat the whole store full of this shit to be full," he said, feeling hungry and cranky, which is probably what happened when you started your day with as much sugar and caffeine as he'd had. "Whoever thought of putting spinach on a pizza should be *shot!*"

Colby tried valiantly to stop it, but he still spit out crumbs on the table when he laughed with his mouth full. He wiped himself off in embarrassment, and Terrell wondered how much he would give, how much he would pay, what part of his anatomy he'd have to chop off, to kiss that boy in public.

Summer of Love, Summer of Fear

WATER boarding might have been a hell of a lot of fun.

If you were both insane and lacking all instincts of self-preservation, that is.

The board they found (and it seemed that every inlet on the stretch of the river had one just waiting for someone to come along and risk their neck) was a basic wakeboard, but someone had drilled out the front, fixed a garage spring to it and a rope to that, and then secured the thing around a boulder about thirty feet upstream. There was another rope, this one with a water-ski handle attached. The trick, Colby told him before plunging into the freezing, fresh-from-the-snowmelt white-capping disaster, was to enter the water upstream so the current would carry you to the board and you could grab on. Once you grabbed on, you stood on the wakeboard, held on to the handle, and rode that thing like a combination water ski and surfboard until your muscles turned to Jell-O and if you held on one more minute you wouldn't have the strength to swim to shore.

That was exactly how Colby described it.

Terrell squinched one eye almost closed and pulled up a corner of his mouth in absolute skepticism. "You are 100 percent shitting me," he accused.

Colby was wearing his board shorts, the red Hawaiian ones, and a T-shirt so he wouldn't burn. He stood under the hard red sunshine, his hands on his hips, and looked at Terrell with a combination of humor and exasperation.

"I swear to God, it's fun, T! It's like water-skiing except harder!"

"It's a way for white people to off their relatives," Terrell said, watching the board bouncing up and down with every fluctuation of current. "I can't believe you do this shit for fun!"

"Well, yeah, beats skateboarding. I kept breaking my arm."

Now Terrell narrowed both his eyes and scowled at Colby in something of an epiphany. "That's why you like me," he said, totally getting it. "You decided your life just didn't have enough goddamned pain! You said, 'Hey! I'll hook up with a socially repressed black man and fuck myself up! It'll be more fun than wakeboarding!' I get it now. So I'll just sit back and watch you fuck yourself up on this thing, and after you break your leg, I'll haul you out of the drink so you can decide you've had enough pain and break up with me!"

By now Colby was laughing so hard he couldn't breathe. "Jesus," he gasped. "Just shut up for a second and watch, okay? I swear—" He burst into another paroxysm of laughter and recovered. "I *swear,* I'm only in it for the fun! You'll see—I swear, you'll see."

With that, he turned and started picking his way across the big river rocks, the kind you had to step on and risk rolling an ankle, and made his way toward the water.

Worry seized Terrell by the scruff of the neck and shook him a little. "Hey… now, Colby, we don't have to do this. We can… I ain't never been up to this part of the river. We can drive into Foresthill—I ain't never been up here. We don't have to do this—"

Colby clambered on top of a boulder that rose up above the water, right where it was deep enough to swim in. He turned around and winked. "Trust me, T. Sometimes it's worth the risk."

And then he jumped in.

Terrell's lungs stopped, frozen in his chest until Colby resurfaced, gasping and shrieking with the cold. He struck out hard and made it to the center of the river before the current pulled him past the board, and Terrell—who had inhaled when Colby did—stopped breathing again until Colby managed to scramble upright on that thing, holding on to the handles, crouching against the brutal current and whooping with excitement.

Colby took a few deep breaths while Terrell was watching, and then he turned around and waved—

And wiped out, flipping up into the air and coming down into the frigid water again on his ass before being pulled under the blackness and down the river. Terrell wobbled to the edge of the water and looked out, fighting for oxygen and against panic. He didn't want to go diving in blindly, but God, where the hell was—

"Woohoo!" Colby cried from about a hundred feet down.

Terrell fought through the terrible fear as Colby swam for shore.

"Oh my God!" Colby crowed, slogging out of the river with water squelching in his river shoes. "That was epic! Did you see that wipeout? Did you *see* it? That thing must have jacked me at *least* five feet in the air!" He laughed as he made his way upriver, and Terrell kept nodding like he got it, like he was all excited by the spectacular wipeout and he was going along with this just fine!

But when Colby got up to him, flipping his wet hair out of his eyes and laughing some more, Terrell's big eyes must have let some of his panic show.

"T! Relax!" he chuckled. "It's a sport—it's fine!"

Terrell nodded, because it was a sport, and it was no big deal, and it was fine. "Fine," he said, trying to keep the little vortex of panic from overwhelming him. "It was great! Yeah. Awesome. Fantastic. Can we go somewhere now?"

Colby looked at him, confused. "Go somewhere?"

"Yeah. Somewhere."

"Somewhere specific?"

Terrell nodded tightly. "Yeah. Anywhere on the planet where your life might not depend on me bailing you out, okay? I don't ever want to see you do that again. Fucking ever. You hearing me? You disappear and I can't fucking breathe. I like breathing. I'd like you to keep doing it too!" His voice rose shrilly, and Colby's smile faded into something… odd. Bemused. Tender.

"I like breathing too, T," he said. "Don't plan on stopping for a while. Didn't mean to freak you out like that—"

"You did," Terrell said shortly. "Freaked me the hell out. Please don't."

Colby grimaced and looked around. They were alone, mostly. There were some people about a hundred meters upstream, but there were a couple of boulders in the way, and there were some people across the river, but those people were behind a boulder too. "The coast is clear, T. Can I touch you now?"

Terrell swallowed. "God, I really wish you would," he said, feeling stupid and useless and cowardly in the extreme.

Colby grabbed his hips and hauled him forward, then turned his head for the kiss. He was cold, God, so cold, until his mouth opened and the heat just pulled Terrell in.

Terrell sank into that heat, and the shivers that he'd held tightly under control came out. Colby wrapped his cold wet arms around him, and Terrell actually *snuggled* into them, and the part of him that was lost in the kiss allowed itself to be terrified at the thought of losing Colby, whether it was under the cold black river or out the door.

"Fuckin' nigger faggots! Get a fuckin' room!"

Terrell might not have even registered the people who came out from behind the rock, but Colby moved a hand off his shoulder and behind him, to where the voices were coming from. Terrell opened his eyes, missing that hand, and saw Colby's middle finger extended while the boy was still lost in the kiss.

Terrell pulled back. Later he'd realize that he hadn't freaked out about people seeing him kiss a man.

"Jesus," he hissed. "You really do have a death wish, don't you! Remember the part about us going somewhere?"

"Yeah, faggots, come over here and *make* me shut up!" the white asshole across the river called out, and his buddies laughed and cheered him on.

"But you didn't get to swim!" Colby said plaintively, and Terrell rolled his eyes.

"Yeah, that's what I'm worried about now. The not swimming. Look, can we go? Those fuckers are dumb enough to try and swim across, and seriously, don't we have better things to do?"

"Nigger lover!" one of the guys screamed, and Colby's face tightened.

Terrell gave a snarl of impatience. "You're going to *argue* with him?" he asked, turning around to grab the towels they'd dropped, and Colby sighed and followed him.

"We weren't doing anything wrong, T!" he complained, and Terrell rolled his eyes.

"Yeah, I know. Lots of people not doing anything wrong get the shit beat out of them all the fuckin' time. Let's find someplace where the assholes don't got a free pass, okay?"

Colby let out a furious sigh, and Terrell hauled ass for the footbridge, hoping the assholes with the free pass didn't decide to go intercept them.

The guys—drunk, long-haired, young as hell—contented themselves with shouting stupid shit as Terrell and Colby tromped over the footbridge and into Colby's car, which was parked on the turnout by the bridge. Colby started up the car, then put it in neutral and pulled the brake.

"Stay right here," he muttered, and Terrell watched as he opened the door, sprinted up to the edge of the drop-off that overlooked the river, cupped his hands over his mouth, and shouted, "Hey! Rednecks! Get a fucking education, you cocksuckers!" before sprinting back to the car. He hopped in and they roared back onto to the little twisty road that led to the highway.

Terrell knew his eyes were big and his mouth was open as the car ripped up the hill, engine whining, and when they got to the split in the road that either went out to the big intersection in Auburn and led to Highway 80, or right across the big scary bridge and into Foresthill, Colby took right.

And Terrell actually found he could talk.

"Now that you've done that damned fool fuckin' thing, is it too much to ask where the fuck we're going?"

"Swimming," Colby said shortly. "There's a turnout for a little lake here. It's hot, and it's my day off, and I want to go swimming."

Terrell shook his head. Stubborn asshole. "Yeah, okay. Let's go swimming. But maybe, since we're up in the hills and you don't know when rednecks are going to go peeking around the corner, maybe we keep our hands to ourselves."

Colby sighed. "I hate this world sometimes," he said, and Terrell thought about it.

"I did," he said seriously. "I got half a hard drive proving I would have set this place on fire and not looked back. But not now."

Colby risked a look sideways before pinning his gaze back on the road, which wound critically around the mountain. "Yeah? What's different now?"

"You, dumb shit. Try not to get either of us killed any time soon, would ya?"

The tension that had possessed Colby since their interrupted kiss seemed to drain out of him. "Yeah. Yeah, no worries. Here—the turnoff for Clementine. We can go swimming, it'll be fine."

And it was.

They swam until the sun went down. There were other people out there, most of them white, but nobody gave Terrell a second glance, and since he and Colby weren't necking, they pretty much ignored Colby too. The lake wasn't hardly a lake—more a deep feeder tributary into the river. At its deepest it went chest deep, and in most spots it went waist high. The bottom consisted of fine red silt in the shallow places and smooth river stones in the deeper ones, and generally, there was a lot of splashing, a lot of swimming, and a lot of hanging out on the towel, drying off, and then jumping back in the water.

It wasn't quite inner tubing, but it was close.

At the end of the day, Colby was getting pink, in spite of copious applications of SPF Flannel Shirt, and Terrell, who had greased up a couple of times himself, felt crispy on the edges.

They got back in the car and drove up the crazy steep hill as the sun was spiking over the mountains, stabbing them in the eyes and turning the entire landscape orange.

They paused for a minute there before turning back to Auburn so they could get some food and then get back on the freeway, and Terrell made a little hum of satisfaction.

"What?" Colby asked. Behind them, another car was making the climb and getting close to their tail. Colby took one more look to his left and turned onto the road, and Terrell just closed his eyes, soaking in the last of the sunshine.

"You were right," he said, eyes closed. "We really needed to go swimming."

Colby's chuckle was deep and resonant and very, very full of Colby himself. "I'm right a lot," he said, and behind his eyelids, Terrell felt the sun dappling orange through the side rail of the California's highest bridge.

"Yeah, you are. What are you right about next?"

"I don't know. I'm thinking we go back to my house, shower, watch a movie, and then I make you a happy man."

Terrell was too content to open his eyes but not too content to change Colby's perception of the day. "You already have," he said, smiling a little. "What happens after the movie will be icing on the cake."

What happened after the movie was that they both fell asleep on the couch. Moira woke them up at three in the morning. Apparently the cats had been pawing at the sliding glass door, and since Colby was usually the one who let them in, she'd gone out to see what was what. Colby was asleep in the corner of the couch, one leg along the back, the other on the floor, and Terrell had fallen asleep in the vee of his legs, his head back against Colby's chest, as comfortable as a kitten in a drawer.

After the two of them stumbled to the bed and flopped in, Colby scooted along Terrell's spine and wrapped his arm around Terrell's waist.

"You know," Terrell murmured, lacing his fingers in with Colby's, "it's scary how much I need this right here."

"Nothing scary 'bout this, T," Colby replied, his voice thick and slurred. "Is all good."

TERRELL had always thought people must get tired of sex eventually, and then get tired of each other, but he was finding out that wasn't always the case. That thing Colby was doing to his ear right when they woke up the next morning? That was *never* growing old.

Neither was Colby's cock grinding up against his backside, or his hands rubbing over Terrell's bare chest.

"We doin' this now?" Terrell asked, only a little surprised and *very* willing. "Usually, you know, toothbrushes, showers…."

"Shhh," Colby murmured before leaning over and taking his mouth. "I'll blow you if you shut up and be happy."

Terrell didn't mind his morning breath, and it turned out he wanted the taste of Colby in his mouth, or the taste of his come, slick and thick, sliding down the back of his throat.

They ended up in a sleepy, languid sixty-nine, the kind where they were both on their sides and they could reach out and stroke any skin they wanted. Terrell liked to play with Colby's balls while he sucked, because he'd discovered that those things were wicked sensitive, and Colby about lost his goddamned mind.

Colby played dirty, though, really dirty, and fiddled with Terrell's asshole, slicking his finger and massaging his rim. A little bit of that had Terrell dropping Colby's cock out of his mouth completely, and Colby laughed softly around Terrell's balls.

"I know what you want," he taunted softly, and Terrell groaned. "And guess what?" Colby murmured, doing some sort of contortion thing to reach behind him into the drawer.

"What?" Terrell panted, amazed, because they'd gone from sleepy to sexy in no time at all.

"Guess who doesn't need a rubber?" Colby punctuated that with a particularly hard suck to Terrell's cock, and Terrell buried his face in Colby's thigh and saw stars with the effort not to come.

"Oh God," Terrell breathed, and Colby scooted up and turned him around so he was facedown against the mattress, his ass up in the air for Colby's hard use.

Colby certainly gave it a workout.

The lube was cold at first, and Terrell hissed, but Colby massaged it in good, rubbing his rim and preparing him. But all the greasing in the world couldn't change the fact that the man was big and solid, and that it was a struggle to get him to fit, but oh! When he slid home, thick and irrefutable, Terrell's breath caught with how much he wanted that thing inside him.

His asshole stretched, it burned, and the feeling of Colby's cock rubbing over his prostate was so good it ached, but oh, please, Colby, move a little faster, God, a little harder, and suddenly those words weren't just in his head, they were coming out his mouth. "God, yes, faster, harder, please… dammit, dammit, *Colby, fuck me!*"

And Colby did, without mercy or delicacy, and Terrell grunted flat against the bed, thrusting backward, needing to be filled, wishing Colby could climb inside him and fill him from the inside out with that glorious, glorious heart.

Colby wasn't quiet in sex, either. He leaned over and yanked Terrell's ass up, muttering, "Come back here," and then he hauled Terrell up totally so he was on his knees, his ass getting reamed and reamed hard while Colby demanded, "What am I doing to you?"

"You're fucking me," Terrell panted.

"Who's fucking you?"

"You are. You're fucking me so fucking… *ah, God, fucking hard!*"

And Colby thrust so hard Terrell saw stars, the good kind, and it was instinct that brought his hand to his own cock so he could beat himself savagely and come, spurting on top of the bedspread while

Colby bit his neck and shot inside him, so hot, so much, Terrell could feel it inside.

He groaned and collapsed forward, Colby at his back, and the two of them just lay there for a moment, catching their breath. Colby planted those absurd, tender kisses across his shoulders, and Terrell let himself need them for a moment.

"Terrell?" Colby muttered, rubbing the sweat falling off his forehead onto Terrell's back.

"Yeah?"

"I hope you know... you know it's not like this with just anyone, right?"

Terrell shook his head, his eyes still swimming with black spots, and he tried not to think about the unbearable sexiness of Colby's come sliding down between his thighs.

He failed, and his cock gave a pathetic little whimper as it thought about getting hard again. "It's special to me," he said honestly. "That's all the fuck I know."

"Close enough," Colby said, kissing his back again, and Terrell closed his eyes. Those words between them were looming high and hard, and he only hoped he had the courage to scale them when Colby got too impatient to just let that scary mountain be.

TWO days off, and it felt like a vacation. Terrell had spent a lot of his vacations working on the Great Black American Circle-Jerk (as he was starting to think of his project now), and once, he'd driven out to Vegas to get laid (the only time he'd ever used condoms. He took the Las Vegas slogan very literally), but even then, he'd come back feeling dirty and sad and tired.

Two days with Colby, and he went back to work feeling refreshed and happy and good about life, dumb rednecks notwithstanding.

He and Colby worked the night shift, and Colby drove them to work telling a string of awful light-bulb jokes that featured his sister, because she'd screwed up cooking stir-fry the night before and they'd had to order pizza, which she'd proceeded to *really* fuck up by ordering with artichoke hearts, *gross!*

Terrell was laughing so hard he couldn't breathe when he heard Colby say, "Oh fuck."

He looked up then and saw the four cop cars in front of the red-and-white-striped awning of Papiano's, and said, "Oh shit. What now?"

They barely remembered to grab their stuff before they walked in, and when they got there, Percy—looking embarrassed and humiliated—was being led away in handcuffs.

"Jesus, Percy," Terrell snapped, pissed off out of sheer reflex. "What the hell did you do?"

"I didn't do *nothin'*, T!" Percy looked miserable and confused, and for the first time, Terrell heard a teenager say that and actually believed him.

"Well, what do they think you did?"

Percy shook his head. "Drug trafficking—that's what they—oh hey, man! I'm just talking to my—"

"Move along," the officer on Terrell's side of Percy said dryly.

Colby, who always had to fix things, started talking. "Percy, don't say *anything*. My sister's a lawyer, she'll be right there! Where are you going?"—this to the guy on Percy's side.

"Sheriff's department," the man said, and Colby nodded, punching up his sister on his phone already.

"Gotcha—how long is he going to be held?"

"The arraignment's tomorrow."

Colby flinched. "Oh shit! He's got to spend the night in there? God, don't make him spend the night in there! He fucking hates jail! Percy, hang on a minute, okay? Don't say *anything!*"

"Oh hell," Terrell muttered. "For that kid, you just asked the one thing he can't give."

Colby looked at him and grimaced. "Follow him, T—wait...."

Oh yeah, it just hit Captain America that he was asking Terrell to risk his job. Terrell grunted. Well, Colby wasn't the only one who could be Captain America, was he?

"Yeah, yeah. Call Suk and ask him to fill in for me," Terrell grumbled. "Here. Give me your keys."

"But I was gonna go—"

"You stay here and hold down the fort!" Terrell ordered. "Beth is gonna fall apart and the whole place is gonna crash. If you can, call Gina—she's not on until tomorrow night. He'll probably be too damned proud."

"Fine." Colby was scowling, which probably meant he wanted to go out and be proactive and shit, and Terrell couldn't do a lot for him. Sometimes life happened to you, and you just had to deal with what you got. Terrell could fix his teeth, but he couldn't fix the black, and thirty years of trying to forget the gay obviously hadn't worked. Some shit you just couldn't fix.

Terrell saw the bad mood rolling off of him and had an epiphany. A touch on the hand, a kiss—any one of these things would have gone a long way toward giving Colby power over *something*. Colby took out his keys and Terrell held out his hand, closing his fingers over Colby's briefly when the keys smacked in his palm.

"I'll be back to pick you up—you first off?"

"Second," Colby said, his scowl lightening up a fraction at the touch of Terrell's skin.

"I'll be here."

Colby grunted and took a step back. "I'll count on it," he said, still angry but now apparently resigned.

Terrell nodded and hopped inside the car.

HE HAD to use his smartphone and call Colby's sister twice to find the sheriff's office and county jail. Once he got there, he waited for Moira, who showed up in her work clothes, which he'd never seen before.

"Not. A. Word." She glared at him while she straightened her white linen jacket and then shook out her straight, above-the-knee matching skirt.

She looked like a marshmallow.

"That is not cute," he said apologetically, and she grimaced.

"My mother took me shopping. She's built like me, but hell, she looks at me and sees a size four. Whatyagonnado?"

Terrell grimaced. "Yeah, well, family. Whatya do."

She shrugged. "I'm fat, Colby's gay—we're just their cross to bear, I guess. They mean well. Now tell me about this kid I'm going to go stick my neck out for. Who is he to you? Is he worth it?"

That stopped Terrell short. "He's... well, he's innocent, how's that?"

Moira's squint was a little like Colby's scowl but sweeter. "That sucks. Give me another reason."

"We're both black when most of the staff is white. We grew up in shitty neighborhoods. He's got an ankle bracelet on, making sure he goes nowhere but his auntie's and his job, and he did absolutely everything we asked of him. Every damned time. That boy would kill himself to knock out the dishes or finish prep or learn a station. Every word out of his mouth was that hard work was better than juvie. They said it was drug trafficking—I think he knows the right people, but he wouldn't do the wrong thing. Not now. I think...." Terrell could see the look on Percy's face when Gina found out he was eighteen. The look when she forgave him. The way he'd been willing to do dishes through a crime scene so the cops wouldn't notice him. The way he took his breaks regular, just like Terrell, so he knew he got his work done right. "I think he likes it at Papi's. I think he's got something to lose."

Moira nodded. "Okay, then. If you think he's innocent, why does he need me?"

Terrell grimaced. God, just as shiny as her brother. "'Cause he's a black man in a white staff, Moira. Colby may not see why that's important, but please tell me you do."

Moira sighed and looked out across the parking lot, where the relentless sun was rippling the light near the pavement. "Yeah, I get it. Can we say you're a friend of the family? If he trusts you, this might be easier."

"Yeah, yeah. Whatever." He had a sudden uncomfortable thought. "Moira," he said, and then mumbled it when he should have at least owned up to his cowardice in the first place.

"What?"

He sighed. They didn't have time for this bullshit. "I'm not out," he said, enunciating and looking, well, not in her eyes but past her shoulder. "At work. I'm not out. Me and Colby—no one knows. Percy won't trust me if he does. We can't tell him that."

"Oh," Moira said, and she looked a lot more upset than Terrell's personal crap should account for. "I'm sorry. I thought... I mean, he's so certain...." She shook her head. "Dammit. Not now. But you and Colby need to have a talk, okay? I'm not sure if he's been entirely straight with you about some stuff, and he needs to be, because... hell. C'mon. One thing at a time."

Terrell wanted to stop her right there and ask her what in the hell she was talking about, but she was right. Now was not the time.

The jail was an imposing phallic presence in the downtown plaza, with white marble and tiny windows. It wasn't until they were emptying their pockets for the metal detectors and X-ray machines that Terrell realized he was still dressed in his Papi's uniform of black polyester pants and neon-green collared shirt, and he grimaced at the bored guard who patted him down. At least the uniform was clean, even if the shoes smelled like too many nights tending bar.

Moira led him down a series of corridors, then up an elevator, which surprised the crap out of Terrell—for some reason, he'd always assumed jails were underground, like dungeons, which was silly, a kid's fantasy, but still hard to shake. A uniformed desk officer led them to a room full of police officers sitting at their desks, and then through that and to a corridor outside of a series of small rooms.

Terrell recognized this place from television. "He's not here yet?"

Moira shook her head. "We were early enough. He's still being processed."

"Good—you got time to tell me whatever your brother's not!" he said, and it wasn't until he said it that he realized how panicked he was.

She grimaced. "Look, T—I like you. I do. You play with the cats. You do the dishes. You buy me pie. And frankly, you're not the loudest person he's had over, if you know what I mean, and seriously, that makes me a happy woman."

Terrell almost choked on his tongue. Damn. He *had* to meet the parents who spawned these two children, because who produced that much mouth? "Well," he said, feeling his face heat to molten, "that makes me happy that you like me. Why are you telling me this?"

"Because Colby has plans for the two of you—and the fact that he hasn't told you what they are worries me. I mean, I've met you. You're a nice guy—but I don't know if you're the guy he's made all these plans for."

Terrell opened his mouth to ask her what that meant, and a cop walked in and handed her a stack of papers.

"Look, T," she said distractedly, "this is the arrest report, and I need to read it. You and Colby can sort your shit some other time, okay?"

Terrell shut up, and the next few minutes he spent writing *What the hell are you hiding from me!* and then erasing it on the text function of his phone. He was just about to lose his fucking mind when another cop came out of the little interrogation room.

"Half an hour," he said. "Then we're moving him to lockup. We'll be outside, the sound off."

"Good," Moira said. "This is confidential."

They walked in and Percy, wearing an ill-fitting orange jumpsuit, sprawled in a chair that was too small for him, looking defiant and miserable and young.

He smiled, pathetically happy to see Terrell. "Oh my God, T! You're like, a lifesaver. I don't know what these fools are—hey. Who the hell are you?"

"This is Colby's sister, and she's doing you a solid for no other reason but that her idiot brother asked her to, so be nice. She's your lawyer. You need to listen to what she has to say."

Moira sat down across from Percy and pulled out a sheaf of paperwork. "Here, Percy—you need to sign and Terrell needs to sign. You're both hiring me for free."

"Why am I hiring you?" Terrell asked as he signed the first sheet of paper, and Moira took it from him and gave him another.

"So you can't be subpoenaed. Here, initial here, here, and here, and hurry. We don't have much time."

She was damned efficient, and in five minutes, she put all the paperwork into her folder and looked at Percy. "Okay—I've read the arrest report, and it looks like they're getting ready to make a case against you for the murder of Will Templeton, but first, they're going to prove that you were Templeton's hookup to the drug underworld. What can you tell me that will make sense but *not* point to you holding that gun!"

Percy groaned. "What? I'm the only person there who knows where to buy drugs? Jesus, half the store confessed to doing blow the other night—they're gonna blame *me*?"

"Well, who are your contacts, Percy? You tell us who your contacts are, and maybe someone else at Papi's goes there, you think?"

"Except I didn't *go* there!" Percy whined. "I knew 'em, okay? They were from the hood, and I grew up with 'em—but like you said. I live with my auntie now." Percy grimaced. "Man, I got a job, and a girlfriend, and she's hella smart and I don't know what she sees in me, but I'm all for that shit! I wouldn't go back and see Edgar—man, that would just be cold stupid!"

"So Edgar—do we have a last name?" Moira asked, taking notes.

Percy shifted. "Uhm, well. Yeah. It's sort of the same as mine."

Terrell groaned. "Cousin?"

"Uncle. But he's as young as me."

Terrell shut his eyes. "Okay. Well, you didn't buy from him, there's nothing to worry about. The question is, did *anyone* from Papi's buy from him? You said doing that didn't make you better than a drive-through. Who asked you to work that window, Percy?"

Percy shifted in his seat. "Now, T—you know I don't snitch!"

Terrell grunted. "This ain't school, shithead! The cops are gonna put you in *jail*. Not juvie, *jail*. And you may think you're all bad now, but those niggas are gonna fuck your flower mouth 'til your teeth fall out!"

Percy grunted and recoiled. Terrell didn't use that word—he hated that word, actually—but Percy did. Percy used it to make being a thug sound all badass and shit. Percy wasn't badass, and Terrell wasn't going to keep himself all pretty if it meant he could get Percy to save himself.

"Juvie was bad," he whispered, looking down. "Down-low is a whole other thing in juvie."

Terrell kept himself from flinching. Aces. That look right there on Percy's face? That was going to make him sex-for-free.

"Then don't go back," Terrell said fiercely. "Look, man. Colby got his sister here because he thinks you're innocent. You tell her everything—and I mean *everything*—and let's see if maybe we can keep you the hell out of jail!"

Percy looked at him sideways. "You and Colby spending a lot of time together, T. You better watch out. Folks'll talk."

Terrell scowled at the kid with one eye narrowed and a lip curled up in derision. "Yeah, Percy, I'm trying to keep you from being Folsom's newest fuckbasket, and you're worried about my rep. Can we try to fucking focus here?"

He looked up and saw Moira regarding him with something like pity, and he began to wish he and Colby had just let nature take its course with Percy. So much he didn't want the world to see, and he was already being scalpeled open and laid out on the table like a dissected butterfly.

"Just sayin'," Percy grumbled. "You know he's a fa—"

"The brother of your lawyer, dumbass," Terrell snapped, not wanting to hear that word. His fault. His fault. He broke open the damned box with the N-word, and this kid was playing in that shitbox with both hands. "Now *Edgar,* Percy!"

"What do you want me to say, T?" Percy burst out, and it was obvious now he'd been stalling. "I worshipped the guy when I was a kid. He kept my ass from being beat! So I start up at Papi's, and I like it there, and Templeton, he's my ticket to staying, right? And he starts asking if I got the hookup!"

"What were you hooking up?" Terrell asked. "Coke or meth?"

"Coke," Percy said, grimacing. "Man, meth is *bad* for your skin. Edgar, he always said coke brought out a better class of client, you know? So I figured if my boss is asking for coke, I can give him the hookup. I just gave him a number, man! Can they really send me to jail for that?"

That last was aimed at Moira, and she grimaced. "Technically yes, but I might be able to talk to the DA here. You're a little fish, Percy. If we can give him a bigger fish, he might throw you back."

"Yeah, well, the only fish I know about is already dead and stinky!" Percy snapped. "I just gave him the number, that's all. Edgar tried calling me, even, tried asking me if I got some more people—I guess Templeton dragged some more folks that way, right?"

Moira made a helpless little sound. "Oh hells. Percy, is there any way Edgar will clear you? Tell the cops that you didn't buy anything or call him? Or get any money from him—"

"Money?" Percy asked, legitimately puzzled. "Why would that fool give me money?"

"A percentage?" Terrell prompted. "For sending folks his way?"

"A number!" Percy cried, almost in tears. "Goddammit, I gave Templeton a *number.* Edgar called me up two nights ago asking me if I had any more like him, because he'd brought in a lot of business. I said I wasn't even doing that. I didn't want nothing to do with that business. I didn't want it three years ago when I got busted being a mule, and I damned sure didn't want it now!"

The passion in his voice apparently broke down his entire shell of "thug," because the face he turned to Terrell was young and vulnerable—and scared.

"I don't wanna be a Folsom fuckbasket, T. I just want to work my suckass job and see my girlfriend. She's making me read a book, and you know? Them things ain't as boring as they were in high school. I'm... I gave a number. That's all." He looked at Moira, talking to her as a person for maybe the first time. "How they gonna say I killed a guy when all I did was give him a number?"

Moira swallowed. "They can't, Percy. Their theory is crap. But I've got to prove it's crap, and I've got to get the DA on my side. Can you give me the name of anyone else at Papi's who might have had the same number? If this is drug related, maybe we can cast a lot of doubt."

"I don't know," Percy whispered, most of the fight already out of him.

"Yeah, that's 'cause you didn't be payin' attention," Terrell said, and yeah, he knew he was bringing the street out in his voice. "She said it right in the middle of Club Papi's."

"Who?" Moira asked quickly, and Percy's eyes widened with realization as Terrell said her name.

"Kelly Gusman."

Moira did a spit take. "Kelly Gusman... as in Assemblyman Gusman's little girl?"

Terrell squinted at her. "How in the hell would I know that?"

"Don't you have a major in *journalism*?" Moira asked, and she sounded legitimately angry. "Jesus, Terrell! Pay attention to your own world, why don't you!"

Terrell blinked. "God," he muttered. "It really *is* like I got that degree for show. Yeah, you're right. I didn't put it together."

"Did you vote?" Moira asked, and Terrell nodded, a little relieved.

"Yeah, I voted. Have I passed inspection yet?"

Percy was apparently pulled out of his misery watching the two of them. "Hey, Terrell—she's fine. You getting' some of that?"

Terrell shook his head in disgust. "Classy, Percy. And no. Now can we focus on keeping your piss-stupid ass free and unviolated?"

Moira looked at Percy with her head tilted, like he was a new species of bug. "So, Kelly Gusman—what do you know?"

Percy rolled his eyes, looking stupid. His chocolate-blond hair was almost long enough to fro out, and Terrell wondered if he was going to do braids, dreads, or pick it out. Just looking at it made Terrell's fingers itch for a razor. Anything to make this dumbass kid look smart and responsible and all of the things Terrell thought might be in there under that unfortunate layer of brain damage left by youth and hubris.

"Man, I don't know anything. She said she was doing blow with Templeton. You need to talk to Edgar, man! Edgar knows who he sells to!"

Terrell rubbed the stubble on his head with his palm. "Percy, really? You're gonna send your pretty white lawyer into the hood to ask a drug dealer who he's selling to? Seriously?"

Moira grunted, but because she was Colby's sister, she made it sound sweet. "We've got investigators we pay to do that. And so does the DA, and it should really be on his dime. Look, Percy. You hang tight. Your arraignment is supposed to be tomorrow, but if I can manage to get the charges dropped by then, they may just release you. If they *do* arraign you, do you have anyone who can post bail?"

Percy shook his head. "No," he said, not even looking at her. "My moms made it more'n clear. I fuck up again, ain't nobody got money for bail."

Terrell sighed. "Yeah, I can post bail," he said and glared at Percy. "Kid, you flee bail, I'll find you and beat you to death with your own arm, you hear me?"

Percy nodded, his relief so thick it had a smell. "Hear you, T. God, just… just get me out of this. I gave a guy a number. I didn't do no drugs, I didn't talk to no one in the neighborhood, I didn't kill no one. Please, man. I'm so fuckin' scared."

Moira nodded. "Here, Percy. You write down your uncle's number, the last place you knew he stayed, and maybe some places he hangs out and deals. I'll see what our guy can dig up, okay?"

Percy took the pen and the yellow pad of paper from her, the manacles on his wrists clinking with his every move. Moira reached into her purse and pulled out a little pack of Kleenex and handed it over without a word. Percy used a tissue to wipe his nose but didn't acknowledge the gift. Yeah, well, maybe if you pretended you weren't vulnerable, that meant it wasn't true. Terrell hoped so, because he felt more and more like that every day with Moira's brother. It was nice to know it wasn't a black thing or a gay thing. Apparently, it was a man thing, and thank God Terrell still had some claim to those.

They left not long after, and Terrell didn't want to think about Percy being heaved to his feet by one guard while another unlocked his ankle chains. His ankles and wrists were still thin with adolescence, and Terrell wanted to scrub that thought out of his memory. *Oh, dammit, Percy! Please, kid, be telling the fucking truth.*

When they got out to their cars, Terrell leaned up against the door of Colby's little Honda Accord and sighed.

"So, whatya gonna do?" he asked, because sure enough, it was completely out of his hands.

"Me? I'm going to go meet a bunch of people and stir up a bunch of hornets and generally piss people off. You? You're going to go back to your job and make nice so you can keep bartending to your heart's content."

Moira gave a tight smile, and Terrell scowled at her.

"You know, I *tried* to get a job in my field, you know that, right? I got out of school, I sent résumés, I wrote pieces, I built a portfolio. I hit every news outlet in California—I wasn't proud. I would have moved. I actually got a bite, you know? Up in Redding? But I'd applied as T. Washington, and I drove all the way up there in the middle of fucking August—my radiator gave around Anderson. Anyway, got there, smoking car, last nickel, and they took one look at me—one look, mind you, no checking out the portfolio, no seeing me in my best Sunday suit looking all shiny and hopeful—and they said that job was filled. Filled. Filled with *bullshit*, that's what it was. Anyway, that's *California*. Where else am I gonna go? Down South? Cause according to those folks, being black in California ain't really being black. Back East? Well I'm just small potatoes back East—and I ain't done nothin' here, so what do I have for them? And it just got *old*, you know? Man, tending bar, I got money, some respect, and I don't got... I don't know... disappointment. No disappointment," he said, but he thought of Colby when he said it, the terrible thrill of knowing that Colby would be there at the end of the shift, and that just kept getting better. Who knew how amazing it could be just to have anticipation instead of disappointment? It was like a drug. He wasn't sure he could ever go back.

Moira nodded her head then and took a deep breath like she was reassessing something. "Does Colby know all this?"

Terrell rolled his eyes. "Yeah he does! We talked together for a year before... uhm...." His face heated, and in the damned Africa hot sun, that was hard. "Anyway, yeah. Your brother's a nosy little shit, you know that? He knows everything. Hell, he can probably name all my cousins, and I've damned near given up on doing that myself."

Moira nodded. "Yeah, Colby's like that. He's always been like that. Wants to know why people do what they do, act the way they do. Why can't we talk to the homeless man, Mom? What's wrong with him? Why would he do that? Why do you shave your legs, Moy? Why only women? What would happen if you didn't? Does people's opinion make you feel pretty, or does the bare skin do it?" Moira shook her head then like she was trying to shoo the memories away. "He just wants to know how people work. It's why he's so interested in this murder thing, I think. He wants to know why someone would do that."

Terrell laughed shortly. "Yeah, well, whyever it was, it wasn't Percy. He's stupid, but he's not desperate."

Moira nodded. "Yeah. We need to figure out who's desperate. But not right now. Right now, I need to hire a supermodel to go flirt with the DA—I don't think he's got Percy's taste in women."

In spite of himself, Terrell smiled. "Yeah, well, maybe Percy isn't so dumb after all. He does have good taste in women."

Moira smiled too, although there was still trouble in it. "And Colby's taste in men is improving, hon. Just…." She sighed. "Just try to dream like he does, okay? My brother? He dreams big. I mean, the world has smacked you down a couple of times, and I can see how you get tired. But Colby—no one's told him he can't. Please don't be the guy who tells him he can't, okay?"

Terrell thought of Colby getting launched into the air by a force of nature and loving the ride. It had scared Terrell senseless, but not Colby. Colby? He was born to do shit like that. "I'll try to be the right guy," he said, but he must not have committed, because Moira's face fell.

"Is he the right guy for *you*?" she asked, and Terrell felt a stab of anger.

"Your brother is the *best*!" he snapped irrationally, and Moira's eyes—big and shiny pansy blue—widened.

"Okay," she said thoughtfully, opening the door to her little red Prius. "Maybe this won't be a disaster. But we're not going to figure it out now. I've got to go try to keep your friend from being a 'fuckbasket'."

Terrell grunted. "Do that. Thank you—I'm grateful."

"So see you tonight, 'kay? If Colby's getting off early, you guys think you could bring home some food? Don't care what it is as long as I don't cook it!"

"Yeah," Terrell said, agreeing before he realized how easy it was, how much they both assumed in that simple request. "We'll get you something, no worries!"

"Thanks!" And with that she slid inside the car and started the motor, and Terrell hoped the AC in the Prius worked better than the one in her brother's beat-to-shit Accord.

He drove back to Papi's to give the news and to wait for Colby to get off, and wondered at how easy—how damned easy—it was to know he was going to be with Colby when he really had spent years of being angrily resigned to being alone.

PAPI'S was all busy again, and he ended up clocking on for the other half of his shift. Beth tried to give him crap about being late and taking off, but Suk shushed her and said he'd been happy to fill in, and so had Tim, the newest bartender, who still sucked and didn't make hardly any tips.

Terrell worked with only half his mind until Sean, the regular with a thousand women, called his name, and Terrell made a sudden realization.

He'd seen the woman with him before.

"Heya, Stacy," Terrell said and noticed that the painted-on neon thing she'd had on earlier in the week had been replaced by something understated and classy in bronze. "You look nice!"

Stacy smiled shyly. "Yeah, well, I only wore that other thing 'cause them skank hoes Sean seems to like to wear that shit. This is what I usually run with."

Terrell laughed. "So you caught his attention with the flash and lured him in with the real—nice! I like it."

Again, that shy smile. She leaned forward over the bar. "You know what the trick is to catching a player, right?"

"Playing him!" Terrell said, garnering a delighted laugh in affirmation.

"You know it!" She had a great laugh—she threw her head back and showed off her straight white teeth.

"You stealin' my girl, T?" Sean asked, putting a possessive hand around the girl's waist.

Terrell smirked inwardly at that and shook his head. "Wouldn't dream of it! Now that you've finally got one you can bring home to the folks!"

Sean rolled his eyes. "Yeah, maybe not off the bat. I wouldn't want to scare her off!"

"Your mom is that frightening?" Stacy asked, a little bit of apprehension in her voice, and Sean shrugged.

"Moms is okay—she's a softy. She's got three girls and two boys and loves us all. But Dad—" Sean shook his head. "Man, my little brother came out last year, and Dad's okay with it on *his* end, but for me? The girl I bring home—"

"Better carry on that family name right, huh?" Stacy asked sympathetically, and Sean nodded.

"Yeah. Man, I swear that's why I held so many damned auditions!"

Terrell snorted. "Yeah. I'm sure your brother appreciates being the cause of all that!"

"Naw, Jerome's got his boyfriend. They bring the best shit to the holiday gatherings—folks love him. He'll take one for the team!"

Terrell swallowed and finished off the mai tai for Stacy with extra pineapple. "You got a real nice family," he said soberly to Sean. "You treat your girl right, treat your family right. You got no idea what you have, man. Here. Glenlivet, comped on me. I'm glad to see the same girl twice."

There were little pulses in his voice that he couldn't seem to get hold of, so he turned away from the two of them and helped another customer, not even checking on their expressions from the corner of his eye.

For the moment, thinking about Percy, thinking about wanting Gi-Gi to meet Colby…. Just looking at them hurt too much.

THE night was chaotic—more than chaotic—because Beth never did call in another manager and spent half the night in the bathroom and the other half talking to anyone who would listen. Everyone with seniority quietly traded with the new people because they could get their shit done and get the place closed without any help from Beth, and the new people—who were tired of getting yelled at for no particular reason—went gratefully.

The seating was… well, disastrous. Terrell kept a weather eye out for Colby and watched him get slammed with one large party after another, and Terrell helped Suk on the back bar for him a couple of times when he stacked his tray with drink upon drink.

The cherry on Colby's shit sundae was five minutes before the kitchen closed, and Colby looked up from getting his food at the expediter's stand to see his entire section full.

"God*dammit*, Kelly!" he shouted. "There are other servers in the goddamned restaurant!"

Kelly looked at him with a wobbling lip, then went tearing off to the girl's bathroom, where everybody in the back of the house could hear her sobbing loudly.

Colby leaned his head back and squeezed his eyes shut. "Fuuuuuucccccckkkkk!"

Terrell looked out from the bar in time to watch Angie walk by and pat his shoulder. "I'll go make it right," she said. "She's sucked donkey balls all night—someone had to snap. You've just got the deepest voice."

Colby gave her a faint smile. "Thanks, Ang. Tell her if she wants to make it up for me, she can fill up my condiments while I work on this, okay?"

Angie nodded. "Will do. My shit's done. I'll help too."

Terrell felt bad for him, but he was also relieved. Colby had flaws. He'd known that from the get-go—all of that energy came with a temper and some excess passion. Terrell had seen it up close and personal. Knowing it was real, and that he loved it too—that was important.

It was at that point that his hand jerked and he dropped a glass, and then sliced his finger picking it up. He carefully avoided thinking about what had made him drop a glass, and then just concentrated on keeping his little world behind the bar clean.

By mutual consent, he and Colby skipped their break so they could just end that fucked-awful night sooner, and when it finally happened, both of them walked quietly out to the car.

"Beth give you trouble?" Colby asked as they neared it, and Terrell shook his head in the easy lie.

"No more'n usual." The bitch had been up his ass like an ugly bug—wiping her fingers along the edges of the bottles, making sure every label was where it should be, counting his receipts twice. It was like her world had spun out of control, and the one thing she could actually mess with was the black guy, because God knew *he* needed his job. "Here, let me put your sister's food in the back. I don't want that shit in my lap."

It was actually better than shit. When Mark-the-window-dick heard about what Moira was doing for Percy, he and the entire kitchen staff kicked in and made her a feast for six. The best stuff—pasta Santa Fe, London broil, three baked potatoes with big to-go ramekins full of all the fixings—it was enough takeout to last Moira and Colby for a week. Four days if Terrell ate there like he had been.

When Terrell had asked what they were going to do about Beth—who had *not* been in on the comp—Mark had shrugged. "As far as she knows, we just dropped all this crap. Don't worry about her—you got Percy's back, we got yours."

Which was nice—and after Beth's rectal inspection, it helped to remind Terrell that humanity was and always had been a mixed bag of fish. Some of it was stinky, but some of it was gorgeous, and some of it made you want to swim.

They both slid into the front of the car, and Colby reached for Terrell's hand but backed off when he felt the bandage.

"What'd you do?" he asked, picking up Terrell's hand tenderly and rubbing his finger over the back of the wrapped gauze.

"Had a big brain fart and dropped a glass," Terrell said. His voice graveled, husky and thick, and Colby brought his knuckles up and kissed them.

"Be careful," Colby said, still looking at the bandage. "You're not supposed to get hurt working a shitty job. You're supposed to get hurt doing something spectacular."

Terrell laughed. "Never thought of it that way," he said, although it figured that Colby would. "So what spectacular thing are you planning to do with your life?"

Colby looked at him levelly. "Don't listen to my sister, whatever she said. You're stage one. Anything else I got goin', it don't go nowhere without stage one, aight?"

Terrell grimaced—but he didn't pull his hand away. "You want to try saying that white, so I believe you?"

Colby rolled his eyes. "That was my best restaurant trash, T—not trying to be black, just trying to be real."

"You've got a master's degree, Colby. You told me that during *sex*, which, as far as I can see, is your favorite thing to do when you're not scaring the hell out of me. It means something to you. You've got plans—your sister keeps hinting at them, even if you don't trust me enough to tell me—"

"That's not how it is," Colby said seriously, and Terrell tried to reclaim his hand. Colby wouldn't let him. "What's the matter, Terrell? Are you afraid someone might see?"

"No," Terrell said, although, yeah. If they had seen Percy's full moon in this lightless vortex, there wasn't any reason to believe their little secret was safe.

"Bullshit. But I get that. I get the whole thing. I get that if you ever brought me to your Gi-Gi's house, you could never go back there. I get that being with me—or with anyone you could love—means leaving everything you've known behind. I *get* that, okay? And I'm not keeping things from you because I want to spring it on you like a big surprise. I'm prioritizing, man. You are priority one. All that other shit is priority, like, six. If you and I are good, if I can trust you not to freak out on me, I'll start working on that other stuff and tell you what it is, and then...."

"Then what? You can go be all Captain America and I'll be waiting here for you?" Terrell asked bitterly, fully aware that he'd earned this. He'd given up his dreams after a few lousy setbacks and devoted his time to nursing his poison on his computer diary like a rabid snake feeding from its own venomous tit. He'd given up the right to help Colby be Captain America, to go do whatever this kid had in mind to change the world. Thirty may not have been particularly old, but it *felt* old, here. There weren't many staff members older than he was at a place like Papi's, because most of them had gone on to find their real lives and left this getting stoned/getting laid circle of nowhere behind.

"No," Colby said softly, surprising him. "This thing I've got planned, it's had you in it all along. From the get-go. You were part of it."

Terrell's mouth fell open in shock. "How long have you been—"

"Since last September. I wanted you to be a part of... hell, everything. Life, work, everything." Colby kissed his knuckles again. "You're skittish, T. It took a while to bring you in. But you're worth it. Can you wait a little while longer until you feel that, like, in your kidneys? That you're worth it? That I want you to be a part of me? 'Cause now you'll say no. You will. Now you'll say no, and there won't be anything I can do to change your mind, and I'm not...." Colby's voice grew thick and gravelly too. "I'm not ready for that. I'm still ready to hope. Can we do that?"

"Hope?" Terrell asked. His voice was thready, barely there. But then, so was the hope.

"Yeah," Colby whispered back. He turned and looked Terrell in the eyes, and Terrell saw that he was exhausted and probably worried about Percy, and now he was worried about Terrell.

"I hope you don't ever regret me," Terrell said seriously, and Colby nodded.

"That's fair enough. I hope you'll want me too much to let me leave."

Terrell laughed a little, and the tension, the melancholy, and sadness that had burdened the car dissipated like moisture on the windows. "You do dream big, don't you, cheese boy? Let's go to your house and feed your poor sister, okay? With any luck, we'll be getting Percy the hell out of jail tomorrow."

LATER—*much* later. Later after a disheartening chat with Moira, and some late-night grub, and a soak in the hot tub. Later with the kind of sex with long, slow touches, where Colby's mouth on Terrell's stomach felt like the thing he'd waited his whole life for. *That* much later— Colby lay with his head on Terrell's stomach while Terrell wiped his come off of Colby's cheek with a shaking thumb.

"That...." Terrell breathed, everything in his body still buzzing. "*That* was...." He shivered again, his entire body just assaulted by a terrible, wonderful languor. "You know when you're a kid, and all the grown-ups are trying not to talk about sex in front of you, so you start thinking it's this big mystical thing and shit, something so amazing, so awesome, that if you actually *had* it, you'd have to die and go to heaven 'cause there was nothing left?"

Colby's silent laughter shook his head on Terrell's tight stomach, and Terrell found he was playing with that dark-blond hair, sorting the bleached sections on the top from the darker layers underneath. "Yeah," Colby said, turning to kiss Terrell right above his nappy pubic buckshot curls. "I remember that."

"Yeah. That thing we just did? That was *better.*"

Colby's laugh was not so silent this time. "Yeah," he said in complete contentment. "That really was."

Terrell stopped separating the chocolate and the vanilla of his hair and swept it all back from his face. "C'mere," he whispered, suddenly *aching* to have that pink, pillowy mouth on his, to know Colby by touch, smell, sound, and *taste.* Colby turned and their mouths met in a sated, content, warm and gentle kiss.

He tasted like Terrell's come, plain and simple, and Terrell had Colby's semen seeping between his ass cheeks and his thighs. He couldn't explain it, couldn't define it, but there was a *rightness* to that, to wearing Colby on his skin, to tasting himself in Colby's mouth. He was saturated in the two of them, and he *needed* it, needed Colby seeping through his body to his bones.

Of course, Colby, being Colby, could not simply live with that. He had to try to make it better.

The kiss broke off and Colby practically purred. He rolled to his back and put Terrell's hand in his hair again, and Terrell chuckled—but went back to playing with it. He didn't bother to separate it this time, just pulled the locks of it between his fingers until it was smooth.

"So," Colby said, his eyes closed, "next time, you want to top?"

Terrell tensed, and Colby sighed.

"No, no—don't get like that. Not a necessity. Just thought... you know. You'd like to know what it was like. To be in charge. To... you know. Fuck instead of be fucked. Bad idea. Sorry, T—won't mention it ag—"

Terrell clapped a hand over his mouth and relaxed again. "Colby?"

"Mmmf?" His lips vibrated against Terrell's palm, and Terrell fought against a giggle.

"I'm happy here. Now, gimme a week, and that little idea'll probably start giving me wood, but right now? I ain't been happy in a long time. Can we just be happy?"

"Mm-hm." Colby nodded, and Terrell took his hand away.

"Do I really make you happy?" Colby asked humbly, and Terrell had another shudder.

"It matters," he said, feeling stupid. "It matters to you that I'm happy."

"Of course."

Terrell smiled. "Colby, I got no words. Just... just know, okay?"

Colby's hand came up and meshed with Terrell's, and Terrell didn't look at them twined together. Yeah, they were black and white, swirled like a mixed ice-cream cone, and the fact was, he couldn't make them any less sweet than that.

THE next day, reality smacked them in the face like a cold, wet, stinky-assed flounder.

"Nobody's seeing sense," Moira said miserably. She was red-eyed and pale, and Terrell was pretty sure she'd gotten no sleep the night before. She was wearing the same suit she'd worn to the jail, but it was a little more rumpled, and she'd changed her shirt underneath.

Terrell made a mental note to ask Colby if they could possibly take her dry cleaning in for her, because it really was the least they could do.

"What do you mean?" Colby asked, because of course he'd need it spelled out. Captain America could never believe in the perversion of justice that race inspired, even in California.

"I mean he's going to be arraigned. I cannot, for the life of me, get anyone to see this kid as innocent. I managed to get some time from the PI, but I don't know when that's—"

Her cell phone was in the charger, and it took that moment to ring. "What?" she snapped, raking her hand through straight blonde hair that obviously hadn't been washed recently. "Oh my God. Yeah. Yeah. Of course it makes a difference. God, it *should* make a difference. Oh fuck. Yeah. Yeah. I'll bring it up at the arraignment, okay?"

She turned the phone off and looked at the two of them. "Percy's cousin? The one he thought would clear him?"

They both nodded, and Terrell's stomach was suddenly heavy and sore. "Yeah," he said, and Colby grabbed his hand for no reason Terrell could think of. Terrell tightened his fingers, though. It helped.

"He was shot and killed this morning. In the back. A .38 hollow point. Edgar Michaels is no more."

Terrell had to make himself blink. "Well, shit. Percy couldn't have done *that*," he said numbly, and Colby grunted.

"Can you use that? Can we get Percy out?"

"Well," Moira said thoughtfully, "it's good and bad. It's good because it makes their crime theory fall apart, and really, they don't have any reason to keep him there. The drug charges are unsubstantiated and negligible, and frankly, without the evidence to convict him, the state has better things to do."

"Then why's it bad?" Colby asked. His hand was still twined with Terrell's. For the first time, Terrell realized that he was being relied on for comfort, and he didn't want to let Colby down.

"Because we've got nobody to substantiate Percy's story," Moira said with a sigh. She shook her head. "It shouldn't matter. It shouldn't. He may have to do some time for violating his parole, but I'll see if I can talk it down. Maybe we can do community service—man, I don't want this kid in jail for another night."

Colby nodded, and Terrell, looking at him, realized that he had faith. God, he had faith—and it was terrifying. Terrell knew the world could let you down, but Colby? Colby knew no such thing.

"Yeah. Do you need us there at the courthouse?" Terrell asked, hoping the answer was no.

"That would be great," Moira said. "The arraignment's at ten—when do you have to be in at work?"

"Eleven thirty," Terrell said at the same time Colby said, "Five thirty."

Absurdly, Terrell's heart fell. Oh. That probably meant he'd be staying the night in his own place, and God, didn't that suck.

"Well, you both come, and if it's not over before Terrell has to leave, he can take your car, Colby, and I'll give you a ride to work."

Terrell tried to do the car math in his head and failed—but what he did know was that odds were greatly improved that he would be staying the night again.

It should have frightened him, how much he was depending on that.

PERCY looked so scared, sitting in the defendant's chair in an old suit of Colby's. Percy was taller and skinnier than Colby, and his wrists and ankles stuck out pitifully. The judge—a stern, balding man with a thin beak of a nose and oily skin—listened to both sides of the case and then turned his glare on the extratanned kid in the suit.

"There was no actual contact nor passing of drugs that involved this man?" The judge tilted his head and listened as Moira (Ms. Meyers, which Terrell thought he should remember: Moira Meyers, Esq.) repeated that no, Percy had simply given his boss a number.

Then the other lawyer, a slick fortysomething white guy with a gray suit, asked to discuss the case up close, and Moira went. When she came back, her mouth was tight and her eyes narrow, and Terrell thought that maybe he'd *better* spend the night at his place, because God, who would want to get in that woman's way?

And that was when things went to shit, and the judge said that they would hold Percy for forty-eight hours pending an investigation.

Percy looked around wildly for something, someone, to hold on to after that, and the person he found was Gina.

Terrell saw it, saw Percy meeting the girl's eyes, and thought, *Oh shit. What's this been? A week? Have they been together for a week? That girl is too smart to stick with this kid, and he thinks she's going to be his saving gra—*

"I'll visit," Gina said. She was sitting to Terrell's left, which made her kitty-corner to Percy, on the bench behind. "Don't worry, Percy. It's two more days. I'll bring you the book, it'll be okay."

Percy's smile about melted Terrell's icy heart. "Thanks," he said simply. Then a spasm of panic crossed his features. "Don't let me down, okay?"

Gina nodded somberly. "I swear, baby. I'll be there."

The judge clanked his gavel as Percy was taken away. Gina leaned forward to get particulars from Moira, and Terrell glanced over at Colby to see if he was ready to go.

He was devastated.

Terrell stood, leaned over Moira's shoulder, and told her that Colby would be taking him now, and then he nudged Colby and made him move.

Colby closed his mouth and stood up, but as they went back downstairs and out the back door to the parking garage, Terrell could see that he was moving stiffly, clumsily, like a blind man who had just figured out that he could slam into stuff if he wasn't careful.

They got into the car and Terrell didn't even bother to look around. Damn Gina and her fucking brave leap of faith. Made Terrell look like a coward, that's what she did. Without thinking about consequences, Terrell reached out and grabbed Colby's hand before he could start the car.

"It's two days, Colby. Gina's going to visit. Percy will be all right."

"He shouldn't have to stay," Colby said grimly. "It's stupid. There's no logical reason—"

"Except he's black, and he's been arrested for dealing before, and that's just the way it is. He's not a saint, Colby. He's not a sweet kid from the suburbs. He wanted to be a thug—well, this is what happens when you jump on that train!"

"He never wanted to be a thug!" Colby snapped. "He wanted to be safe! Just like you do. And you've got a right to be safe without having to... I don't know, mule for your uncle Edgar or... pretend your dick doesn't exist!"

Terrell had to laugh at that one. "Well, thanks to you, I'm pretty sure mine is up and working!"

That worked. Colby's grim expression twisted a little. It wasn't a smile, but it wasn't a scowl either. "It's working fine," Colby said, running his fingers through his hair. Since he wore it brushed forward from the crown of his head, that made it do all sorts of stupid shit, and Terrell grunted.

"God, cheese boy, let's comb that mess before your Captain America thing is tarnished by bad hair." He fished in the glove compartment of the car for a minute and came back with a comb, but not before he saw the passport.

He gave Colby the comb and curiously pulled out the passport. "Wow. You've got one—look. It's recent! Damn. You planning to go somewhere?"

Terrell looked up at Colby, expecting a smile and some sort of explanation about a trip for graduation, but what he saw was the same expression Colby had worn when he'd told Terrell that the other shit in his life was not a priority.

"Not at the moment," Colby said grimly, combing through his hair and setting that long-haired Caesar thing he had going all back to rights. He took a deep breath, and the smile he turned toward Terrell was warmer and stronger than Terrell expected. "I'll let you know when I'm ready, okay, T? And don't worry. I'm not planning to walk out the door unless you're ready to come with me."

Terrell blinked. "Where in the hell would I go?" he asked, startled, and Colby grimaced.

"With me. Isn't that the only thing that matters?" And with that, he started the car and drove.

Traffic was tense downtown, and Terrell let him negotiate it without a lot of talk. The radio was playing—white people's music, but Terrell figured he'd get to listen to Linkin Park all he wanted if he was driving, and Terrell got lost in the sound of it too. When they pulled up in front of Papiano's, on the corner of Howe and Hurley, they were both a little more relaxed, and the smile Colby turned toward him was simply distracted, not distraught.

"I'll see you tonight, T—I'll get here a little early, you can take the car and then come pick me up."

Terrell nodded, and then Colby reached out and stopped him before he could slide out.

"Doesn't it worry you?" Colby asked seriously. "What people will think? They see us come to work together all the time, giving each other rides. I know you're paranoid about this shit, T—why haven't you said anything?"

Terrell shrugged. "I'm pretending," he said after a moment. "I'm pretending, for as long as I can, that this thing ain't no one's business but ours."

Colby thought about that and nodded. "You know, there's worse answers. Have a good shift, 'kay?"

Terrell nodded and slid out of the car.

IT WAS an okay shift. Erin was running it, and he was working with Tim, the new guy, so there were all sorts of fuckups that could have been avoided. They let the kitchen guys go early, so when an unexpected rush happened, they had to comp all sorts of food for being late. Erin hustled Tim out of the bar before he could stock his shit, and that was always fun because Terrell was running out and working the holy hell out of the bar-backs, and that was interesting too. But finally the afternoon mellowed out and Mark-the-window-dick slouched up at the bar, eating dinner in his dress whites before he left for home and pumping Terrell for information.

"So why'd they keep Percy? Shouldn't all that shit, I don't know, like, absolve him or something?"

Terrell rolled his eyes. "Yeah, but Percy is young, stupid, and black. He's going to be kept until they're ready to get rid of him."

Mark grunted. Terrell knew that grunt. It was the sound of a man who didn't really believe that it was the black thing and who probably thought that maybe Percy had this coming to him. Terrell didn't blame him, really—Terrell had thought the same thing about Percy until right about now.

"He's a good kid," Terrell said sincerely, soberly, and Mark looked up. He was blond too—his hair was actually a little paler than Colby's, and he wore it the same way, pulled toward his forehead from the crown. But Mark's eyes weren't quite as blue, and his skin never tanned because he was one of those guys who got sick if he had too much sun.

Terrell had never, ever gone soft and wanting and sweet for Mark the way he had for Colby, almost from the beginning.

"Yeah," he said after a minute. "You know, you're right. That kid did everything we asked of him. We need to get him out."

Terrell breathed a little better. A mixed bag of fish, isn't that what he'd thought? Well, maybe this guy wasn't a bad fish. "Yeah, but first we've got to do what Colby's wanted to do from the get-go. Figure out who did it."

Mark shrugged. "It should be easy, really. It's someone wearing black sneakers—which sounds like all of us, except I think if it was a kitchen person, you'd know."

"Yeah, we already thought of that—you guys would be sliding around if you tried to run down the back dock."

"Yeah, and you would have recognized the stench. They do *not* smell good after a few shifts. It had to be someone from the front of the house. And it had to be someone who went *into* that office with that guy a lot, because *nobody* noticed who it was, and that's a hell of a thing not to notice."

"Well," Terrell defended, "that could be damned near any girl in this place! You may or may not have figured this out, but that man played the fuck around!"

Mark nodded. "Well, yeah, but we know it's not Angie, for instance."

Terrell thought about it. "Yeah, and Gina wasn't working that night."

"It could have been Erin," Mark said reasonably. "Or Beth—"

"No, she was in the bathroom. Besides, Erin and Beth both had those stiletto heels on, which is why we didn't think about them or either of the Do' Hos in the first place!"

"Well then, Trish!"

"No, dammit, because she found the damned body, you know that!" God, Colby was *so* much brighter than this guy.

Mark grimaced. "No, really don't. Remember? I wasn't there!"

Terrell grunted, and at that moment Beth called his name. Erin was gone, which meant she was checking out, and damned if that woman didn't want him to organize the maraschino cherries by size or something. "Yeah, yeah. Well, me and Colby will have to put together a chart or something. This is his hobby, and his sister is the one getting Percy out." Terrell sighed, the thought seeping in that all this would be for moot. "Of course, even if we *do* put it together, it's not like the police are going to listen to us anyway!"

Mark sighed and wiped off his fingers with the napkin, acknowledging that their conversation was at an end. "Yeah, well, you let me know what you two figure out." Suddenly Mark blinked, and looked at Terrell, and then blinked again. "T, you and Colby—you're spending an awful lot of time together."

Terrell scowled. "So?" he asked, his voice hostile, and Mark nodded neutrally again, and Terrell's heart fell. No. Not so soon. He wanted to deal with this later. Much later. When he felt brave and shit.

"Nothing," Mark said quietly. "None of my business."

Terrell was going to open his mouth then and actually *be* brave, but Beth called his name again and he let it go.

But he was ready now. He started running those things through his head, the things that were the whole truth but that shut people up in a damned hurry. He might be forced to say something he never thought he'd say, but he didn't have to host an episode of *Dr. Phil* or some such bullshit. Not on *his* shift!

Venom Den

"CAN we go to your place tonight?" Colby asked without preliminary as he slid into the car. "Moira's been working her ass off, and I think we should stay out of her hair."

Terrell nodded. "Man, it's like you read my mind. Did you eat?"

Colby shook his head. "Naw, why? You don't have anything at your place?"

"No, Colby, because I've been living with *you* for two weeks!" The sarcasm in Terrell's voice made *Terrell* wince, and Colby patted his knee.

"Aw, T—whatsamatter? Didn't you get your nap?"

Terrell grunted and tried to make sure the car was in reverse. He'd driven it to the jail and back the day before, and to his apartment and back to work to pick up Colby tonight, and he wasn't as comfortable as he could be with stick shift. *His* car was automatic, and that's the way God intended for all cars to be, he was sure of it. "Clutch" his skinny *ass*. It didn't even *sound* like a real car part. Car parts had names like "exhaust manifold" and "carburetor." A "clutch" is what a girl brought to a dance!

"Yeah, yeah—I got my workout *and* my nap, thank you very much. I'm just...." Well, shit, he wasn't anything that Colby wasn't, was he? "I'm just being an asshole. Ignore me, dammit. I'm sorry."

Colby patted his knee again. "Would it make you feel any better to know that Gina visited him today? She left his book and said he wasn't doing badly. The guards took pity on him, kept him isolated, and he's bored but not too bugshit."

The lump in Terrell's throat caught him by surprise. "She… God. I'm glad. I can't believe she's sticking with him."

Colby grunted. "Yeah, well, maybe that thing we saw in the parking lot was a long time brewing. Sometimes it's like that. You want this person for so long that when it finally happens, it's… it's the real thing."

"Yeah."

"Yeah? Is that all you've got to say?" Colby's eyebrow was twitching up skeptically.

Terrell couldn't help a small smile. "Well, yeah. It's been known to happen," he said mildly. "Sometimes. When it's special."

Colby laughed, but the sound was strained, and Terrell caught his breath. He sounded tired. Tired and sad.

Terrell put a hand on his knee and squeezed before shifting again. "You're not worried now, are you? I mean, you're Captain America—you're winning, right?"

Colby's response was uncharacteristically sober. "Am I winning, T? I need to know. Tonight, especially, I need to know I'm winning."

Terrell went to reach for his hand, forgot he needed to shift it into first around the corner, and stalled the engine. Colby burst into surprised laughter, shouted, "Clutch, T!" and Terrell did what he said no question. The car's momentum jump-started it before they slowed down, and Terrell sped up into third.

"Maybe we should—" Terrell started at the same time Colby said, "Yeah, have this convo another time!"

They both laughed at that, and Colby's energy returned, filling up the car, becoming larger than life, because that was just who he was. Terrell took the final turn to his apartment building and found a miracle guest spot to park.

He and Colby were pretty quiet on the way up to the room. Terrell opened the door and was in the middle of saying, "Do you want to take a shower?" when Colby stopped him at the door and pressed him back, kissing him almost violently.

He slid in the door and kicked it closed, and Colby pressed him back again, devouring him, needing him so badly, Terrell wondered if he was enough, and then gave back to him again.

Terrell was used to being gentled, and to Colby being kind, but there didn't seem to be any room in Colby for that this time. Terrell, who had just learned what it was like when your skin was fed properly, felt inadequate, lost, in the face of Colby's ferocity.

"What's wrong?" Colby whispered when Terrell backed away to catch his breath.

"You're... I'm not enough," Terrell gasped, and Colby shook his head.

"You're everything. Everything... just kiss me. Just don't stop."

He held still for a moment as they leaned forehead to forehead, and Terrell brushed his lips against the corner of Colby's mouth, against his chin, against his ear. Colby gasped then, obviously loving that, *needing* it, and Terrell played with his lobe, nibbled and sucked on Colby's little gold ear studs, because that seemed to turn his key.

Colby made a sound that was all consonants, and Terrell took his cue, took his power from that sound, and kissed his way down Colby's shoulder and chest. He pulled away for a second to drag Colby's uniform shirt off his body and then suckle on a dark-pink nipple.

"Bed," Colby gasped, and Terrell backed him up to the bed in the corner and suckled him until his knees gave out. He moved to the other nipple as Colby dug his fingers into Terrell's shoulders, and Colby's moans grew louder and more insistent, Terrell surged ahead aggressively, kissing his ribs, his stomach, and then, after dragging down his jeans, licking the crease of his thighs and his cock.

Colby let him this time, let him take over and kiss and explore and play with that amazing foreskin. Yeah, Colby was still sweaty from work, still smelling like grease and run-off-his-ass, but Terrell didn't care. Not now, not with Colby who needed *him*—Colby who was splaying out that string-muscled body for Terrell to devour. Colby's cock was *sweet* in the back of his throat, and Terrell swallowed him, deeper, deeper, deeper, until he was gagging on it. He came up quickly and went back down, unable to get full enough on the taste, on the feel, on knowing that *Colby was inside of him*, and Colby flailed, squeezing his shoulders, his biceps, begging for more, for harder, for *everything*.

He needed.

Terrell swallowed him down one more time, squeezing his balls gently and allowing his fingers to play with Colby's taint and a little below.

That's all it took, one touch to his asshole, and Colby arched off the bed and thrust so deep into Terrell's throat that Terrell almost gagged completely. He slurped up to halfway and grabbed the base and sucked *hard* on the head until Colby let out one of those *deep* groans from the pit of his stomach. He shook in every sinew of his body and poured himself down Terrell's throat.

Terrell kept swallowing, kept sucking, kept fondling and teasing, and Colby didn't stop coming until Terrell couldn't swallow anymore and Colby actually bit the outside of his arm to muffle a scream.

At last it was over—Colby was replete, panting on the bed, and Terrell was lost, dazed in what he had just done, just made happen in his lover's body.

Colby gulped some more air and then threw out an arm. "C'mere," he said.

Terrell went willingly, needing some sort of reassurance, because until that moment, animal passion hadn't been in his repertoire.

"Good?" Terrell asked, leaning over to kiss Colby's sweaty shoulder. The boy was naked, glistening with sweat, and Terrell's shirt and shorts were sopped through.

And not, embarrassingly enough, with sweat.

"You ready for me to return the favor?"

"Naw," Terrell muttered, hiding his face in Colby's sweaty pit, because it was better than the alternative. "I came in my shorts."

That drew Colby up short. "Yeah?" he said, raising his head off the bed to look down.

"Yeah," Terrell muttered. It had happened pretty much when Colby spurted down his throat, and it had given Terrell the passion to swallow and not let the whole thing dump on his face.

Colby moved that reassuring arm out from under his neck and kissed Terrell's cheek, and then his neck, and then rucked up his shirt, all in an effort to get down and strip off his basketball shorts and drawers. There Terrell was, still semierect, his cock smeared with come, and without warning, there Colby was, licking it up with a flat pink tongue.

Terrell gasped because his cock was hella sensitive, and that tongue—not too rough, just thorough, cleaning the shaft, the balls, the crown, the slit, oh God, and back down the shaft again—was turning Terrell on.

"Ahhh! What are you going to do when that thing gets... oh Jesus, hard again?"

"Put your hands on your nipples, T—they're sensitive."

Terrell did, giving himself an almost vicious pinch when Colby went down to engulf his shaft in a working throat, and Terrell bucked, thrilled and oversensitive and ready to come again.

Colby looked up at him, happy and flushed from coming and from being aroused a second time. "I've got a plan," he said, and Terrell half laughed and half groaned, because part of that plan involved taking T down his throat again.

Colby popped up, grabbed his hand, and wrapped it around his own dick. "Here—hold that thought." He disappeared for a moment, rooting around in the drawer underneath the pedestal in the bed, and came up triumphant.

"A*ha!*" he practically giggled.

"Yeah, I got lu-*ube!*" Because that shit was still cold and Colby dumped it right on his cock.

"Yup," Colby said happily. "Anyone as repressed as you were must have jacked off *constantly.*"

"It was my best sport," Terrell muttered, and his voice would have been sour, but… oh my dear Lord! Colby squirted some of that shit on his fingers and then put his hand behind him. The look on his face—twisted, beyond pleasure, almost into pain, but also wanting, needing, *craving*, and oh God, he was going to let *Terrell* fill that for him. If anything, the thought made Terrell's cock ache more.

Colby knelt next to him for a moment, pleasuring himself with his fingers in his own asshole, until Terrell groaned, turned on from watching him. Colby turned and kissed him, swinging one knee astride Terrell's hips before he reached around his back, grabbed Terrell's erection, and carefully sat down.

Colby went slowly, moving up and then lowering whenever things got too tight. Terrell just watched him, trying to put the look on Colby's face together with the feel of his cock in Colby's body. Colby's ass radiated heat, and every inch he slid down was more and more scalding, supernova heat, which lit up Terrell's sex nerve endings like a pinball machine so that when Colby, very gingerly settled into that long glide down, with Terrell's cock firmly buried inside of him, Terrell could do nothing but dig his fingers into Colby's thighs, arch upward in ecstasy, and let the molten, excruciating, gorgeously pleasuring heat pour over him.

"Good?" Colby panted.

Terrell nodded. He managed to gasp, and he was going for "Yeah," but what came out was "Ynnnnggggghhh… ah…." Colby laughed but then gasped too.

That was when Colby *really* started to ride up and down, the tight rubber-band muscle of his entrance gripping Terrell so hard he didn't dare move, and Terrell could barely gasp out another "Yesnnnnggghhhh!" before that slow glide went faster.

And faster.

And Terrell needed it *faster,* so he grasped Colby's thighs again and started pistoning his hips upward, rabbit-fucking fast. Colby braced one hand on either side of him, gripped with that tight rubber-band muscle, and held on for the ride.

Terrell had never felt so out of control and so powerful all at the same time. Colby's inner thighs were shaking with the effort of holding him just so, and Terrell's *whole body* was shaking with the effort of fucking. He saw Colby's erection bobbing with his frenzied movement, and Terrell wanted to see him come.

"Grab it," he managed, and Colby didn't need more words than that. His hand was a blur as Terrell's hips practically vibrated with speed, and suddenly Colby moaned again, yelling, loud and unapologetic, as he spurted, white and hot and messy, all over Terrell's stomach and chest.

The sight of Colby's white come and the sensation of Colby's painfully tightening body—those were the things that sent him over the edge himself.

He came, moaning, flooding Colby's insides and thrusting convulsively until Colby collapsed across his chest, ignoring the sticky mess the same way Terrell had ignored Colby's sweaty body, both of them exhausted and replete and done.

Colby's breathing was still harsh when he shifted, and Terrell's cock fell out, gushy and warm. Colby hmmed but didn't seem to notice beyond that—he was too fascinated with kissing Terrell's shoulders.

Terrell managed a half laugh, and then Colby stuck out a pink tongue and licked some of the sweat off and smiled.

"Ew." Terrell managed the word, but he couldn't manage the scowl that should have gone with it.

"Naw. Sweat." Colby licked his shoulder again. "I always thought it would taste different on your skin," he said thoughtfully.

"Black sweat?" Terrell asked, amused but not offended.

"Licorice sweat?" Colby smiled. "Chocolate sweat? I don't know. I just…." He nuzzled some more. "I just always thought the color was amazing. Rich and… just more."

It seemed like such an odd thing to say. "You like my skin color."

"Well yeah!" Colby grinned up at him now, obviously enjoying his surprise. "I do! I mean, it wouldn't make me love you if you were an asshole, but, well." He flushed and hurried on, and Terrell's mind didn't hardly have time to stumble on the big bad word. "But you're not."

"So you like it?" Terrell felt dense. Attraction. That's what Colby was talking about. Attraction. It was a simple thing. Such an animal thing, Terrell almost forgot that Colby would need it. But he *would*, wouldn't he? He'd need to feel something simple and animal to do what they just did, right?

Colby blushed now. "I didn't want to sound like... I don't know. One of those stupid groupies, right? One of those people who only want a black guy for the novelty? 'Cause they think he's hung like a donkey and it'll piss off the parents or something? I just...." Colby giggled and blushed some more, and Terrell found himself mesmerized by this new Colby, this actually boyish Colby who played with Terrell's skin and seemed to treasure Terrell's good opinion.

"You just?" he teased.

"I just *like* the color of your skin. Like I *like* your voice, or, you know"—he licked Terrell's neck—"the way you smell after sex or"—his smile grew thoughtful—"the way you kiss me."

Terrell's big metal smile wasn't getting any smaller. "You want me to kiss you right now?"

Colby's flush of embarrassment wasn't going away. "Very much," he whispered.

"Anything," Terrell said soberly.

"I'll hold you to that."

And Terrell put him out of his misery and pressed their mouths together and tasted him, warm and red and wet, and loved him.

Of course, all that warm/happy lasted until the come started to dry and Terrell ran to the bathroom for a clean washcloth.

"I don't get one?" Colby asked as Terrell came out of the bathroom, and Terrell grinned at him but shook his head.

"No, 'cause I'm gonna feed you, and if I'm gonna run out smelling like sex, you're gonna stay here and make sure your balls don't smell like Papi's by the time I get back, are you hearing me?"

Colby grinned back and looked away, embarrassed again. "Yeah, yeah—I hear you. Look at you, all bossy and shit. A guy tops once and—"

Terrell cut him off, kissing him, framing his face with both hands and feeling that soft blond stubble under his palms. "You gonna shave while you're in there?" he whispered.

Colby pulled back and grinned. "You want me to?"

"Naw—I don't mind a little razor burn on my balls."

Oh God—Terrell would never get over hearing his boy giggle like a little kid.

Ever.

GOING to get him food meant he ended up in Safeway at twelve-o'clock at night, hoping no one noticed the razor burn on his neck because apparently that's just where it wanted to be. He spent some time praying that nobody would know, speculate, visualize, or theorize about what might be on his balls. Nope, nuh-uh, no thank you, because Terrell had been mighty perfunctory with that washcloth, and now he was regretting it.

Besides. It wasn't really anyone's business, now was it?

Of course, it never paid to overestimate the discretion of bored slobs just doing their work, now did it? Because there he was, in line with a little premade tray of fruit, some sourdough bread, some presliced gouda cheese, Dijon, corned beef, and a half gallon of milk, and the damned sales clerk started talking to him while he was counting out his tip money and thinking he should probably make a bank deposit so he'd have rent in two weeks.

"I hope she fine," the boy said, and sure enough, he was black as Terrell, his nose was flat, and his teeth were pointing sixty-three different ways. Terrell had a moment of shock, though, because he realized that for all that, the boy wasn't bad-looking, just needed a little bit of dental work and a pass with the razor on his head and he might be presentable.

And then he realized what the boy was implying.

"Hope who's fine?" he asked as the groceries added up.

"That girl who left those out*standing* hickeys on your neck, brother. 'Cause I'm telling you, it takes a lot of work to get something to stand out on *our* skin, so I'm hoping she was fine!"

The total rang up, and Terrell gave the boy some cash and decided he wasn't all that attached to this store anyway. "I don't know who *she* is," he said, "but *he's* pretty enough to make your balls ache if you swing that way. And I do." At that moment the change machine spit out his thirty-seven cents, and he grabbed his plastic grocery bags by the handle and stumped out of the store.

The look on the clerk's face was something he was going to treasure for a *very* long time.

WHEN he got back, Colby was sitting at his computer, surfing the Web, and Terrell had a bad enough fright to almost drop his groceries in the doorway as he entered.

Colby turned around, though, and grinned. "Heya! I hope you don't mind—nothing was on television, and I got bored!"

"You never heard of a *book*?" Terrell asked, indicating the bookshelves which were the only other things in nonkitchenette side of the apartment besides the couch, the coffee table, the TV, and the bed.

"Well, yeah, but I just got out of school, and my brain hurts. I need something mindless before I get back into that again. I was hoping for porn."

Terrell grunted. "Then you are in the *wrong* apartment, boyfriend—you would have to admit you were gay to have gay porn. All my lubing was done pretending I wasn't thinking about guys who looked like you!"

Colby preened for a minute. "Yeah? You were thinking about guys who looked like me?"

Terrell's face heated. "Yeah, but only after I met you. It was like wanting some other cheese besides American. You had to taste it first to know that's what you wanted."

Colby chuckled, his smile smug and cocky as it ought to be, as he surfed. Terrell started working, putting together a sandwich and some fruit on a plate and pouring a glass of milk. God, he was glad it looked like Colby was going to be there in the morning. He *hated* the taste of milk, and Colby was going to have to drink what was left.

"Hey, T—what's this folder here, and why don't you want me to see it?"

Colby's voice scared him badly, and he dropped the knife on the cheap green Formica counter only to have it bounce, rebound, and slide down onto the cracked brown tile of the floor.

He swore, bent down to pick it up, and then rinsed it off, wincing when the pipes made that god-awful burbling sound, because this place was *not* classy.

"That's my video diary," he said, trying to keep his voice steady. Telling the truth—he and Colby had always been really good at telling the truth. "And it's about me being an angry black man, and I don't want you to see me being stupid and pissed off."

Colby made a sound like he was choking on his own smirk, and Terrell looked over his shoulder and scowled.

"What?"

"Did you think I didn't know you were an angry black man, Terrell? Do you think this shocks me?"

"Yeah, don't mind that guy. He thinks he's pretty 'cause he's white."

"Jesus, Colby—you could be the only white man I've known who didn't think he had a free pass to the Do' Ho's jeans."

"No, that guy don't piss me off, because I can come back here and be white with you!"

All of the stupid-ass shit Terrell had said when they were just out on the back dock talking came back to haunt Terrell now as he was trying to make a corned beef sandwich. And then he remembered how bad—how *truly* bad—his video diary got before he'd managed to pull himself back, and he tried really hard not to cut himself accidentally because he'd once been mentally handicapped on purpose.

"Yeah," he said, his voice low and humble, "well, in spite of that, you and me are here together, but what you heard on the back dock? That wasn't hardly anything, Colby. That guy on those diaries, I'd just as soon you didn't know he ever existed."

Colby stood up and walked into the kitchen. He was wearing a pair of Terrell's boxers, and that was it, and Terrell thought all of that tanned skin, from the bare chest to the furry shins, was probably the classiest his kitchen had ever been.

"Do you think I'll leave you if I know how bad it was?" Colby asked seriously, and Terrell shrugged.

"I don't think showing someone you were a freakin' sociopath is aces in the romance department, no."

Colby nodded and took the plate with the double-decker sandwich on it, wisely guessing that the single-decker was for Terrell, because Terrell just didn't eat as much as Colby. He paused, though, and bent and kissed Terrell on the shoulder, and then cupped the side of Terrell's head in one large-palmed hand while kissing his temple.

"You were pissed," Colby said quietly. "All that education and you couldn't get a job. Stuck at Papi's with the who's banging who and getting drunk three times a week and which manager is gonna take from your drawer for their drug buy—it pisses you off. Don't think I can't see that."

Terrell shook his head. "Man, it was so much worse than that," he said, thinking, *This is it. This is what's going to end it. Goddammit, I was finally fucking happy.*

"I want to see," Colby said quietly, and Terrell shook his head.

"Please," he begged, hating himself. "Please, no. Not tonight. Please."

Colby put his sandwich plate down and wrapped his arms around Terrell's shoulders. "Don't you want to know that I can see the worst in you and still stay?"

Terrell shook his head. "Can't we wait just a night before you leave?"

Colby sighed eloquently, and Terrell wondered one more time if it was a family gift. He picked up his sandwich and made his way back to the couch, where he dug in with a lot less enthusiasm than Terrell had hoped for.

Terrell sat on the opposite end of the couch, leaning up against the vee made by the arm and the back, because it supported the muscles in his lower back better.

Colby looked up at him when he was halfway done with the sandwich and said, "Is your back hurting you?"

Terrell shrugged. "Always." But in Colby's arms, he managed to forget.

"Will you let me rub it this time?"

Terrell stopped midbite. How long ago was that? A week? A week and a half? Really?

"How'd you get so patient?" he asked, not because he didn't want Colby's hands on his skin, but because admitting it now, when he was pretty sure he'd be losing Colby in the very near future, just didn't seem worth it.

Colby closed his eyes and growled low, like a bear. "Terrell?"

"Yeah?"

"I love you. I'm in love with you. I'd fucking die for you. I want to be with you forever. I want to watch you do amazing things and be at your side. I want to watch you grow old, and I want you to be with me when I grow old and think that's not a bad thing. I want to take you bungee jumping, and even if we don't jump off that cliff or bridge or helicopter, I want to hear you scream bloody murder and tell me I'm stupid. I want to touch you every night, even if we just fall asleep together. I've been in love with you for almost a year. I've turned down offers and given up dates and switched shifts on my sister's birthday and my mom's birthday and given up a trip back East to see my grandmother just so I could take a ten-minute break with you on the back dock. I worked last Christmas, through my mom's cooking, and that's pretty fucking impressive, so I could give you that damned Easy button, and all I've asked for, ever, just once, was for you to just give it a chance and kiss me back."

Terrell had set his sandwich down with the first sentence. It sat forgotten on the plate while he stared at Colby and wondered when his head was going to explode, and his chest, and maybe his eyes and somewhere in there maybe his heart.

"Damn."

At least Colby could still laugh. "Until now. Now I'm not asking you to say 'I love you' back, because I sprang this on you damned quick, and I'm not asking you to declare undying devotion or fly up to Washington and get married, because I know you're not ready for that. I'm asking two things from you. One is that you trust me enough tomorrow to let me look at that file. The other is that you let me rub your goddamned back."

Colby loved him. Colby had always loved him. This last year, standing by his side, doing the high-five dance, taking that blessed, blessed time together on the back dock, had been love.

Terrell had been in love too.

He swallowed hard against something tight in his chest, and blinked rapidly because his eyes were watering, and then he swallowed again. "A back rub," he said, feeling like it was inane and stupid. "Yeah. Sure. Would love one. Let me know when you're done with your sandwich. Thanks."

Colby's smile was weak, but it was still there. "You, uh, going to finish your own sandwich there, T?"

"No," Terrell said, thinking he might never eat again ever. "My stomach just got all jumpy. Do you think I hear that sort of thing every day?"

Colby grimaced and took a bite of his sandwich. "I hope no'," he said through a full mouth, and Terrell grunted.

"I told the night clerk at Safeway my boyfriend gave me a big hickey. I thought that was a real big fucking deal. So here I am, thinking potatoes, and you're thinking french fries, Irish potato famine, emigration patterns, food groups, carbo-loading, overcropping, pesticides, why we should give the Idaho potato in particular a fucking break and farm something else and how the other kinds of potatoes could solve world hunger, and I'm still back on 'We can *fry* this shit?'."

Colby was holding his hand over his mouth so he didn't spray his sandwich all over the damned table while he busted up. "Pretty much, yeah. So, can we fry this shit?"

Terrell looked at his sandwich and decided he might have a bite after all. "I prefer mine with lots of fucking butter and some bacon, but I'll give fried a try," he said.

Colby nodded and smiled and wiped his mouth on the back of his hand.

"Sour cream," he said like it was of utmost importance. "Can't have a loaded baker without sour cream."

Terrell wrinkled his nose. "That is way too goddamned close to milk. I don't know what's wrong with white people. It's like you want to put milk on everything. You cheese it, you sour it, you yoghurt it, and you know what that shit is?"

"Milk," Colby said, still grinning.

"It's *milk*! And you know what that shit does to me?"

"Makes your stomach bubbly," Colby filled in, and Terrell looked at him sideways.

"You really have been paying attention."

"You were my best homework assignment *ever*."

"Yeah, well, you were my first trip to school."

Colby took another bite and chewed it thoughtfully. His hair was drying, and without the product he normally put in it, it was doing a sort of dark-brown wave from his crown to his forehead. Terrell liked it. Maybe he could let it grow out and give up on that Caesar thing. It was big in the bigger cities a while ago, but too many guys did it, and it wasn't working now.

"You're doing fine, T," Colby said after he'd swallowed and washed down the sandwich with half a glass of milk. "But I think maybe you're ready for the advanced classes."

Terrell regarded him with the sort of helpless sense of a man who thought he was getting on the kiddie roller coaster but who ended up on something with three double loops and one of those four-story drops instead. "Uhm, since I was originally in romance special ed—"

"Did you want me too?" Colby asked seriously, and Terrell couldn't lie to those Captain America blue eyes.

"Every damned day," he said, his chest tight again.

"Then you were doing just fine. No special ed romance for Terrell. He's ready for grown-up-level work."

Terrell took another bite of his sandwich. "Says you," he grumbled. "Teachers tell you that shit all the time, but really, they just want you to write more goddamned papers."

Colby's laugh was deep, strained, and a little bit evil. "You have no idea," he said, and Terrell shook his head and finished his sandwich.

LATER, after they cleaned up and watched a little bit of television (some rerun cop drama called *Cold Case* that left Terrell everything but a blubbering wreck and made Colby get all red-eyed and sniffly too, goddammit! Why did people just do that? Walk into the house when they knew the psycho was there with a gun? Confront a murderer with a suspicion when they were all alone and not a cop in sight? Did people have *no* fucking sense?), Colby had Terrell take a quick shower and then lie facedown on the bed, buck-frickin'-naked.

"Does it have to be naked?" he asked, thinking that they'd let the bed air out, but it still smelled like down-and-dirty after what they'd done a few hours ago.

"Yes," Colby said shortly, although he was in his boxers, like he was getting ready for bed.

"Why?"

"Because I like looking at you naked. Do you realize you have an *amazing* ass? The dark skin is only part of it. It's all smooth and globular and—"

"Just shut up about my ass," Terrell muttered, not able to look at him at all. "Any other reason? 'Cause I'm getting tired here, and I'm pretty sure we've had all the sex stuff out. If I'm gonna fall asleep, I want to do it in my shorts!"

Colby glared at him. "You," he said deliberately, "are killing my buzz. This is *my* fantasy, and I want you naked."

Terrell shook his head. "You *fantasized* about giving me a massage?" he asked, and his voice was dubious, but he climbed into the bed anyway. Well, the man said he liked Terrell's ass—who was Terrell to question? "All the things you could be dreaming about—traveling, parasailing, saving the fucking world in a hang glider, and me, bare-assed naked, that's what you came up with?"

"Ugh! God, you're stubborn." Colby swung up behind him, straddled his thighs, and dumped some cold hand lotion on Terrell's back. Terrell hissed, and Colby let out a sound of satisfaction. "If you could stop complaining for one damned minute, I'd warm that up for you." Colby started working the lotion into the small of Terrell's back, and his movements were firm and healing—but not sensual.

"I just can't believe rubbing my back was an—ah, God, that's fucking *awesome!*—fantasy!" It was like he knew what to do with each muscle, the ones bunched around his spine and his shoulders, and he knew just where to press to make them relax. Push, push, push, knead, sculpt, dig, release… ahhhh….

"It wasn't the rubbing, dickhead. It was the…." For a moment, Terrell thought he stopped because he was working particularly hard on that spot right between Terrell's shoulders.

"The what?" Terrell asked, curious in spite of himself when he realized Colby wasn't going to finish his sentence. His body felt floaty, half-connected to his brain, and he realized how much of his attention every night was centered around coping with the pain in his back and his legs and his shoulders, *especially* on the days he didn't go swimming.

"The making you feel better. The knowing that for twenty minutes of your life, I made you happy. I was the only thing you were thinking about, and you were all good."

Colby hit a muscle group up near his shoulder, and Terrell grunted. "Mission accomplished, dickhead. Except you got that part done about a year ago. The sex finished it off. The massage, that is just... mmm, *hell* yes! Icing on the cake."

Colby laughed, and some of the self-consciousness that had saturated his voice fell away. "A year ago? What happened a year ago?"

"You started working at Papi's, genius." Colby scooted back and started to work in his thighs then, and Terrell buried his face in the pillow and let out a long-drawn-out moan. "Oh my *God*, that's good! But seriously, how could you not know that?" He sighed as Colby soothed over the muscle he'd just released. "God, and you say I'm the stupid one."

Colby laughed and continued to work, and Terrell sank into the touch and the well-being, trying to remind himself that Colby was going to leave him behind and this good feeling would be all gone in the morning. The thought kept trying to pester him, to bother him, to chafe at his happiness, because he knew, somewhere in the gnatosphere of his little warm glow, that Terrell Washington did not get this much joy.

But the gnatosphere was where the thought stayed for that night, because Colby was right *there*, touching him, easing his pain, making him trust the world, and that's when the inevitable happened and he fell asleep.

HE WOKE sweating in the weak AC, to the sound of his own voice, with the tinny overtones of his computer's shitty speaker, spewing dumbass crap into the world, and the gnatosphere became the atmosphere, and it sucked.

So this kid, a black girl, stands up to ask her new superintendent what their school is doing to minimize the achievement gap. She has figures, facts—man, this kid did her fucking homework. You would see it on MSNBC, right? And you know what this old white man replies? He says, "As of yet, this so-called achievement gap has not been sufficiently documented to implement a solution."

Do you know what that is? That's the white man's lie. Any kid who has been to a school like that, who has had forty kids in a third-grade classroom, who has had to use ten-year-old graffiti-ridden text books, that kid knows what the achievement gap is. The achievement gap is the white man's way of keeping the rest of us in our place. Turn us off of education, and we don't learn enough to know he's fucking us over. You turn us off of education by implementing tax loopholes for the rich and making the poor fork over twice their share, and you know who the poor people are in this country, right? They're the black and the brown and the yellow people—not the white people. And that shit just fucking goes on and on and on—

"Jesus, Colby, could you shut that shit off?" God, having Colby leave him because he was apparently functionally brain damaged would be better than having Colby see him spew this vomit into the air.

"Why?" Colby asked. He was hunched over the computer, staring at it raptly, like his favorite pop star was buck naked, doing the nasty and saying his name. He was also wearing nothing but his boxers, and sweating in the heat.

"Because it's crap. Have you tried hitting the AC unit? Sometimes that makes it work better."

"No, I'm fine. Why's it crap?" Colby paused it and stood up, then headed for the AC unit and smacked it until it started making noises like it was at least trying. He walked back to the computer and cocked his head for a moment, waiting for Terrell's answer.

Terrell shook his head. "It's crap because who do you think graffitied up all those schools, tore up the newer textbooks so they had to use the old. I mean, the achievement gap is a two-way street—yeah, sure, the white people started it, but the people in those schools don't always live up to our end!"

Colby blinked and smiled a little. "Well, that's awfully nice of you to let us white folks off the hook, T, but remember that poverty breeds despair. If education isn't a way out like it should be, why should people respect it?"

"Because all you gotta do is shut up and listen! Man, if people would just sit down, shut up, and do what the teacher says, everything could be wine and fucking roses—"

"Except you know people aren't that simple! My classroom had an entire corner of toys just to teach math, so all those squirmy little kids who didn't want to do fractions could play with blocks until fractions made sense. You told me yourself you had worksheets—only, like, a third of the people out there, maybe, can learn easily with worksheets alone. So all those squirmy little kids in *your* class got told to sit down and shut up and they didn't see the purpose, and then they lost hope, and then—"

"Well yeah, but you know, in the homes where the parent tells the kid to sit down and listen to the teacher, they can get over it. But my place, with Gi-Gi? It was always 'Those teachers, those people, they just don't think black!'."

"Well, they didn't! You told me so yourself!"

"Yeah, well, that was no reason to put the teachers through what we put them through—"

"No, no, it wasn't, but that doesn't mean there's not a whole lot of education reform that needs to go on!"

"But who's going to pay for that! Because the white people in office sure ain't gonna vote for no tax raises to educate...." Terrell's voice was escalating, and his breath was coming in passionate pants that had nothing to do with sex and everything to do with some of the basic political realities he had never been able to escape. "Why are we arguing about this shit?" he asked in irritation. "The next election isn't for, praise *God*, another three years. The last thing we should be bitching about is—"

"Is how a white guy and a black guy are going to have a life together? Yeah, Terrell, that's the last thing on *my* mind, that's for sure!" Colby was being a sarcastic little shit—but he was also smirking, and Terrell could tell by the crinkles at his eyes that he was giving Terrell crap.

"Yeah, but why does that discussion have to start with me being a dickhead on the computer?" Terrell asked, fighting a smile. It was hard to be mad at Colby when he was saying all the shit that Terrell had said himself on his video diary years ago.

"Because you weren't being a dickhead," Colby said. "I mean sure, I wouldn't have wanted to hang out with you back then, but I see where you were coming from. What happened to mellow you out— *that's* what I want to know."

Terrell's reluctant smile died an abrupt death. "I'm gonna go to the gym and swim. And if you're still watching this shit when I get back, I'm gonna go get the car tuned. And if you're still watching this shit when I get back from *that*, I'm gonna have your head examined, because you should be out of here finding some guy with a law degree and not hanging out with me."

Colby's sarcastic twinkle faded too, and Terrell missed it. "Which part don't you want me to see, Terrell? You put me there while you go swim, and when you get back, we'll talk about it."

Terrell shook his head, fighting against the heat behind his eyes. "You're not going to want to—"

Colby held open his arms, and gave a "c'mere" gesture with his hands, and Terrell jerked back.

"You want me to—"

"To come here and let me hold you," Colby said calmly.

Terrell regarded him through one squinted eye and one wide-open eye. "Why aren't you coming over here?"

"Because if I go over there, we're going to end up having roaring sex again, and you need to know I can take the worst."

Terrell nodded and thought that maybe a good-bye hug wouldn't be a bad thing. He dragged the sheet over his groin and walked over to Colby, who wrapped his arms around Terrell's thighs and rested his face against his middle. Terrell closed his eyes and held him there, and ran his hands through that hair, tousled and soft now, and wished that this was something he could really have.

"I'll be here when you get back," Colby said against his stomach. "We'll talk. I swear."

Terrell grunted and bent down and kissed the top of his head. "I really do love you. Make sure you lock the door before you leave."

Colby bit his stomach.

"*Ouch!*"

"Don't be stupid. Now get me to the place you hate the most, and put on your suit, and leave. After we're done hashing *this* out, I've got something else we need to talk about, so one way or another, you've got a big day."

"August 17, three years ago, and the week leading up to it," Terrell snapped, and then he stalked off, more than partway pissed because he was pretty sure Colby wasn't going to be his... what? Lover? Boyfriend? What the hell ever. Colby just wasn't going to be his when he got back, and he'd wanted that moment, dammit, to pretend that boy had really belonged to him.

BUT swimming laps was not solace; even as his joints relaxed in the water, his muscles and chest were still tense. His legs might be bandy and his teeth were still an achy metal mess, but there wasn't nothing wrong with his memory.

August 17, three years ago, had been a week after Terrell had driven to Redding to be turned down with one glance at his skin.

It had been three days after a drive-by shooting had killed Monique's best friend in middle school.

It had been two days after he'd heard that the state assemblyman who had voted to kill the education budget for nearly ten years was speaking at the state capitol on August fucking 17.

It had been one day after he bought the gun.

Yeah, he knew how to use a gun. When he'd been a kid, everyone had one. He'd been in third grade when some kid's father had shown anyone who'd walked into his house how to lock and load an AK47. Terrell even knew the places that would forge the ten-day waiting period, but he didn't need to go there. All he'd needed to do was ask a militant white guy at work if he could borrow a gun, and the guy had forked it over, no question. It was weird how much that man had thought he and Terrell had in common after that—skin color was a bad thing, unless you were planning on killing people? It still didn't make any sense.

So he remembered exactly which day it had been, and he remembered what he'd been doing and what he'd looked like. He'd been exhausted and angry, and he'd let his hair grow to about three inches deep. He'd been wearing a red-for-Bloods T-shirt and a red baseball cap and a brand-new pair of oversized jeans, because he was making a goddamned statement, now wasn't he. And he'd loaded that thing in front of his computer's camera, and he'd sat down and recorded what he thought was his last will and testament.

So see, this world ain't getting any better. My people ain't ever breakin' free. We need to do something, something real. Education was my ticket out, but I'm locked in this same shithole with the rest of them niggas, and they don't even know it stinks in there. I know it stinks. I know who's makin' it stink. And I'm gonna go put a cap in that motherfucker. They'll probably drop me right there on the capitol, and this right here—it's set to get mailed to the press at six o'clock tonight. The whole world can see. They'll see me graduate from college and think I have a future, and they'll see how I got beaten down. They'll see me try and try and try and fucking fail.

And some folks will say I had it comin', 'cause I must not have been that smart, but somewhere out there, someone will see this and think that things will change. God, I need things to change.

TERRELL walked in just as his image on the screen uttered those words, and he found himself frozen like Colby, staring at the screen, waiting for the next image to show up.

It did. The computer clicked on and he was there, sweaty, weeping, and bare chested.

Violence is not the answer. Pacifism isn't the answer. Education isn't the answer. God... just... what in the fuck is the answer!

Colby paused the image and turned toward him, and Terrell waited, everything in his body tightened like a watch spring in the freezer, brittle and taut and waiting to snap in the frigid cold.

"What happened to the gun?" Colby asked calmly.

Terrell swallowed. "I threw it in the delta and paid the guy I got it from twice what it was worth. He didn't ask any questions."

"Well, I know you didn't assassinate whatshisname, because I helped vote the guy out of office last year. So good choice there. What happened?"

Terrell sighed and thought about going to get his car tuned up, but he couldn't. Colby was *there*, still there, in his computer chair, in his apartment, still talking to him. Answers. For that alone, he deserved answers.

"What happened?" Terrell laughed and walked through to the bathroom to hang his towel up. He was still wearing his suit, but it had dried on the way back from the pool, and he had a tank top on over it. He thought he was hungry, and he wanted more than water to drink since it was nearly twelve in the afternoon, but he couldn't stop this now, this conversation he and Colby were having. It had a momentum all its own. He had the day off, but Colby worked tonight. Great. He wanted Colby to have the day off too, so they could hammer this out and finish it before either one of them had to go and face the people at work. He needed this finished so his real life could start again, as bleak as it really frickin' was.

"Yeah, T. What happened?"

"What happened was I walked out the door, and there was my neighbor, Mrs. Perkins, and she's white and she's got a walker, and she was trying to wrestle her laundry downstairs, and so I help her, because that's what good boys do, right? They help their elders, and my Gi-Gi taught me right.

"And then, while I'm down there helping her with her laundry, here comes three kids and their mom. And moms is exhausted and blonde and blue-eyed and snapping at all three of the kids, and the kids are hungry, and two of them are white, but the oldest one had a black daddy, and it's real fucking clear this woman had to make a choice today between clean laundry and a trip to McD's, and that wasn't because her kid was black, that was because her crappy job cleaning houses just didn't pay enough. And the oldest kid, he gets mouthy with her, and she slaps him across the face and then just bursts into tears.

"So I get Mrs. Perkins set up, and McD's, it's… you know where it is! It's just right next door to the frickin' Laundromat, so I've got that goddamned gun wedged into the back of my pants under my T-shirt, and it's hot—really hot—and it's uncomfortable, and I go into McD's and buy those kids some fucking chicken nuggets and four extra-large sodas and then bring them into the Laundromat, and mom, she starts to cry she's so grateful. And this whole time—this whole goddamned time, I'm thinking, 'I've got a gun. This woman thinks I'm a good guy, and I've got a goddamned gun in my pants.' And by the time I could get the hell out of there, that politician, he was already out on the steps of the capitol, and here I am, all my militant black shit, and goddammit if things aren't really tough all over."

Colby must have fixed the AC. Terrell was shivering, feeling cold and vulnerable, and he wiped his hand across his eyes and pretended it didn't come away wet.

"I was stupid," he said, feeling it. "I was all the things I get mad at my neighborhood kids for being, that was me. I was twenty-seven years old, and I had a degree, and I didn't have any goddamned excuses, and I was just piss stupid."

Colby stood up this time, and Terrell found his salt-stinging eyes were being kissed, and Colby's big, capable hands were at his shoulders.

"Is that all you got?" he asked softly. "'Cause when I was eighteen, I bought a Southern flag because I liked some rock star who was from the South. Took me three years to realize that most of the people who flew that thing had Nazi shithead tattoos on their bald heads, you know?"

Terrell laughed softly. "Is that all you got?"

"My uncle told us these horribly racist jokes when I was ten. I thought they were funny as hell, because I just had this vision of all these kids held up against the ceiling by Velcro in their hair. I told a friend in high school—who was black, by the way—and he didn't talk to me for a week. He finally sat me down and told me he was hella offended, and I felt like shit. That's when I realized what racism was, and then I realized how subtle it is, and how ugly it is, and how stupid it was to think anyone was immune. And then I wanted to know why we were that way."

Terrell found himself laughing softly, imagining Colby wanting to share something, not realizing how inappropriate it really was. "God, we're stupid when we're young."

"Yeah. Do you forgive me for being stupid?"

"My shit wasn't the same." A gun. Terrell had loaded a gun and walked out with the intent to kill.

"No, your shit was a lot scarier. I'm so glad you came back."

Terrell nodded and leaned into him, accepting him, accepting his comfort, needing him suddenly, needing him too much to shy away or try to be strong. "I am too."

And God, he really, really was.

They stood there for what felt like a long time, long enough for Terrell's back to start hurting, and he must have shifted, because Colby steered him to sit on the couch.

"So," he said quietly. "We're done with that. I've seen that. I'm still here. Do you trust me now?"

Terrell shrugged, thinking that he still didn't believe it, but he'd tell Colby that he did to humor him. "Yeah, sure. Why?"

"Because I'm about to give you something you really need, but knowing you, you're going to need to be nagged into taking it. It'll help if you trust me."

Terrell was wrung out. God, a nap? Some lunch? Something? He needed something. He wasn't sure he could have another conversation like they just had so soon on the heels of that one, but Colby didn't do things by halves, did he? He was like the killer boxing combo of human beings. *Pow! Pow! Still standing, T? Good, 'cause I've got a haymaker in my rep, and I think you can take it!*

Well, Captain America, bring it on.

"Can we eat when we're done?" he asked, feeling pathetic.

Colby grinned. "Here. I'll make us some sandwiches, and then— then I'm gonna offer you a job."

And there it was. The haymaker. By the time he finished talking, Terrell thought it was a good thing he was sitting down, because his knees were more than wobbly, and his head wasn't sitting quite right.

The Long and Winding Road

TERRELL chewed on his sandwich and wondered at the human capacity to eat when food really should be the last thing on a body's mind.

"You haven't even seen me write!" he protested, part of him angry about this and part of him figuring that this was just Colby, because Colby just *made* the world to his requirements, because that was what Captain America *did.*

"I don't care if you write in crayon and use druidic symbols, T. Do a video diary. Do YouTube installments. I *wrote you into the grant*, dammit, someone with a degree in journalism. You satisfy the requirements. I want it to be you."

Terrell was so bemused, he started talking to his sandwich. "He wants it to be me. Did you hear that? He wants it to be me! He makes it sound so easy! Hey, Terrell, I love you, you love me, let's run away together to… where the fuck was it?"

Colby ducked his head over his own sandwich, probably to hide his smile. He was unsuccessful. "Germany, Belgium, the Netherlands, and South Africa."

"You know those places don't like black people," Terrell said blankly, pretty sure this was right. There was not good history there.

"I understand South Africa is trying," Colby said apologetically, and Terrell scowled.

"Yeah. South Africa. How close is that to Uganda, by the way? Because you may say South Africa is friendly, but in Uganda? You and I would be put to death right now. And that is *not* exciting me."

"We'll stay the fuck away from Uganda, Terrell, I promise. There is *no* Uganda on the itinerary—"

"Which you *have*?"

Colby actually managed to blush. Oh my God, the world's whitest human, and *that's* what it took him to blush? "Yes. I had to. I was writing a *grant*—they need that shit!"

Terrell took a deep breath, and took another bite of sandwich so he could gather his thoughts. He should have known. He should have known Captain America would have a plan to save the world.

"You were writing a grant—when were you writing this shit?"

Oh. Good. Colby blushed again. "After Christmas," he mumbled. "I gave you the Easy button. You used it every frickin' day. I had hope. Fucking sue me."

"You had hope? You had hope, so you *wrote us a grant*?"

Colby stopped blushing and glared at him. "Okay, I may not have seen your diary of shame yet, T, but even then, I knew—you *need* this!"

"I need a trip to Uganda?"

"No! You need a trip to the *anti*-Uganda! You need a trip to all the places being gay doesn't suck so you can come back here and realize that the world is a bigger place than this stupid city!"

"So that's your plan. We visit all these places, you write the big important paper, I do the daily documentation, and we collaborate on the book."

"Yes."

"You and me."

"That's what the grant says."

"Who gave you *money* for this?"

"Rich gay white men."

Terrell almost spit out his sandwich. "No. Really."

"Yes, really. Well, I don't know if they're white. Or even gay for that matter. I just know I researched groups that were interested in this kind of data, and then found one and wrote a grant application, and they said yes. They'll pay for both of us—maybe not the greatest hotels, but they'll pay. Six months in Europe and South Africa to figure out what those countries with all the gay-friendly policies have that we don't over here, then six months to come back and assemble all our data and write it down. See? We can go travel, then we come back, move in with Moira, and play with her cats."

Terrell scowled. "I want my own—"

"Or we can come back, buy a house, rent an apartment, whatever, and get our own cats. We'll figure it out, T. But I want you to be with me when we do."

Terrell looked down at his sandwich and then around at his apartment. It was nothing, he thought hollowly. The walls were stark and white, with the exception of the one behind the couch, which was faux brick. He'd lived here for eight years, and he'd replaced the sheets and comforter a couple of times, and that was all. He wore basic clothes, bought the expensive orthotic shoes, and really?

It was a bolt-hole, a hiding spot—there was nothing different here than any other apartment in Sacramento, except right now, there was a man across the couch from Terrell who was offering Terrell the world.

"I've got family here…." It sounded weak to his own ears. He could leave the country and come back, and Gi-Gi wouldn't ever know. And besides that—

"Are they really your family, T?" Colby asked, his voice pained and gentle. "Really?"

Terrell looked away. "Man, you can't just spring this on me. I mean… Jesus, last week, I wasn't fucking gay!"

"Oh bullshit!" Colby snapped. Terrell had obviously hit his temper spot. "You were just as gay then as you were last night with your dick in my ass! The difference was, last week you thought that meant you'd have to be alone forever, and now you know it means you could be *happy*." Colby set down his plate, and just that sudden, he was on his knees—on his *knees*—in front of Terrell, and Terrell swallowed on his sandwich as quickly as he could and tried to let Colby do this right, because at the moment? He was the only one who knew how.

"C'mon, T—this is… it's *perspective,* that's what it is. It's a chance to see how other places in the world work, and to see that being gay and being black—they don't have to be bad things. And once we see how it works where it's working good, we can come home and we can start… start suggesting how to make changes that will make it better *here*. Three years ago, you picked up a gun and then realized that's not the way to make changes. I'm giving you a chance to pick up a pen—which is something you *trained* for, remember? And to grab my hand and go out and try to make those changes a better way."

Colby's hand was on his knee, and Terrell covered it automatically, because it looked naked and vulnerable there, all pink and cold.

"I've…." Terrell took a deep breath. "We need to call your sister," he said, thinking of Percy for the first time all day. "And then I need to go do some shit."

"And think about—" Colby looked desperate. He looked *disheartened*, and Terrell didn't blame him.

"Do you even imagine I'll be thinking about anything else?" Terrell asked, and he squeezed Colby's hand. Colby nodded, and Terrell shook his head. "What were you going to do if you tried to kiss me and I clocked you?" he asked, just in awe of this much confidence.

Colby shrugged, and his smile was a little bit sad, but it wasn't defeated, because that wasn't Terrell's boy. "I knew you'd kiss me back," he said, nodding. "But this other thing—I still don't know how far you'll go."

Terrell sighed. "Well, before I go transatlantic, I should probably start by visiting my own backyard, you think?"

Colby grimaced. "Tell her I said hi," he said, and Terrell shook his head.

"I most certainly will not." He closed his eyes. "Are we done with our sandwiches now?"

"Yeah, why?"

"God, Colby. Do you even have to ask?"

They left their plates on the coffee table, and Colby turned on the television. It was hot and humid and almost too sweaty to touch, but Colby sat back in the corner of the couch and Terrell lay on him. They sat there in the quiet, not watching the bad cop show on television, and held each other until the sweat soaked through their clothes and slicked their skin together.

Eventually, Colby would call Moira, and Percy would still be in jail, and Colby would have to go back to his place to get some clothes since the Laundromat was out of order at T's. But that was in an hour. Terrell had just gotten this way, just gotten to where he could hold somebody and it was all good.

He needed it to be all good before he chose a path for all great or all bad.

COLBY had to get up and leave, but before he walked out the door, he stopped and pulled Terrell up to his feet. Instead of moving away then, he palmed the back of Terrell's head and brought him forward until he could feel Colby's breath on his face, until he could smell his own soap on Colby's skin, and the sweat, and the worry too.

"You need me, T," Colby said, but his voice was a little broken, and a whole lot of Terrell screamed, *Yes! Yes, I need you! You gave me everything, and how can I turn my back on it now!* Because dammit, Colby's voice should always be Captain America's, and *nobody* should hurt Colby so he sounded like that.

"Don't give up on me just yet" is what he did say, but he sounded lost and he knew it.

They were close enough that he felt Colby's little starting smile before Colby pressed forward with the kiss.

Ah... God, Colby's open mouth on his was a miracle. It was oxygen and joy, and Terrell pushed against him, taking all of it, and then, near the end, when he thought Colby was going to pull back and he wasn't ready, giving too. In fact, he gave until his hands were framing Colby's face and Colby was pushed back against the front door, their bodies hard and straining together. Colby had shoved his hands down the back of Terrell's shorts and was digging hard fingers into Terrell's buttcheeks, and Terrell raised one leg, leaning his knee against the door behind Colby and angling his body for any closeness, any at all, that would make them one person, so close there was no telling where one's skin ended and the other's began.

It was Colby who broke off the kiss, breathing hard, and he kissed Terrell's temple, sweat and all.

"I'm going to take that as a sign of hope," he panted in Terrell's ear, and then, while Terrell was trying to get his bearings, he slipped away.

When he was out the door, Terrell leaned his head against it, hearing the sound of Colby's footsteps as he padded down the Astroturf on top of the concrete in the hallway, and wondered what in the hell he was going to do in another country, where the sound of Colby's footsteps would have a totally different timbre.

TERRELL didn't have a lot of fond memories of Hiram Johnson High School, although he understood it had undergone a lot of renovations and staff improvements in the past few years. It didn't matter. The three teachers who had really encouraged him had been laid off or fired for stupid shit that didn't really matter, and he had no reason to go back there.

But he did. He tooled down 65th Street, looking over at the school as the football team labored voluntarily in the sun. He'd never been a fan of the football team, or the players, or all of that beating-the-chest macho bullshit that seemed to go with it, but now, in the late afternoon of the summer solstice, he could appreciate the dedication those kids brought with them. It had always seemed a shame to him that all that dedication, all that need to improve, to do better, to be the best, had so very often amounted to little more than a good story when someone was drinking with his buddies at the bar.

Wasn't all that hard work supposed to lead up to something? Shouldn't it give you something bigger than a memory?

Sure—some kids would tell you about dedication and perseverance and how they learned good adulthood lessons when hitting a practice dummy with all their body weight in the brutal Sacramento heat. But a lot of them would just tell you that the coach was a dick and they should have been out getting them some poontang (like any smart girl would give it up to those kids!) and that they don't remember why it was so important.

Terrell parked on the residential street for a moment—not long enough for the cops to get suspicious—and watched those kids sweat, watched them bruise themselves against the obstacles they willingly fought, and wondered, just wondered, what all that effort was for.

He asked himself again, wasn't it supposed to lead up to something? Shouldn't it be bigger than a memory of suffering?

Dammit, what *had* those eight years of college, the scraping for classes, the waiting for the one required course that was only taught every other year, the scrabbling for student loans, the living on two hours of sleep—what *had* that been about, if it wasn't for him to go out and do something with them?

He pulled away when that last one hit the brainpan, but that didn't stop it from splatting around in there and making a hell of a mess.

He made his way back toward Stockton Boulevard then, back toward the med center and Parker Avenue, almost wistfully wishing he'd brought Colby with him.

Yeah, man. That's the hotel where that one politician got busted having himself a little crank and ho party—you remember that? Yeah, the Greenbriar Hotel—we heard all them cop cars that morning, and then we laughed our asses off when we saw it on the news.

And that right there—God, that was scary. Yeah, that house with all the boards over the windows? That was an honest-to-God crack house—junkies on the mattresses, guys with guns in the doorways. The night they cleaned that place out, cops came and knocked on our doors and told us to sleep on the floor.

Yeah, this place looks good now, with the church all moved into the old movie theater and the new whitewashed paint job, but it didn't look so good when it was an X-rated theater, you feel me?

And you would not believe what this corner here used to be. It's like they fixed it up one corner at a time, and each time they did, the other corner got worse with the old condoms and the old needles and the junkies dying on the weeds. Man, it looks good now, but we used to walk down this street to get to the store, and it scared the holy shit out of us then.

And then, right down Yosemite Street, he saw the damnedest thing.

He saw a couple—young, about his age, so probably part of that new urban reclamation he had missed when he'd moved out—of all things, walking a tortoise.

There it was, crossing in front of his car, one plodding horny foot at a time, and the young Hispanic man about Terrell's age looked at Terrell apologetically like an indulgent father would look at someone when his child accidentally cut in line.

Terrell shrugged, charmed, and the young woman behind the man gave the wagon she was hauling a little jerk. The wagon had been built up—new wooden slats on the side and a wooden ramp that folded down and hung off the back—and it was obviously some kind of tortoise conveyance for when the big guy wasn't walking across the road.

Which the tortoise would do, eventually, Terrell was sure of it.

Finally, finally, the poor guy got to where he was going, and the young man turned and waved thank-you for Terrell's patience, and the girl did too, and together, dragging the wagon behind them, they followed their pet across the lawn of what was apparently a stranger's house.

Terrell thought of that tortoise and how he wanted to tell Colby that story. He wanted to make it funny and make Colby laugh.

And Colby would tell him he could make something bigger out of that story. It didn't just have to be about a really fucking big reptile crossing the road in the orange light of sunset. It could be about getting where you're going eventually, even if you had to take your time. It could be about how maybe you had to look at the place you came from with different eyes, because everything changes, and if you could see a tortoise crossing the street, the stuff you used to assume was true might not be true after all.

It could even be about how you never knew what was around the corner, but you had to maybe have faith that the things you loved would give you some joy right back.

That story could be a whole lot of things, but Terrell knew that none of them would be as good if Colby wasn't there to hear them.

When he pulled up in front of the battered, weed-eaten, oil-stained driveway of his Gi-Gi's house, Terrell knew which way he'd tell that story when Colby was ready to hear it.

TERRELL'S uncle's old car was rotting in the driveway, and nobody had mowed the lawn in ages. It figured. Gi-Gi had always been begging, ordering, asking, pleading, or bribing the men to do the big jobs in the house, but after Terrell had bailed, nobody would listen. When he was younger, he used to think that it was just a matter of all those black men doing their Gi-Gi wrong after she'd gone and given up so very much for them to have a place to sleep and food to eat, but as he grew older, he came to realize that it was a whole bunch of stuff that added up to it.

Gi-Gi wasn't great with enforcing the rules. She tried, but she was tired—she was raising anywhere from three to eight grandkids, and she worked too. It wasn't like she had a lot of time for understanding and time-outs and all of that fun rich people's stuff. She needed to keep them fed, keep them from hurting themselves, and teach at least one of them in the house to do laundry and cook so that one could help with the others. That alone was an exhausting job, and she did it by herself. Some shit had to slide. Making sure the boys mowed the lawn when she asked them was some of that shit.

Growing up at Gi-Gi's, a man had to be a man, a girl had to find a man, and a baby had to be quiet or he or she would get a random smack from a weathered hand.

But as much as she'd been spread thin, she *had* loved them.

She protected her kids from the law, she protected them from the schools, and when they stayed off of them, she protected them from the streets. There had never been a time when they hadn't had enough food, or hadn't had clean clothes, or hadn't had a roof over their heads.

As much as Terrell had tried to make things about black and white when he'd been younger, there was nothing black and white about his grandmother. She wasn't all bad and she wasn't all good— she was just the woman who had raised Terrell, and that was what was and he couldn't change it.

He wondered when she had guessed he was gay.

It had been bothering him since he'd been told not to bring Colby by. He tried to mark a time when she had changed toward him. Had she ever grown cold toward him? Directed him away from looking at boys? What had she said when he'd been a kid to let him know that who he was was not okay?

He couldn't remember. Try as he might, no moment stood out. He couldn't remember a spanking or a sharp word or even being banned from watching reruns of Will Smith when his hair was funny. He just knew he was not allowed to be gay, and so he'd spent most of his life not being that way and having dirty, furtive sex in filthy, obscene places, because that was the thing he was. Dirty, sneaky, and obscene.

He thought those words to himself and closed his eyes, and saw Colby.

Any Colby—Colby from a few days ago, hanging on to the damned wakeboard or triumphant after he'd been tossed; Colby from a year ago, tired and a little overwhelmed, but still able to crack a joke on the dock behind Papi's; Colby from two weeks ago, hauling some racist little prick out of Papi's to defend Terrell's honor.

Colby, who was going to write a paper and change the world.

Colby with the glorious body and the sublime touch, who did things in private that seriously made Terrell think God was living and breathing and didn't see skin color but only the color of a man's soul, and Colby who never, even when he was buried in Terrell's body and screaming to come, could be called something like "dirty" or "sneaky" or "obscene."

Colby, who wasn't invited to Gi-Gi's house because just being who he was meant he couldn't eat at the table.

If Terrell was dirty, Colby was dirty, and Terrell just couldn't buy that lie anymore.

Gi-Gi was cleaning up the battered outside toys and gathering them to the small pavement porch in front of the empty brick flowerbeds. She wore a faded housedress and flip-flops, and her hair was cut short and straightened, carefully curled, and set with product to frame her face.

"Terrell!" she said in honest joy, standing upright with an effort and rubbing her lower back. "It's amazing to see you, boy! You didn't tell me you were planning to visit!"

"I wanted to come last week," he said, his bitterness falling away. God, she couldn't help the things she'd been raised with any more than he could, could she? "But I wasn't going to come without Colby."

Her face darkened, and she turned away. "Well, I'm glad you came to your senses. White boy doesn't have any place here—"

"Gi-Gi, you know that's not true. There's white people all over this neighborhood. Don't know why Colby would be any different—"

"Because he would be and you know it!" she snapped. She looked genuinely upset, and for a moment, Terrell thought about maybe just going back to the way things had been. She didn't even have to know he'd left the country. He could just keep sending stuff and telling her he was busy.

But then, how was he going to say he had family, if that was all they were to him?

Terrell nodded. Funny how Gi-Gi had never tolerated lying, but it seemed like she'd spent his whole life encouraging him to do nothing but lie.

"You're right," Terrell said, smiling a little. "It would be different. Gi-Gi, how many days a year do you see me?"

Gi-Gi looked sad for a minute. "Maybe three, four. You come, you say you've got to work, you go. You always bring presents. We got the crib for Monique's baby. That was thoughtful."

Terrell shifted where he stood. He realized that after Colby's massage the night before, his back hadn't given hardly a twinge. Not all day.

"Thank you, Gi-Gi. Don't you ever think you'd like to see more of me?"

Gi-Gi shifted now. "We don't want you to put yourself out, baby. We know you busy."

Terrell tried again. "Don't you *want* me to spend more time here?" he asked, feeling a little desperate. This woman *raised* him!

"What are you asking me, Terrell? Are you asking me if it's okay that you're nasty with that white boy—"

"How would you even *know* that's how it is?" he asked, a little desperate to know, and to his disgust, Gi-Gi waved her hand and made a "pfft" sound.

"Terrell, you been looking at boys since you were in kindergarten. I had to beat you to stop telling me you wanted to kiss a boy in the first grade. That boy would have grabbed his father's gun and *killed* you, and nobody here would have blamed him. What did you want me to do? If I let you be that way, you woulda got yourself killed before you even had a chance to grow!"

Terrell shook his head. "I do *not* remember," he muttered, exasperated. "How hard did you beat me, Gi-Gi?"

Gi-Gi looked embarrassed. "Mostly I spanked you, but you were standing up and ran into a wall. You were only out for a second, Terrell, and after you were done crying, it seemed to be all gone."

Terrell broke out with half a laugh. Oh, of all the—he had literally had the gay *beaten* out of him? "Not all," he said, wondering what sort of story he could make of *that* to tell Colby.

"Oh, I know it. You were *way* too interested in Will Smith. You wore that DVD about the alien invasion about out!"

Terrell chuckled, feeling exhausted and worn-out and ready to be amused by the fucking world. "Yeah, Gi-Gi, he was a hottie. So you knew all that and you just hoped it would… what? Go away?"

Gi-Gi gestured weakly. "Terrell—you don't want to be that way around here."

"But I'm not around here anymore, Gi-Gi, and the guy I want to bring here, he wants to take me away. He wants to take me to places where it's okay to be ga—"

"Don't say that here!"

"It's okay to be me, then, Gi-Gi—how's that?"

"There's nothing wrong with you!" she protested, and he closed his eyes.

"Nothing except who I want to spend my life with," he said.

"You don't know that!" She was looking more and more upset, and he didn't know what to do about that.

He took two steps forward, wanting to hug her, but she flinched back from him, because apparently having this conversation made him real to her when he'd only been a wayward child before.

"I do," he said quietly. "I do. I'll keep my cell number, Gi-Gi. If you want to invite me and Colby over for dinner, you let me know. But don't call me if you need something and you're not willing to do that. If you're going to be my family, you need to be my family. If you're just going to tell me I'm nasty and I don't even get a hug? I'm not someone you need to be taking gifts from anyway."

It hurt. Both of them. Her eyes filled up, and she held out her hand in protest. "Terrell—"

He flinched back, and she covered a sob with her hand.

"Give me a call for that dinner invite," he said. "My boyfriend and I would appreciate it."

And then he turned around, got back into his car, and drove away in the wizard-hat purple twilight of the smoggy Sacramento sky.

Bam!

HE WAS restless after that.

He texted Colby to tell him to drive to Terrell's apartment after work and pick him up, but that wasn't big enough, or soon enough, to see Colby and tell him…

Just see him.

He didn't even want to think about what he'd commit himself to when Colby was right there, laughing, encouraging, touching. Anything. He'd commit to anything. He'd commit to the world.

He *would* commit to the world.

And for once? He was ready for that to just happen. He was ready for Colby to just take him by the hand and lead him somewhere.

He was ready to fly.

Without conscious thought, he found himself in the parking lot of Papiano's. Colby was working second shift—he'd be getting off about now.

He parked close and stumped through the foyer, waving at Erin, who was wearing her manager's clothes and all ready to seat.

"Heya!" he said chirpily. "Is Colby—"

"He's off—he's back by the lockers," she said, and she didn't even blink. For all he knew, she had a mental slideshow of what she *thought* they might do on their spare time, but she didn't let it show.

He realized that it didn't matter. She could speculate to her heart's content. If she didn't want to hang with him and Colby if she knew what they were doing, that was her problem. Not that he was going to *tell* her or anything, but suddenly, he was about done with what folks thought.

His feet thudded on the dark and shiny wood of the floors, and he walked confidently to the back of the house. He passed the threshold for the servers, where the wood turned to tile, and stayed well clear of the expediter's station, where the food was prepped and prettied before it could be served. People came in back all the time off duty—leaving shit in your lockers was like the sign of the true veteran.

The back of the house was full of the usual sounds: the clatter of plates and crockery always sounded obscenely loud when it bounced off the tile floors and white walls, and the calls of the window dick made an odd counterpoint. Percy wasn't working fry, and Mark was being a complete asshole to the rookie working his station, and Terrell felt a moment of sympathy for the guy before he turned his attention to what really mattered.

Back by the lockers, Colby was in the process of taking off his little apron and pulling his "covering the greasy hair" baseball hat out of the locker. His smile when he saw Terrell walking back was gorgeous and blinding, like sunshine to a man in a dungeon.

Terrell walked up, and natural as could be, they started the high-five, low-five, come-here-my-brother dance they'd been doing almost since their first day. But when they came in for the clasp of hands at the chest, Colby held him still for a moment, just by his voice.

"You look happy."

"You'd better make me that way," he said quietly, and when he stepped back, Colby grinned at him again.

And then the person behind him said, *"Terrell!"* in exasperation, and he turned around apologetically. He wasn't going to start making out with Colby, for all his newfound freedom. He wasn't planning on changing all that goddamned quickly, was he?

"Sorry, Kelly," he said, and she rolled her eyes and smiled tiredly, going to her locker right behind him. Her curly brown hair was more of a frazzle than usual today, and he wondered if she was still doing blow with the baby or if she'd gone and had her "procedure" yet. None of his business either way, really, but she sure did look like hell.

He turned back around to Colby and shook his head. "Here—you follow me to my house, 'kay?" he said, and then Colby nodded.

They turned to walk around Kelly, who was slipping off her high-heeled shoe, and Terrell, for no good goddamned reason he could think of, realized she had tennis shoes in the front of her locker, sitting right there, in front of her purse.

Black tennis shoes. Like the servers wore.

He turned, dreamlike, to Colby, who was right on his heels, looking into Kelly's locker too.

Their eyes met, and they had the same goddamned thought at the same time.

"What?" Kelly snapped, reaching past her tennis shoes to her purse. "It's not like I've got tampons or anything sticking out, is it?"

"You wear server shoes," Colby said, and Terrell glared at him. Goddammit, two straight days of watching crime dramas, and didn't that boy learn nothing?

"So what?" Kelly said, her back toward them both, and Terrell heard the click before he saw what it was.

But Terrell had started hearing that click when he was in middle school, and he didn't even need to see what it was. He turned around, grabbed Colby's shoulder, and tried to haul the dumbass into the front of the house before he opened his mouth and got them both killed.

"So nothing," Terrell said, and Colby made a sound of impatience.

"So," Colby hissed in his ear, "you remember—oh fuck. Darlin', what in the world are you doing with that thing?"

A .38 caliber Saturday night special pointed right at Colby as he turned around to greet it.

Terrell started to edge forward so they were standing shoulder to shoulder, because he didn't want Colby anywhere near that thing. "*That*," Terrell said evenly, heedless of the fact that it was now pointed at him, "is a big mistake. Why you gotta do that, sweetheart? No jury in the world would convict you."

"Not for the murder!" Kelly said, gesturing with the gun a little wildly. Terrell and Colby both swayed out of its way, but that didn't make them feel any safer. "For the fucking drugs! Goddammit, Percy's in jail because he gave Will Templeton a *number*! What are they going to do to me when I used that shit and bought for me and my dad!"

Terrell didn't even have to look at Colby to know that both of them had the jaw-dropped, boggle-eyed look of a soon-to-be-deceased possum.

"There is so much that is fucked up about that," Terrell muttered, while Colby said, "Oh, sweetheart, you can *so* get a lighter sentence—"

"But Percy is in *jail,* and he didn't *do* anything!" she almost sobbed, and Terrell decided someone had to speak up and tell her the truth.

"Honey, Percy is a black gangbanger with *priors*! You're a white princess with a bad daddy—you've got it made!"

"Got it *made?*" she screeched. "Got it *made?* My dad's got me doing lines on the goddamned coffee table with his politician friends, and I've got it *made?* I've got a fucking *death sentence*! Nobody wants me to talk! I won't even make it as long as Percy!"

And oh God, that gun went round and round and round like a fucking roulette wheel, didn't it? Round and round she goes, where that bullet goes, nobody knows!

"But what are you going to do with that gun to make it any better?" Colby asked, and Terrell wanted to step on his foot. *Oh, for fuck's sake, don't piss off the crazy woman, Colby! Goddammit, Captain America, not everybody can be reasoned with!*

"I don't know!" Kelly shouted, and Terrell saw it in slow motion as the weight of the gun slid up against her trigger finger and Terrell moved right in front of Colby so Colby didn't have to look at that thing and—

BAM!

And then his shoulder exploded in red and black, and he fell back against Colby and dropped his urine as he slid to the floor.

He didn't even see Beth the stoned manager. Apparently she slunk out of the manager's office with the Taser they kept back by the safe, and zapped Kelly in the back of the neck. He heard about that part later, much later, after he'd finished bleeding on Colby's lap.

The pain was… oh hell. It was nauseating. And his pants were wet and he couldn't even believe that didn't bother him, because—

"Oh *fuck*! That crazy bitch *shot me!*"

"Oh Jesus! Jesus… *Terrell!*" Colby screamed, and Terrell wanted to wave his arm and make him stop that shit.

"I can't move my arm," he said, not feeling lucid at all. "What in the fuck? She *shot* me!"

"You jumped in front of me, you dumb motherfucker!"

"You would *not* shut up, Captain America!" Terrell complained. "Jesus. How many shitty cop shows you gotta fuckin' *watch*!"

"Mark, you asshole, call a fucking ambulance!"

Terrell couldn't even see Mark, because his vision was getting really black and fuzzy around the edges, but he heard his voice. "The door whore shot Terrell?"

"Yes, and he's bleeding!" Colby's voice was cracking, breaking. "You are *bleeding*! You dumb asshole, you come here, and you're all happy, and you give me fucking hope, and you stepped in front of a *gun* for me? Oh for fuck's sake!"

Terrell tried his other arm and raised it to wipe Colby's cheeks, because he was *crying* and Terrell wanted him to be happy. "Man, don't fucking cry. That's not what I wanted!"

"Why, because people will know?"

"Aw, who gives a fuck," Terrell said, and his vision was getting blacker and blurrier, and Colby was doing painful things with his shoulder and a big pad of clean rags.

"Good," Colby muttered. "Good. You stepped in front of a bullet for me, asshole. You'd damned well better step out of the fucking closet."

"There are no closets in my apartment," Terrell said seriously, and it was about the last coherent thing he said.

HE WAS aware of a bunch of different stuff then, but at the same time, it was all horribly removed from where he was. There was pain, and it seemed to put a big barrier, a big brick wall between everything he felt and everything he was doing and everything people were doing to him.

He remembered getting in the ambulance, though, because he didn't let go of Colby's hand. That was good, Colby's hand in his, but then the guys who'd put him on the gurney pushed Colby aside so they could move the gurney too damned fast. Colby got in the ambulance, though, and Terrell had vague memories of his hands on Terrell's head, steadying, being calm and kind and bitching at him for all sorts of stuff he could not possibly fix at this point of the day. He passed out before the ambulance came to a stop then and there was lots more pain and some confusion and a mask over his head and then there was some blissful damned peace.

HE CAME to in a hospital room. His black arm was stark against the white sheets, and there was an IV needle stuck in it that looked even more wrong. There were also all sorts of monitors beeping, and a window that looked like it belonged in a solitary confinement room in a mental institution piping in some stark goddamned sunshine.

And there was Colby, dressed in the Papi's clothes he'd been wearing the last time Terrell had seen him, only covered in blood, which he didn't remember. He was propped up in one chair with his long legs extended and resting on another, and asleep on his elbow, snoring in a way that was not subtle at all.

Terrell opened his mouth to ask for water and what came out was a dry amphibian croak that startled Colby so that his arms went out wide and his legs splanged sideways and he stood up abruptly, knocking over both his chairs.

Terrell was tricked into laughing, which hurt, and for some reason, that made him laugh more.

"Do *not* laugh!" Colby sputtered with all the dignity of a wet cat. "Do *not* laugh." He stalked forward to a portable tray where a plastic pitcher with a straw rested, and then, with motions that seemed practiced, held the pitcher down so Terrell could take a sip. He pulled it back too early and said, "Just enough to moisten your mouth, T. You're still woozy from the anesthesia."

Terrell narrowed his eyes. "Ya think?"

Colby rolled bloodshot eyes at him. "Don't get shitty with me! You're the one who jumped in front of a bullet, dammit! I'm just waiting for your full recovery before I lay into you like you have never been laid into before!"

Terrell would have laughed if his mouth hadn't been so dry. "Don't tear me a new asshole," he said, proud of himself. "You get plenty of use outta the one I got!"

Colby's eyes went huge, and he leaned forward in absolute exasperation. "Awesome," he muttered, stalking around the little space next to the hospital bed and picking up chairs. "*Now* you get comfortable with your sexuality. You got anything else you want to drop on me while you're giving orders?"

"Yeah," Terrell said, because he'd been thinking about this all day, when he wasn't breaking up with his family or getting shot at. "I want our own damned cats."

Colby must have been tired, because he dropped into the chair he'd just righted and pulled close to the bed so he could stroke the back of Terrell's hand with cold fingers. "Our own cats."

"Two gay men owning two cats named Pussy? Someone'll take away our gay card. You'll see. If they can't make us not be gay, they'll make us not able to have cats."

Colby closed his eyes and shook his head. "Okay, so we'll have our own cats. That's good to know. It's part of a plan. We'll name them Rooster and Richard, it'll be great. Anything else you want to tell me while you're stoned and I'm fucking insane with worry?"

Terrell thought about it, and it was hard. His brain was not working all that well, and he was surprised. No matter what had happened in his life, he'd always been able to depend on his gray matter to make it clear. "I don't have a passport," he said, working hard to enunciate. This was important. He needed a passport.

It apparently meant something to Colby too. He grabbed Terrell's hand and started to cry. "We'll get right on that, T. I hear you. One passport. Me and you, we've got plans."

"Damned straight." At least he thought he said it. It was the last thing he thought before he came to again.

THIS time when he woke up, he felt well enough to reach for the water himself. And he spilled it all down his front.

Moira was there picking it up, grabbing a cloth from some sort of closet, and getting close enough as she dabbed it off for Terrell to see that she was wearing a T-shirt and stretchy shorts and that her long blonde hair looked greasy.

"I'm sorry, T," she muttered. "Colby told me to keep an eye on you—I was doing a shitty job."

"Was nice of you," Terrell said. He looked around and saw that the hospital room was bathed in late-evening light—and full of cards and flowers and all sorts of cheery weirdness. "Where'd all this crap come from?" he asked, surprised.

"Everyone at work, for one," Moira said seriously. "And Percy—we got him out of jail last night, and I think he had Gina buy an entire florist's for you. There's even some here that Colby said were from customers. You must be a kick-ass bartender, you know that?"

"I'll getya drunk," Terrell affirmed. The water was mostly sopped up, but none of it was in his mouth. "I'm thirsty. Where's Colby? Why would you name a cat Rooster?"

Moira laughed, filling his little plastic pitcher from the sink. "He said you were a handful on the painkillers. I'm getting your water, Colby's home because he needs a shower and a change of clothes, and you'd name a cat Rooster if you wanted to call him Cock."

Terrell giggled, and Moira offered him water and held the pitcher herself as Terrell tried again.

"Good," he said. "Told him, no Pussy cats in a gay man's house!"—and then he laughed until his stomach hurt while Moira shook her head and laughed with him.

"That's fucking hysterical," she said when he was done. "Do you have *any* idea how much my brother loves you?"

Terrell nodded, feeling comfortable and sleep ready again. "We're going to Europe together," he said complacently. "I'm gonna help Captain America save the world."

Moira laughed. "Way to go, T. You surprised me."

"Uh-huh!" Terrell told her soberly. "And then I got *shot!*"

"Yes you did. And that surprised *you!*"

"Didn't do a lot for Colby either," Terrell muttered. "He's not stable. He *cried.*"

Moira shook her head and got a little closer. "So did I. You've been living at my house for almost a month, sweetie. Did you think I wouldn't cry?"

"Gi-Gi didn't cry," Terrell said solemnly, and to his surprise, Moira looked guilty and angry at once.

"No, she cried, T. But she didn't come to the hospital either."

Terrell fought against the fluff in his head. "How do you know that?"

"Because Colby stole your cell phone and called her. She heard you'd been shot, said you should have known better, called Colby a faggot, cried a little, and hung up. I'm sorry, T. I shouldn't even have mentioned it. You're a mess, but... but you didn't see my brother's face. He was... he was so hurt for you."

Terrell grunted. "Well, I'm hurt for him. Don't tell him you told me. I'll tell him something that'll make it better." He sighed and yawned and found himself whining. "But when does this sleeping shit stop? I'm done with it. I want to be awake when your brother gets here!"

"Yeah, well, go to sleep now, T. It's late afternoon, he'll be back in an hour."

Terrell yawned again. "You make sure he wakes me up. Good seeing you, Moira. Think your parents will mind that he's bringing home a hoodrat and calling him a boyfriend?"

Moira did a spit take and was still cracking up when Terrell fell back asleep.

HE WOKE up a couple of more times and was woozy and (apparently) hella amusing, and finally, *finally*, they changed his pain meds in the morning when Colby was there again, and he could have a reasonable conversation with the man.

It was informative. He discovered several things.

Colby told him that Beth had been the one to zap Kelly and stop her little crime spree, and that when they'd taken Kelly away in handcuffs, Beth had literally walked out of Papiano's and into rehab. The GM that corporate sent when Erin had called them in hysterics told the entire staff the next morning, and among every frickin' other thing, that had been something for folks to chew on.

Colby also told him that Percy had been let out of jail within hours after Terrell had been shot—apparently nobody wanted the hue and cry Moira was raising about keeping an innocent man in prison when a girl had unrepentantly confessed to doing the crime. Terrell was glad to hear that—glad to hear that it hadn't even been one more full night in jail, and *really* glad to hear that Percy was living with Gina now. He didn't see it lasting, but he didn't see it hurting either one of them, and that was good.

Kelly hadn't gone down quietly. Her father and a couple other of his politician buddies had been raided and the coke had been everywhere, and since Kelly was nineteen and could confess to being a user with her pops for a couple of years, it looked like they were going to jail for a long time.

She'd also implicated her father in the murder of Percy's cousin. He hadn't pulled the trigger himself, but Moira said they'd found some ballistic evidence that made it clear one of the guns registered in his name had been the weapon. A politician and murder for hire—people would remember this case for at least twenty minutes.

Colby also told him that Kelly had miscarried her first night in jail, and that had brought Terrell up short.

"That's sort of a good thing," he said apologetically, and Colby had shrugged.

"Yeah, I wasn't seeing a happy ending there," he agreed. "Are you sure you're up for this? You were like Sleeping Beauty yesterday. Except funnier, because the weirdness you spewed was fucking hilarious."

Terrell eyed him sourly. "Someday, I'm going to make you a Rabid Hamster and see what shit *you* say. No, I'm better today. The pain meds are basic ibuprofen this time round, not the serious IV crap that was taking me out yesterday."

"Well, good." Colby plopped into the chair next to Terrell's bed and just looked at him.

"What?" Terrell asked, but he knew.

"Are we going to talk about what you were going to tell me the other night before life just got fucking weird?"

Terrell smiled. His teeth hurt, because he hadn't brushed or flossed in three days and the metal did that to you, but he figured he could get one of those plastic toothpicks off of a nurse before he fell asleep that night. They'd taken out his catheter earlier that morning— before they switched up his pain meds, obviously—and oh yay, T could go pee.

But right now, he just flashed all his metal teeth in a smile and took in a tired, worried Colby who was no less vital than a fully functioning conquer-the-world Colby usually was. "Yeah. Yeah. You said we'd get me a passport. I thought you'd have some idea."

Colby looked down at his feet. "I wanted to hear it," he said softly. "I *really* needed to hear it from you, T. Especially now. Now that... now that I had your blood on my clothes and... and I had to sit here during surgery and... I just need to hear it now." He wiggled his toes in his brown leather flip-flops and looked back up. "Is that so bad?"

"I love you," Terrell said baldly. "That's not the pain meds. That's all me. When I came to see you, I'd just gone to see Gi-Gi. I told her that if you weren't welcome at her table, then she didn't need me for anything. That's just the way it was. I'm tired of having family that's not really family. You and Moira put out your hands, and damned if I'm not taking them. I'll take your damned job and I'll go off to save the world with you. How's that, Captain America? Is that everything you needed to hear?"

Colby smiled and took his hand, his good one, which was the one with the IV, but, well, what were you going to do. "I love you too. Can you maybe not scare me like that again? I can't even go wakeboarding and you step in front of bullets? What in the fuck is that, T, that's all I'm sayin'!"

"Hey, man, what the hell is Captain America if he doesn't have his shield?" Terrell joked feebly, and Colby just sat there, clinging to Terrell's hand and looking down.

"Lame, T. Completely lame. Man, I'm overfuckingjoyed we're going to Europe together, but I'm telling you—don't rip my heart out. That's all I'm saying. Don't rip my heart out. It's a simple goddamned request."

Terrell squeezed his hand and promised, and they talked about Percy and Gina and about Erin getting promoted and about stupid shit and people they wouldn't really remember in a year and they both knew it. Terrell didn't have words then, and wouldn't have them until later that night as he was lying in the semidarkness, missing Colby and trying to fall asleep. They were weak, and not really what he wanted to say, but he had them. Clutching the words, the things he wanted to tell Colby when they were in the same bed and the darkness was all around them and they were safe against the world, Terrell fell asleep and dreamed of the clear blue sky of someplace beautiful he had never heard of.

HE HAD to wait a week before they'd let him out of the hospital, and he was *not* pro with that. Colby took pity on him and went to his apartment to bring him a boatload of books so he didn't go out of his goddamned mind, which was nice, and Moira went one better and brought him an iPad with some bells and whistles, including a Kindle account in his name, which was also nice. She said it was on loan, but she didn't say when she needed it back, and when Colby saw it later in the day, he smirked.

"What?" Terrell asked, enjoying the hell out of *Angry Birds*. Colby hadn't said anything about his moratorium on video games, either. He figured a man was allowed to change his mind when he'd been shot.

"She bought that for you special, did you know that?"

Terrell was so shocked he stopped playing. It was the day after they lessened his pain meds, and he was beginning to think *all* television was a lie at this point, because if he'd been in any one of his favorite cop shows, he'd be thinking about getting laid right now, but *that* was not happening.

"She did not!" he protested. "She got this from… it was a beta-testing thing at work and…. I mean, I don't know, she said it was some sort of giveaway, but I didn't get the details, but… oh hell."

Colby closed his eyes tight before opening them and grinning. "Yeah, T. She did. She bought it for you special. I saw her with the bag this morning and didn't know what it was for."

"Then why all the bullshit!"

"Because she really likes you—"

"She thinks I'm going to break your heart," Terrell said flatly.

Colby nodded and sat down on the edge of his bed, lacing and unlacing his fingers. "She could be right, but that doesn't mean she doesn't like you. You wanted to fight for Percy, fight for the underdog. It's all she's wanted to do her entire life."

"Yeah, just like her brother. Where did you two come from? Was there a two-for-one sale under the hero tree or what?"

"You want to meet our parents?" Colby asked seriously, and Terrell didn't even hesitate.

"Yeah. I mean… *yes.* I mean… even if they're not all excited about *me*, I want to see *them*, because, they're like… they *made* you."

Something odd happened to Colby's face then. He was always so in control, always so thoughtful, so energized, and suddenly his control dropped, and he became liquid, gentle, soft, and young. "I want you to meet them too. I want you to come home to my home, and stay there, and never go back to your shitty apartment again. When we get on that plane, I want it to be *us.* Forever forever. You'll like my parents, T—I have no doubt. But I need you to tell me again that you'll like my life and share it with me."

Terrell set the iPad to one side and grabbed Colby's upper arm. "I brushed my teeth," he said, seemingly at random. "See?" He smiled, showing off all his metal. "I wanted you to kiss me today."

Colby's smile was slow and whole. "So is that your way of saying you will?"

"Do you think I brush my teeth for just anyone? No, Colby—you are…." He was going to make this so playful. But he couldn't. "You're everything. I told you I love you, and I'm not sure how much of that sank in. But I love you. You're… you're Captain America most times, but I've seen you just be Colby, and I love him too. Just… just don't ever stop being just Colby for me, will ya? The world needs Captain America—but Captain America almost got himself shot. *I* need Colby. That other guy saving the world is nice, and I'm pleased to know him, but… but *you* gave me an Easy button and tried to seduce me on the back dock of Papi's, and you ate sandwiches on my couch and watched stupid cop shows that you don't ever pay attention to. *You*, Colby. I'll go anywhere with you, *do* anything—just as long as it's you."

Colby's smile was shy. *Colby's* smile was shy, and his kiss was gentle, the kind where you closed your eyes before your lips touched, and kept them closed and moved slowly.

Terrell leaned forward, against the advice of everything at his shoulder that told him moving was not a great idea yet, and when he winced, Colby pushed him back, his lips still gentle, and brought one hand up to cup his cheek.

Their breathing quickened, and Colby pulled back with reluctance.

"Yeah," he said, leaning his forehead against Terrell's.

"Yeah?"

"Worth waiting for. So worth waiting for."

"Yeah, well, you are worth getting shot for. What are we gonna do with my apartment?"

"Give it to Percy. His auntie didn't let him back in the house when Gina brought him home. Her place isn't big enough for two."

Terrell started laughing, but quietly so Colby wouldn't move. "You got it all planned out, don't you? You *are* Captain America."

Colby pulled back and regarded him soberly. "I really wish you wouldn't call me that."

"Tough. Shit. Are we really gonna have a cat named Richard?"

"And one named Rooster too. And Moira will watch them when we're off on assignment."

"You're so fucking amazing, you'd leave Captain America in the dust."

Colby looked down at his hand, which was resting on Terrell's thigh. "As long as you come with me, he can find his own guy."

"Good, 'cause I'd fight him for you. Get my black ass beat into the pavement, but I'd fight him!"

Colby's grin was playful and a little sad. "We'd have to try option B, then, T. I've seen about as much of your blood as I ever want to. Deal?"

"Deal. So tell me about your parents."

"You'll meet 'em during Fourth of July. They promised to bring the RV up this summer, and you'll get home just in time."

"RV?"

Colby's smile was less sad this time. "Yeah. Let me tell you all about it...."

It was still a long time in the hospital for Terrell's taste, but Colby visited every day, and that made it pass much faster.

Things You Can't Change

FOURTH of July had never been Terrell's thing.

His Gi-Gi had always loved it, gathered the family, made all the men grill while the women brought things like potato salad and frog-eye salad and three-bean salad to the table. They'd let off fireworks, and nobody ever mowed the lawn, and it was often dry, so more than one year they'd had to hose off the weeds when they'd caught fire. And afterward, nobody—nobody in Terrell's neighborhood, that is—cleaned up their trash. The excuse was "It's a free country," but Terrell had always thought of the Fourth of July as the day the country trashed itself, right up until he hit college.

When he hit college he saw things like the country's unemployment rate, and the achievement gap and racial profiling, and he started to think of it as the country's biggest lie.

But this year, he came home from the hospital on the first of July and participated in the Great Dust Disturbance at Moira's house until Colby made him go lie down because not only was he sneezing, he was dizzy and exhausted to boot.

The next day, he was part of some sort of bizarre jam-making movement that Colby had never warned him about and that might have made him rethink the whole gay thing altogether if he'd known about it. They cooked from early in the morning until nearly sunset, and for about three quarters of the time, he thought they were rabid-rat crazy. Then, in the late afternoon, Colby gave him a spoonful of actual *jam* from strawberries picked and bought the same day, and Terrell declared that this might have made up his mind just a little bit faster, because *damn*, that shit was good.

"You never cooked with your Gi-Gi?" Colby asked as he pushed the strawberry goo through the strainer for what must have been the sixth time.

"Men didn't cook," Terrell said, shaking his head. "Women didn't go to school. Yeah, I know. It doesn't make much sense to me neither."

Colby grunted and gave Terrell the clean jam mixture to spoon into the jars that were mostly submerged in the double boiler. "I looked it up on the GPS, you know. It's maybe five miles away, but man, it feels like it should be on the moon."

"Yeah, well, here I am, earthbound cosmonaut, making jam." Terrell transferred the jam pot to his left arm at that point and let out a noise like a wounded cat, and Colby hopped to his side and whisked the pot away. Then Colby made him sit down and started to give him that invalid shit.

Terrell glared at him and petted Dewey Folds, who liked to wrap himself around Terrell's ankle at any opportunity and purr. "What in the hell am I supposed to do when your parents get here?" he asked irritably. "If you two don't let me help, all I'm going to be able to do is sit there and stare at them while they wonder what in the hell their son is doing with *me*!"

Colby sighed and kept spooning the jam into the jars, because that was something timely and you couldn't make that wait. "Terrell, my folks knew I was gay before I did. I told them when I was twelve, and they showed me a picture Moira had taken two years before, of me playing in her dollhouse with my G.I. Joes. They went out, fought a battle, came back and made dinner, kissed each other good night, and woke up and went to war again."

Terrell held his hand up in front of his mouth to keep from spitting--he was laughing *that* hard. The cat had long since hissed at him and taken off for parts unknown.

"So see? They never had any doubts about who I was going to grow up and fall in love with, and I lucked out in the gay department, because Dad's an environmental engineer, Mom's an environmental lawyer, and they're both about as left-wing as a free bird can get. So you? They're going to see you as some sort of proof that they raised me right, and that their little boy does not give a ripe shit about where his lover grew up as long as said lover makes him happy. Are you all caught up now on my backstory? It's not as sad and angsty as growing up in the hood and getting the gay beat out of you"—Colby was still pretty appalled at that, actually. Terrell didn't have the heart to explain to him that he still thought Gi-Gi might have saved his life with that one—"but it *is* a plausible explanation for why you should chill the fuck out and, just once, forgive your fucking country for having a holiday to celebrate its own goddamned possibility, okay?"

Terrell was pulling in air now, because his laughter had subsided and his shoulder hurt and things were starting to make sense. "You like this day," he said after a moment. "And you like that I'm going to have to meet your parents before we go off to do whatever Captain America thing you've got planned."

Colby delicately dropped the seals on top of the jars one by one before answering. "Yeah, T. I don't know if I'd be real big on getting married even if it was a thing in this state. Too much like getting a stamp of approval from people who really don't matter. But I'll tell you who *does* matter. You, me, Moira, and my folks. So yeah. I want them to come and see us as a couple, and then we'll be real."

Terrell nodded and watched for a few more minutes as Colby grabbed a pair of tongs, fished the jars out of the boiler, and put them on a cooling rack on the counter so the seal could form.

"What are you thinking, T?" Colby asked, setting up the next stand of jars with the tongs.

"I'm thinking that there is not a person on the planet I would trust more to do shit right," Terrell said after a minute. "Can I get up and help now?"

Colby shook his head no and went to wash his hands. He came back and—gingerly, because he was still sticky most everywhere but his hands—kissed Terrell's temple. "You look tired and you opened your stitches again. Go back to bed, T. Go read, go watch television, go sit in the tub from the pits down if you want. But let me finish this and shower, and then we'll spend some time not getting all psyched up, and we can talk about what research you need to do before we leave in September, and we can decide if you want to go back to Papi's before then or not."

Terrell squinted at him. "That's a hell of a lot you're expecting me to do after you told me to go lay down and rest."

Colby grinned. "You'd be surprised what you can do when you're not freaking out about stuff that should be no worries."

Terrell grumbled to himself as he went to take a cool shower and lie down, but deep down? He was actually starting to like the thought of this damned holiday, and no one was more surprised than he was.

When Colby slid in bed next to him, it was nearly nine o'clock, and Terrell had just taken a painkiller and was ready to lie on his chest (tilted toward his good arm) and fall asleep watching stupid cop shows. For some reason they were even more fun to watch now that both of them had actually *been involved* in something that looked like one. There was no more "Well that fool should have known better than that!" because they'd both been the fool, and they had a little more sympathy now.

Terrell had just rolled over to do the leaning—and to appreciate the time touching Colby skin to skin, because in the two days since he'd gotten out of the hospital *that* hadn't gotten old—when Colby blindsided him with a kiss.

It wasn't a kiss for show, or for tenderness, or for "Oh my God! I'm so glad you survived!" It was a deep-in-the-back-of-the-throat, I-want-you-so-bad-I-*hurt*-with-it, suck-your-tonsil-through-a-straw *kiss*—and Terrell was down with that and at more than three-quarters mast before Colby came up for air. Terrell had time for one gasp, and opened his mouth again as Colby went in for round two.

Round two was better, wetter, harder, and when Colby's mouth disappeared from his, it was to kiss along his throat, down his bare chest, to kiss his nipples, suck in soft skin from his stomach and mark him. Colby kept kissing, kept nipping, until Terrell's hips were rocking back and forth and he was about begging with every shallow thrust.

Colby pulled back right when he was about to pull down Terrell's shorts. "You want it, T?" he asked, and Terrell managed to gasp, "Please," just once, before Colby took him in his hot mouth.

It wasn't subtle, the thing Colby was doing. It wasn't a virgin's blow job or a thing you'd do to a man who was unsure and experimenting with his sexuality. Colby had Terrell deep in his throat and was squeezing his balls with just enough pressure to make Terrell ache but not enough to make him hurt. Terrell felt it, felt his touch, his need, his demand—Colby was making love to a *grown-up*, a man who knew what he wanted and was unafraid.

Terrell was unafraid.

He clutched at Colby's head with his one good hand and cocked his knee up so Colby could play with his taint and his pucker, and Colby took him up on it, clenching Terrell's thighs to him so tightly Terrell had no option but to thrust forward and trust that Colby could take him, take his sex, take his come, before Terrell grunted, groaned, and gave it to him.

Colby didn't disappoint.

Terrell was still panting as he brought his good arm up to Colby's sweaty face so he could cup his cheek as Colby swallowed and caught his breath and swallowed again, and wiped his mouth on the sheets.

At last, he was able to come up and face Terrell, his face still all pink and spotty with sex blotch and his mouth still glazed because he didn't get all that off.

His smile was beatific.

"You proud of yourself?" Terrell asked, wondering if his heart was ever going to calm down.

"You have no idea."

Terrell palmed the back of his head and brought him in for another kiss, this one slower, gentler, and full of blessing.

"Want me to return the favor?" he asked, and Colby shook his head.

"Naw, man. Not tonight."

Terrell blinked and ground his groin up against Colby's to discover that he'd come in his shorts. "Well, God, aren't you Johnny-rockets," Terrell murmured, but his voice was low and affectionate, because Colby was a sexual creature from his nose to his toes, and that right there was a high fucking honor.

"Jesus, T—I'm just so damned glad you're here."

And something cracked in his voice, and Terrell suddenly knew the price you had to pay for a lover who would service you and not ask for a damned thing in return.

"I'm so glad I'm here too," he whispered. "And not just alive. Right here, right here with you. It wasn't much fun being alive without being here."

Colby nodded and closed his eyes tight, and Terrell saw, of all things, tears leaking through the corners. Terrell kissed them, one, then the other, and pulled Colby close. "You're not going to fall apart on me, are you, cheese boy?"

"You know us white guys," Colby muttered against his good shoulder. "We're a bunch of pussies."

"Yeah, yeah," Terrell murmured, but he kept Colby tucked up against his chest for a good long time. He figured if Colby had gotten shot, his world would have ended too—it was only fair he give Colby the benefit of believing Terrell getting hurt would mean the same to him.

The next day Colby and Moira's mom and dad drove their ethanol-powered low-emissions recreation vehicle from their small home in Marysville and into the driveway. After they'd parked, they proceeded to bring out potato salad, frog-eye salad, and three-bean salad. (Terrell was happy to see frog-eye salad—they called it "salad" but it was really dessert, complete with fruit, whipped cream, and tiny balls of pasta.)

Gina and Percy—at Moira's invite—parked Gina's old SUV behind them, and brought beer and Papiano's buns, which they'd smuggled out and which Colby forgave.

Terrell was not allowed to participate in the getting ready. He was not allowed to clean off the picnic table that he'd not ever seen in their backyard, and not allowed to help set it. He was not allowed to put food together in the kitchen or stand with Mr. Meyers and his daughter at the grill.

Hell, he wasn't even allowed to drink beer, because it would have messed with his damned pain meds.

All he was allowed to do, while Colby and Percy got the food ready, was sit in the shade with Mrs. Meyers and Gina, play cards, and talk about Mrs. Meyer's two favorite people: Moira and Colby.

Yeah, she knew about the case, and Gina got to tell her that Moira had pulled some strings mighty quick to be getting Percy out at o-dark-thirty the night Terrell had been shot. Mrs. Meyers—*call me Anne, won't you?*—was short and plump and blonde and blue-eyed and just the prettiest little ol' middle-aged American ideal mommy with a twinkle in her eye and an apple pie sitting in the other room to cool. So it was a real mindfuck when she nodded her head at the end of the story and asked, "And what happened to the skank ho bitch that shot you?"

Terrell spit out his diet Coke, and Gina spit out her beer, and Colby came out in time to set down the frog-eye salad on the table and kiss her cheek.

"Aw, Mom, are you impressing my boyfriend again?"

"I don't know," Anne Meyers said, grinning at Terrell. "Did it work?"

"Ma'am, you can call that woman whatever you want, as long as you call her incarcerated."

"Where she'll be for a good fifteen years," Moira said from next to her dad. "That was *fun*! They let me press those charges. I wanna do that more often!"

"Does it involve me getting shot again?" Terrell asked. "Because if so, I think you'd better find yourself another goddamned hobby!"

Mr. Meyers, who was tall and hale with most of his hair, most of it even Colby's dark-blond color, took a swig of his beer and said, "I'll drink to that! So, Moy—maybe take up dating or something, since we don't want any more holes in Terrell than he's already got?"

Moira groaned. "Thanks a lot, T! I thought you liked me!"

"I love you like a sister!" Terrell returned, and then quietly realized that it was true.

That night, Terrell found himself standing next to Percy as the whole family sat on the flat part of the garage roof and looked up toward Cal Expo, where they could see the big fireworks display.

He hadn't talked to Percy much that day, and he'd wanted to see how the boy was doing. Percy seemed fine—even drank soda all day so Gina didn't have to freak out about giving alcohol to a minor—and as they stood there, looking at the pretty lights, Percy sighed.

"T?"

"Yeah?"

"You're sorta fuckin' gay, aren't you?"

Terrell had to blink, and he realized that the last time they'd talked, that had been a big sticking point for Percy. "You think, genius? Colby's only grabbed my ass sixty thousand times tonight."

"Yeah, that's fucking gross, T. But that's not the point."

"What's the point?"

"All them lights up there, I used to just think they were for white people."

"Me too."

"Think maybe they're for us?"

Terrell sighed. No, he wanted to say, but he couldn't. Like Colby had been saying all along, it wasn't a perfect world, but nobody got that. You just tried to make it better. "Sometimes," he said. "More of them for you than for me, if you feel me."

Percy sighed and drank more soda. "Don't ask a brother that when he's not cool with the gay thing, T. Just saying. But I hear you."

"I'm not your brother, asshole," Terrell snapped, annoyed.

"You are tonight, T. We're the only black people for six blocks."

Terrell looked at him, his face turned up to see the pretty fireworks, and saw that he was kidding, and then burst out laughing. "You are the dumbest motherfucker on the face of the planet, Percy. But I am damned glad you are not in jail."

"I'm glad you're not dead."

Yeah, all right. It was not peace on Earth, goodwill toward men, but as Colby came over and grabbed his hand and they both ignored Percy's groan of disgust, Terrell decided it would have to do.

IT TURNED out that Terrell was both lucky and unlucky in the whole "getting shot" department. The bullet had been a through-and-through—which all the cop shows made look like someone could just go back to work and wear a white sling and be all good in a couple of days. Terrell had already figured out that this was not really the case when you had major surgery on your shoulder to keep from bleeding out, but the next few weeks confirmed it.

He was not allowed to go back to Papiano's for nearly six weeks, and then he only had a month to work before he and Colby took off.

He spent the days doing research on all of those places he and Colby were going to visit, and he reminded Colby for maybe the millionth time that South Africa and the Netherlands and Belgium and Germany may have been all excited about the gay thing, but they were going to spaz out about the black thing.

"Hey—since you're gay, maybe that will get you a pass!" Colby joked, and Terrell scowled at him, narrow-eyed, until Colby kissed him hard and possessively and said, "Well, T—that's important too. We can always hope there's a perfect place out there, some place that's as egalitarian as one of those sci-fi shows, but until we make one on planet Earth, it's important to figure out what we're doing wrong. We can be a part of that too."

Terrell pulled himself out of the kiss with the firm conviction that Colby would have him wearing the red-white-and-blue uniform eventually, and Colby laughed at him and told him he'd rather have Terrell naked.

Terrell did a lot of that during his recovery too.

The last night he and Colby worked before they left for Europe—they called it a leave of absence, because burning the bridge of a job that had a location in thirty countries around the world when you were planning on being a world traveler was not a smart move—the staff reserved the bar and threw them a send-off the likes of which nobody had ever seen.

A lot of their regulars were there to see them off, and people who didn't have to work came in to buy them drinks (which they shared, because otherwise someone would have had to pour them into the car, and they hadn't brought a driver with them, so they had to be moderate), and people like Erin and Angie came up to them and told them they made an adorable couple. Of course Jason came up and told them that his church would take them should they choose to repent, and Mark told them he was glad they were okay but he didn't want to shake hands in case of that AIDS thing, but Terrell had perspective now. He'd been shot defending the man he loved—for some reason, the small bullshit did not get under his skin anymore.

Maybe it was because Colby liked the color of that skin—Terrell was reluctant to let it get all bubbly.

At the end, as they were walking out to their car after being hugged and handshaked and congratulated until they were exhausted with it, Colby looked up at the still-sweltering September sky.

"This time tomorrow," he said whimsically, "we'll be on a plane."

"Yeah," Terrell said. "We'd better go home and have sex now while we can."

Colby grimaced. "Romance, T—you has it!"

Terrell suddenly grew sober when he didn't think he could. "You know what we are right now, even before that plane takes off?"

"What?"

"We're legend. Man, those people are going to be talking about us until that place goes out of business."

"How's that feel?"

Terrell thought about it. "Big," he said after a moment. "It feels big. We are bigger than Papi's. We're bigger than that little hidey-hole on the back dock. We're bigger than my shitty apartment that Percy's living in."

Colby nodded seriously, and they regarded each other over the top of the car. "We're bigger than black and white and gay," he said, and Terrell heard him.

"Hell yeah."

Colby grinned as they slid in the car and started toward their future. "Not bad for our first step out the door."

AMY LANE is a mother of four and a compulsive knitter who writes because she can't silence the voices in her head. She adores cats, Chi-who-whats, knitting socks, and hawt menz, and she dislikes moths, cat boxes, and knuckle-headed macspazzmatrons. She is rarely found cooking, cleaning, or doing domestic chores, but she has been known to knit up an emergency hat/blanket/pair of socks for any occasion whatsoever, or sometimes for no reason at all. She writes in the shower, while at the gym, while taxiing children to soccer/dance/gymnastics /band oh my! and has learned from necessity to type like the wind. She lives in a spider-infested, crumbling house in a shoddy suburb and counts on her beloved Mate to keep her tethered to reality—which he does, while keeping her cell phone charged as a bonus. She's been married for twenty-plus years and still believes in Twu Wuv, with a capital Twu and a capital Wuv, and she doesn't see any reason at all for that to change.

Website: www.greenshill.com
Blog: www.writerslane.blogspot.com
E-mail: amylane@greenshill.com
Facebook: www.facebook.com/amy.lane.167
Twitter: @amymaclane

Also from AMY LANE

A Knitter in His Natural Habitat

Amy Lane

http://www.dreamspinnerpress.com

MOURNING
Heaven

AMY LANE

Also from AMY LANE

http://www.dreamspinnerpress.com

Also from AMY LANE

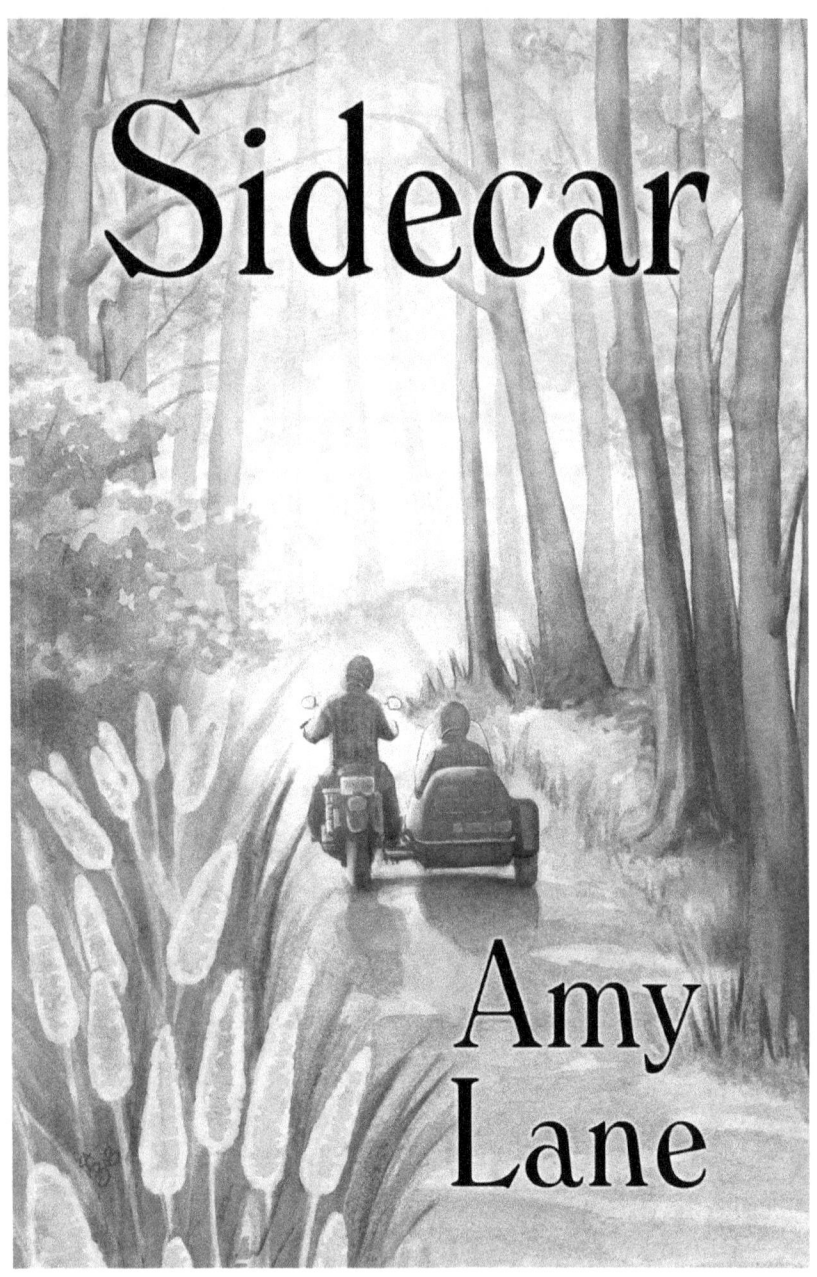

Sidecar

Amy
Lane

http://www.dreamspinnerpress.com

www.ingramcontent.com/pod-product-compliance
Lightning Source LLC
Chambersburg PA
CBHW070057260626
47160CB00004B/1239